Wind Rider

A Novel
By
Linda Abels

Dedicated to
Andrew Thomas Warren
September 28, 1986 to June 2, 2000
A young life taken far too soon.

Acknowledgements

Many thanks to my husband, Wayne and, children and grandchildren for your patience and consistent encouragement over the past six years while I worked on this story.

Thanks to Jerry Jenkins, DiAnn Mills and the Christian Writers Guild. Without their teaching, mentoring, and guidance this story would never have begun.

Thanks to Kelly Sumner, Scott Woodson and all my other critique partners over these years for your patience and encouragement.

Thanks to Juliet Kennedy, my friend, critique partner, mentor, and editor for finding all those misplaced and missing commas and sharing your vast storehouse of knowledge of the mechanics of writing.

Thanks to Deb Warren for creating the beautiful cover and sharing your heart wrenching story of the loss of your beloved Andy.

Thanks to Foothills Community Church in Arvada, Colorado, the pastors and staff who led me to Christ and continue to encourage and support me in my walk with our Lord.

"So do not fear, for I am with you;
do not be dismayed, for I am your God.
I will strengthen you and help you;
I will uphold you with my righteous
right hand."

Isaiah 41:10

Wind Rider

*"He heals the brokenhearted
and binds up their wounds."*
Psalm 147:3

Chapter 1

I'd flown over a thousand miles to begin a new life I didn't want in a place I didn't want to be. I'd spent my entire life of sixteen years on our family's ranch in Evergreen, Colorado.

Although I loved my aunt, uncle, and cousin very much, I did not want to begin a new life with them in a place far removed from the beauty and serenity of my Rocky Mountain home.

San Francisco International was an enormous airport with crowds of travelers moving in every direction. Conveyor belts carried people down the center of gray-carpeted walkways that disappeared into forever. I didn't know which way to go, and I recognized no one. Then from a distant corridor, Aunt Carol ran toward me. Relief overwhelmed me as I choked back tears. Rational thought pushed away childish need, and I fought the yearning to fall into her arms and cry.

Aunt Carol's cheeks flushed, and she trembled as she pulled me into a hug. "Oh Brittany, I'm sorry I'm late. Are you okay?"

"A little tired."

She released me and wrapped an arm around my waist as we crossed through the bustling terminal. Tears rolled down her cheeks. It was obvious from the graying of her hair and the lines on her face that her grief ran as deep as mine. "I can't believe they're gone."

My throat constricted to where I couldn't reply. Mom and

Dad and my little sister, Tiff, were gone. I'd never see them again. Though I didn't want to talk about it, no one understood my grief better than Aunt Carol. She and my mom were identical twins. She inhaled a deep breath and released it. "You look wonderful. How are you feeling? We can get you a wheelchair."

"I can walk."

"Do you still have pain in your arm?"

"It's a little stiff, but I'll be fine."

She embraced me, and her voice caught. "The last time we saw you, you were still unconscious."

I pulled away. "I didn't realize you saw me—like that."

"The doctor had you sedated, and you slept most of the time. We came by to visit you every day." She wiped away a tear and forced a smile. "But you're here now, and Uncle Jim and David can't wait to see you."

We walked side by side through the concourse. She dabbed at her eyes with a wadded tissue. I reached for her hand. With tremulous fingers, she clasped my hand in hers, and we continued for several moments in silent understanding.

We rode a train to the main terminal, maneuvered escalators, and then traversed a labyrinth of wide corridors to reach the baggage claim.

Next to the baggage carousel, with arms outstretched to greet me, stood Uncle Jim. His towering height and dark hair speckled with silver set him apart. He pulled me into a tight embrace. "Oh, baby, I'm so sorry." He rested his head on my mine. "But you're here now, and we're going to take good care of you."

My cousin, David, teetered back and forth in an oversized 49ers T-shirt. His scruffy blonde hair peeked out beneath a backwards ball cap as he offered a high-five. I returned his gesture, and he flashed a pearly white grin. "Hey, Cuz." His words were hesitant. With eyes downcast he fingered his ear buds. "If there's anything you need, I'm here for you."

Uncle Jim patted my shoulder. "We need to get this young

lady home."

He hoisted my duffle bags and led the way to the parking garage. We walked through damp air for what seemed an eternity. Uncle Jim stopped behind a silver blue Mercedes. He popped the trunk and dropped my bags into the gaping black hole. I settled in the backseat and stared out the window into the dampness and gloom.

Mist-shrouded highway signs buzzed past us.

Aunt Carol turned in her seat and smiled at me. "Are you hungry? We can stop somewhere and grab a bite."

The thought of food nauseated me. "No thanks."

"Maybe you'll change your mind later. I'm sure Millie can whip something up for us."

Millie was their cook and housekeeper. She'd been with the family for as long as I could remember. She was a very sweet grandmotherly lady who kept the family well fed and organized.

The rain stopped, and the sun peeked through the clouds as we wound our way up tree-lined avenues with steep grades. A hodgepodge of buildings lined the streets, from storefronts to restaurants to elegant restored apartment buildings. Rows of ancient houses sat side by side with enormous palm trees dotting the minuscule yards on the properties that had a yard. Uncle Jim pulled up in front of their gray Victorian embellished with burgundy and gold scrollwork. "Here we are. Home sweet home."

Our little group passed through a wrought-iron gate and then mounted stone steps to gold-inlaid, carved double front doors. Millie opened the door to the right. A wide smile lit up her soft brown eyes. She draped an arm across my shoulders. "Come along, Ms. Brittany, I've got your favorite meal warming on the stove and a special treat for dessert."

Chapter 2

Morning light peeked through the blinds, and the sun's teasing fingers reached across the familiar quilt. I stretched and took in the surroundings as a wave of homesickness overshadowed my appreciation for what Aunt Carol had done.

My pictures and posters hung just as I'd left them in Colorado. My trophies, ribbons, and photos of Mariah covered one wall.

I explored the room and ran my hand across photos of Mom, Dad, and Tiffany, as deep sorrow filled my heart. I closed my eyes, and the nightmare returned—the icy road, the blinding snow, everything moved in slow motion as the car skidded out of control. Tiff screamed from the backseat. Dad grabbed the wheel. We slid over the drop-off and slammed into a rocky cliff side. I blacked out.

I opened my eyes, willed the thoughts to leave and then dropped into the desk chair. The portrait Mom and Dad had made of me barrel racing on Mariah hung on the wall above the desk. Tears rolled at the memory of my beloved horse I'd had to leave on the ranch in Colorado.

A knock interrupted my thoughts. "Brittany? Are you awake?"

I wiped my eyes. "Sure."

Aunt Carol slipped in. "How did you sleep?"

"Fine." I shrugged. "I love the room. Thanks."

"Lisa took pictures of your bedroom on the ranch, and she

shipped your things while you stayed with Nana Masters."

"It's looks the same as back home."

"Our decorator is fantastic."

Sitting on the edge of the bed, I ran my hand along the stitching on the quilt Nana made for my twelfth birthday. "I can't believe I slept so long. What time is it?"

Aunt Carol glanced at her watch. "It's eleven thirty. Since it's your first day with us, we let you sleep. We've been to church, and now we're going to Fisherman's Wharf. It's a beautiful day, and we hoped you'd join us."

Her invitation surprised me. I had hoped to spend the day in my room alone. "I don't know."

"Please come with us. We'll have lunch on the wharf. It will be fun."

Mixed feelings surged through me. I was glad they had not insisted on me going with them to church. She was being so nice. What could I say?

"The bathroom across the hall is yours. Millie put out towels, soaps, and shampoo. If you need something else, ask Millie."

"Aunt Carol, if you'll give me time to shower and change, I'd like to go with you."

"Great. We'll wait for you in the kitchen."

She left the room and shut the door behind her. I pulled out jeans and a T-shirt from one of my bags. Someone knocked.

"Ms. Brittany?"

I rolled my eyes and smiled. "Come in, Millie."

As she eased open the door, she poked her head through the gap. "I can come back."

"Did you need something?"

"I heard you and Ms. Carol talking. Since you're awake, I can put your clothes away and make the bed while you shower."

"You don't have to do that."

She pulled back my quilt and stripped the bed of the sheets. "Oh, Ms. Carol will have a fit if she hears I let you make your bed and put your things in the closet and dresser."

Though I was uncomfortable with her making my bed and unpacking my bags, I gathered my clothes and headed to the bathroom.

Beneath the soothing hot water, I lathered on lemon-scented soap and tried to ignore the bright pink scar on my right shoulder. Showered and dressed, I girded myself with resolve and hurried downstairs to join the family in the kitchen.

Aunt Carol's orange pants and peach-colored blouse looked the same as the clothes Mom wore last summer for my birthday party. I stared in disbelief and forced back threatening tears.

"Brittany? Is something wrong?" Aunt Carol said.

She crossed the room. With her blonde hair tucked behind her ears, a few strands refusing to stay in place, the long, dark lashes surrounding azure eyes, she looked so much like Mom.

Uncle Jim joined us. David pulled out an earbud and stared. Millie turned to face us. My uncle slipped his hand beneath my arm. "You're upset. Come sit."

The pain in my heart became a sick and fiery gnawing as the realization that Mom was dead, and I'd killed her, twisted inside me. With tears washing my face, I ran from the kitchen.

"The Lord is with me; I will not be afraid.
What can mere mortals do to me?"
Psalm 118:6

Chapter 3

Monday morning came far too early as the remains of dense
fog surrounded the ominous building. Aunt Carol turned her
black Lexus into the parking lot of Kennedy High School, and
my stomach churned. The school counselor scheduled the
appointment for nine-thirty. The clock in the car read nine-
fifteen. I swallowed hard. "What time do classes start?"

Aunt Carol silenced the engine with a click of a button.
"First period began at seven-thirty."

A small group of girls wearing torn jeans and colored T-
shirts stood next to the school entrance. Several of the teens
stared in our direction. I slumped into my seat and sighed.

Several long moments passed before I slid out of the car
and shuffled to the sidewalk. Aunt Carol took my face in her
hands and locked her eyes on mine. "It will be okay. I
promise."

Despite the embarrassment over her physical display of
encouragement, I managed a smile before entering the school.
Double doors opened into a hallway where gray morning light
filtered through high set windows of the modernistic-designed
building.

"The office is right here," Aunt Carol said as she hurried
ahead and entered through double glass doors.

Quickening my pace, I joined her. She spoke in soft tones
to an older woman in a red dress. The lady offered me a toothy
grin. "So, you're Brittany?" The woman rounded the counter
and stood in front of me. "Welcome to Kennedy High School.

We are so glad you're here."

I stifled back a nervous giggle. "Thanks."

A young woman, who looked not much older than a high school student, emerged from a door to our right. Her shoulder-length, auburn hair set off her deep green sweater, and she welcomed us with a soft southern drawl. "Brittany and Mrs. Harper, won't you join me?"

Aunt Carol motioned for me to take the lead. "Brittany, this is your guidance counselor, Ms. Chatham."

Ms. Chatham took a seat behind her desk and pointed to two chairs facing her. We sat as she opened a thick manila folder. "You have an impressive academic record, Brittany. We should be able to keep you in the same curriculum you took in Evergreen."

My mind congested with doubts and fears.

She stopped studying the documents and met my gaze. "Do you have questions?"

I sucked in my bottom lip.

Aunt Carol laid her hand on top of mine. "Are you okay?"

"Does she know?" I said

"She knows about the accident."

"I haven't been in school for over two months."

Aunt Carol nodded. "You will be fine."

Ms. Chatham slipped a stack of papers inside a blue folder. "You have been an exemplary student throughout your educational career, and I understand you've been with a tutor since the accident. I am confident you'll be able to jump into your classes with no problem."

I wished I was as convinced of my abilities as she was.

She handed me the folder. "You'll find everything you need to begin tomorrow morning, and the school secretary has your books ready at the front desk. You can pick them up when we come back from our tour."

I stammered. "Tour?"

"I will give you a tour of Kennedy. I'll show you where your locker is, your classrooms—those things. It will be fun."

The woman had to be crazy to think I'd enjoy parading around the high school with her and my aunt. As we exited the office, a period bell rang and students surrounded us, pushing, laughing, and ignoring us. Lost in a sea of unconcerned kids, maybe the tour would not be too embarrassing.

"Britt?"

I recognized the voice and spun around to face my cousin. "David?"

"Where you headed?"

"We're going over to the student commons," Ms. Chatham said. "And you, Mr. Harper, are due in class. You'd best move along if you don't want to be late."

David cast the counselor an ornery grin. "I'm going." He gave a slight wave and then bolted around the corner.

An hour later, Aunt Carol and I returned to the main office. I gathered my books and papers, and we headed for the car. I plopped in the front seat, snapped my seat belt, and stared at the huge edifice before me.

This was crazy. Evergreen High fit in this building three times.

The late morning sun warmed my skin, but inside a tremendous chill permeated outward.

"We must learn to regard people less in light of what they do or omit to do, and more in the light of what they suffer."
-Dietrich Bonhoeffer

Chapter 4

The past week I existed in a vacuum. I missed my horse, Mariah. I was homesick for Nana, Uncle Scott, and the Bar K. School and homework occupied part of my day, but the evenings were long. Every night after dinner, I excused myself to the solitude of my room.

On Saturday morning, I joined the family for breakfast, and when I finished, I excused myself. I lay on my bed staring out the window with unseeing eyes. My thoughts escaped to another place and another time when a knock at my door interrupted my musings.

"Hey, Britt. It's me." I stood, stretched, and groaned. "What do you want, David?"

"Let me in."

"Go away."

"No. Let me in for five minutes. Then, if you want me to leave, I will."

Why couldn't people understand I wanted to be alone? I pulled the door open. "Five minutes and you're out."

He scrunched up his nose as he entered. "Don't you think your room is creepy?"

"What?"

"The way Mom did your room. It looks like your room on the ranch."

My room was the only place where I didn't feel *creepy*. "I

like it. What do you want?"

"You want to go for a ride?"

"No."

"Flying down the California highway with the wind blowing through your hair."

Now he had my attention.

"Just you and me?"

"Mom and Dad went to a meeting at church. I told Millie we were going for a drive. She said we could go, and she'd pack us a cooler."

It was obvious he would not give up, so I agreed to go.

As we crossed through the kitchen, Millie handed David a large, red cooler and winked. "Have a great time."

It seemed like more food than just the two of us would need. But who knew what Millie might have put together? She was always baking, cooking, and fussing over David and me.

"You're the best, Millie," David said.

His older model, dark blue convertible sat in front of the house with its top down. He set the cooler on the backseat and vaulted over the car door. The engine roared to a start, and music blared from the stereo. David shouted above the booming bass, "Are you coming?"

I climbed in and fastened my seat belt. "Nice car."

"Thanks." He ran a hand along the leather bucket seat. "She's a 1966 Chevy Impala Super Sport. Three hundred and fifty horsepower. One hundred percent muscle car." He turned his attention back to the road.

He talked about his car like I talked about my horse, Mariah, and appeared to love it as much.

A few quick turns and we were speeding down the hill toward the bay. Sunlight reflected off the water as orange, steel bridge abutments whizzed past. To our left the Pacific Ocean beckoned. To our right barges and sailboats dotted the bay.

Moments after crossing the bridge, David turned into a drive that led past green hills and through shading clumps of forest.

I ran my fingers through my mass of tangled hair. "Where are we going?"

"To see my friends."

We rounded a curve and then pulled into a parking lot where a large sign read, "Golden Gate Recreation Area."

Rivulets of sunlight filtered through branches of mammoth pine trees, casting a patchwork pattern on the ground. Several boys played Frisbee, and a cluster of girls sat on the ground talking. Groups of older men sat at picnic tables playing chess or checkers.

I climbed out and shut the door as a man in tattered jeans walked in our direction. "Hey gang, it's David," he announced.

"It's David," several other voices shouted.

My cousin grabbed the cooler from the backseat and hurried toward an unkempt crowd of people forming around one picnic table. Filled with a sense of uneasiness, I followed close.

A young woman with unwashed dreadlocks and facial piercings scanned me through dark-lashed eyes. "Who's the girl?"

David opened the cooler and passed out a couple dozen sandwiches. "This is my cousin, Brittany. She's from Colorado."

The smell of body odor overwhelmed me as the group gathered in to collect their sandwiches. Many of them gobbled up the offering as though they hadn't eaten in days.

A wrinkled old man with missing teeth and shoulder length, stringy, unwashed hair stepped toward me. "So, you're from the great state of Colorado?"

I stepped back as he came closer. "Yes, sir."

"Did you hear, gang? The little lady called me sir. That is very nice of you. No one has called me sir for a long time. You can call me Larry." He moved a dirty hand toward my hair, and I sidled out of his reach. "With that blonde hair and those big brown eyes, you could pass for David's sister."

The old man frightened me, and the young woman staring

at me made me uncomfortable. I turned and strolled beneath a shading canopy of foliage, venturing far enough from the crowd to be out of earshot of the chatter but close enough to see David. In the low crook of a tree, I leaned my back against the trunk and lost myself in the serenity of nature.

My cousin played Frisbee with four other kids and then sat at a picnic table. He sipped from a bottle of water and then draped an arm across the shoulders of a boy with dark hair and a coppery complexion. Dressed in a clean black T-shirt and khakis, he did not appear to be one of the homeless people. The way he and David laughed and talked; it was obvious they were buds.

Frequent glances at my watch did not help pass the time. With the sound of the wind rustling through the pines and the screaming of the gulls, I leaned back and closed my eyes.

Two hours passed before David grabbed up the empty cooler. He waved a hand in my direction and shouted, "Hey Britt. Let's go."

I joined him as his *friends* gathered around; several patted him on the back and offered a thank you for the sandwiches. Taking me by the hand and drawing me closer, David introduced me to his bud, Kody Diaz.

"Hey," I said.

There was a heart-rending tenderness in his gaze, and his dark, penetrating eyes caused my heart to skip a beat.

"Hey yourself," he said.

As he followed us back to the car, Kody talked with David about their band and a Sunday morning gig.

I fastened my seat belt as David and his friends shouted their goodbyes.

Rounding a curve and pulling off to the side, David brought the car to stop at the entrance to the park. "Don't mention our coming here to Mom and Dad."

I'd heard stories about homeless people in Denver. A spider-tangle of impulses gripped me. "They don't know you hang out with these people?"

David stiffened. "These people, as you call them, are people who have fallen on hard times and are looking for someone to care."

"I've never been around anyone like them."

"You don't have homeless people in Colorado?"

"I've seen a few on the streets of Evergreen. But you are avoiding my question. Do Aunt Carol and Uncle Jim know you come here?"

"They know I come to the park with the youth group for stuff like the barbecue next Saturday, but they don't like me coming here alone. Mom and Dad think one of my homeless friends will pull a knife on me, shoot me, or rob me. They don't understand."

I didn't want to argue with him, but I felt uneasy about him coming here alone. "And you do?"

A shadow of annoyance crossed his face as he revved the engine and cranked up his music. "Yeah, I do."

". . . as far as the east is from the west,
so far has he removed our
transgressions from us."
Psalm 103:12

Chapter 5

We returned to the highway, and David slowed as we passed a sign reading "City Limits of San Rafael." He turned left onto a road lined with white stucco homes and palm trees.

He'd not said a word since we left the park, and so as not to agitate him, I'd remained silent until now. "Where are we going?"

"Dillon Beach."

His response held a note of impatience confirming that my reaction to his homeless friends had upset him. As one who avoided confrontations, I figured my best course was to act as if nothing was wrong. The farther we drove from the confines of the city, the lighter my mood grew. "This was a good idea."

A smile teased at the corner of his mouth. "What?"

"Leaving the city behind us. Flying along the highway. It's like riding the wind."

"Sometimes you have to cut loose." He gripped the steering wheel. "Riding the wind?" He laughed. "We're Wind Riders."

Having the freedom to float on the wind without a care in the world sounded good. "Wind Riders."

"We'll be heading to the summerhouse after school lets out. But I thought you might like to get out of the city and spend some time there now."

To our left, the bay sparkled in the afternoon sunlight as sleepy sailboats drifted across its surface. For the next thirty minutes, I soaked in the warmth and welcomed the ocean breeze.

David maneuvered the Chevy along curving roads that descended closer to the beach. "Do you remember it? You guys usually came at Christmas. But one year you came in the summer and we spent a few days here."

"I'd forgotten. We must have been about seven or eight." I stared in disbelief at the shoreline encroached by enormous black stones battered by ocean waves breaking into thunderous crashes. "It's awesome."

We pulled into the drive of a simple-designed, modern home. David led me to the back of the house where I gazed across the deep green ocean to where it met the horizon. "Do we have to go back?" I inhaled the tangy smell of saltwater and wet sand. "Can't we stay?"

He climbed the steps onto a raised deck and unlocked white French doors. "We'll be staying soon enough. Mom likes to leave the city in the summer."

We crossed through a living area with a worn leather sectional that filled one side of the room. Magazines and leather coasters littered several occasional tables, and on the far side, floor-to-ceiling windows framed spectacular views of the Pacific Ocean.

The house sat on a high point that ended at what looked like a sheer cliff. Stepping closer to the window, I pointed down the hill to an inlet beach of white sand. "How do we get down there?"

David nudged me to the door, and then he took the lead as he walked across the front yard toward the road. "The public beach is at the bottom of the hill."

We followed the steep downward grade and then turned off the road at a parking lot and picnic area.

At the edge of the pavement, with two swift kicks, I removed my boots. I pulled off my socks and tossed them on the soft, white sand and then rolled up my jeans and scurried toward the shoreline. I dipped my toes in the icy water and gasped.

David snuck up behind me, gave a light push, and came close to sending me toppling into a cold bath. I splashed him and ran along the beach kicking at the surf as it lapped at the shoreline. This was the best I'd felt since leaving the mountains.

My cousin caught up and teased, "Wow, you run faster than most girls."

He splashed me, and I splashed him back as we laughed and jumped around in the surf for at least an hour.

I stopped to catch my breath, then stood on dry land and squeezed out the corner of my shirt. "Want to race?"

Reminiscent of a wet yellow dog, David shook water from his hair and body. "No way. I hate getting beat by a girl."

With a near unbearable excitement, I ran up the beach and weaved between looming rocks and through crags filled with debris left behind by the tides. At a wall of multicolored stone, I stopped and turned back to see if David had caught up with me. He said he didn't want to get beat by a girl, but I thought he would take the dare. He sat at the water's edge, staring out over the ocean.

Puzzled by the abrupt change in his mood, I called out to him. "David?"

He turned and waved.

I hurried to his side, and he shot me a crooked grin. He was quiet and introspective, and I stared at him in bafflement. "What are you doing?"

Resting his elbows on his knees, he gazed off toward the horizon. "Thinking."

I settled onto the sand next to him and dragged my fingers through the soft surface. "About what?"

"God."

Strange, disquieting thoughts raced through my mind. "What about Him?"

He shrugged, and his focus on the ocean told me I may have said something wrong—or he understood something I did not.

As I quieted myself, my thoughts spiraled into a dark empty place. "Do you have thoughts about death?"

His eyebrows arched. "No. Why?"

"If there is a God, why did he take my family?"

He jolted to his feet. "If there is a God? Why would you say that? How can you look at the ocean and say, 'If there is a God'?"

I sucked back a sob and bolted toward the parking lot. My thoughts raced as I argued his point to myself. David could never understand. He talked about a God I couldn't see and touch. And he thought his God had all the answers.

My cousin grabbed my arm. "I'm sorry I shouted at you, but it's so hard to watch you and know."

"Know what? Know I killed my parents and my sister? If an all-powerful God exists, why would he let that happen?"

David met my gaze. "You didn't kill them. It was an accident."

What could I say? How could I make him understand that the *accident* would not have happened if I had not been driving?

He kicked at the sand. "Get over this, Britt. Stop blaming yourself. *S*pend more time caring about other people."

"What do you mean?"

"You only care about yourself." Cold sarcasm and disdain echoed behind his retort.

My pent-up tears threatened to burst forth. "How can you be so insensitive?"

"I'm being insensitive?" He swiped sand from his wet shorts. "You don't care how anyone else feels. And you're ungrateful."

"That's a lie. Why would you say that?"

"What would you call the way you've acted ever since you got here?"

I refused to answer and kicked sand as I crossed the beach to the edge of the parking lot. I dropped to sit, swiped sand from my feet, and pulled on my socks. David stood over me balling his hands into fists.

My lower lip trembled. "I'm not ungrateful, David Harper, and I care about other people."

"Oh yeah? What about Mom?"

"What about her?"

"Do you know how she feels about losing her twin sister? Mom cried for weeks after Aunt Cali died. She sits and stares and goes off by herself for hours."

I pulled on my boots. "I'm sure she is sad, but how have I been ungrateful?"

"Mom planned this great welcome to make you feel at home. She decorated your room with your stuff from Colorado. Mom went to a lot of trouble to make you happy, and all you've done is pout and run off every chance you get."

Tears streaked my cheeks. I did not want David to see me cry. I needed to be alone, so I hurried toward the road that led back to the house.

He caught up, grabbed my arm, and pulled me back. "Britt, I am not trying to be mean. I'm trying to understand."

"What don't you understand?"

"Today at the park—you acted like my friends were diseased or something. They're real people with real feelings just like you."

I pulled from his grip and choked out, "I'm nothing like them."

"You're right. You're not. They care about each other. I expected you to show compassion and hoped you'd see what I see."

He pushed all my buttons, and I no longer cared if he saw my tears. Was he nuts comparing me to those homeless people? "How can you call them your friends? You have nothing in common with them, and most of them are old enough to be your parents or grandparents."

He stormed up the road in front of me, muttering as he went.

As I rounded the corner of the house, I found David

slumped in a wicker chair on the back deck. I'd had time to compose myself on the walk home, but I didn't want to resume the conversation we'd left hanging at the beach. Gazing out at the darkening sea, I slowly walked to the back of the property where the yard ended at a rocky cliff side. A few hundred yards out from the stone face, foaming white waves smashed over black rock formations.

The angry surf mirrored the turmoil roaring inside me. David said I was selfish and ungrateful. He was right. I was wretched. I killed my family. I didn't deserve to live.

Stepping to the edge of the drop-off, I looked down at the jagged rocks littering the sandy shoreline. One long step and— I could end it.

As I reached out one foot, an arm surrounded my waist and yanked me from the edge.

"What do you think you're doing?" David said. "Are you crazy? Are you trying to kill yourself?" He gripped my shoulders and turned me to face him. "Brittany?" His skin went from ashen to flushing pink as he shook me. "Brittany? Answer me."

I jerked from of his grip. "What?"

"What did you think you were doing?"

A shock of defeat held me immobile.

I couldn't let him know what I'd been about to do. He had stopped me this time. I grinned and straightened my shoulders. "That drop-off is amazing. It must be two hundred feet. The power of those waves breaking over those rocks is awesome."

"You are one crazy girl."

I forced out a chuckle and walked toward the house. "Yeah, I've heard rumors."

We took seats opposite each other in the living room. David's face remained flushed.

Crazy? Taking my life seemed like the sanest thing I could ever do. But I felt bad for frightening him. "Sorry if I scared you."

"I don't get it."

How could he understand? He was right. I was into myself. I was all I had.

David answered the musical ring of his cell phone. "Yeah, sure," he said. "Yeah, I'll be home in time. Pick you up around eight?" A grin spread across his lips. "See you." He clicked off the phone. "I don't want to fight."

"Me neither. Who was that on the phone?"

"Sara."

"She your girlfriend?"

"Sort of."

"The Lord is close to the brokenhearted and saves
those who are crushed by the spirit."
Psalm 34:18

Chapter 6

The next morning, I forced my eyes open and peeked from under the edge of my covers. A cloud gripped the house in grayish-white gloom. With eyes transfixed on the scene, cocooned in my quilt, I curled up on the window seat and stared in amazement.

Nothing existed beyond my window except a dense apparition. The ominous creature had swallowed us whole.

Aunt Carol's voice carried through the closed door. "Hush. If she's not up, we don't want to wake her."

Uncle Jim's calming voice of reason replied, "I understand, dear, but she's part of our family, and I want her with us."

Shuffling my bare feet across the soft carpet, I opened my bedroom door and yawned. "Morning."

Aunt Carol stood in front of me in a pink terry robe, her dark blonde hair sporting a bed head. "Oh good, you're awake."

I stretched beneath the wrapping of my quilt. "I've been up for a while."

Beads of perspiration ran down Uncle Jim's face and his sweat-soaked jogging suit revealed he had just come back from his morning run. "We want you to go to church with us this morning, and we wanted to give you plenty of time to get ready. It is seven o'clock, and we should leave around eight. We thought we'd stop for breakfast at one of our favorite restaurants and attend the ten-thirty services." He peered over his wire-rimmed glasses. "Okay?"

After a long pause, during which I fought the urge to refuse their invitation, I drew in a deep breath and squeaked out, "Sure."

Aunt Carol scurried toward their bedroom. "That's wonderful, dear. We'll see you downstairs in an hour."

Forty-five minutes later dressed in a dark floral broom skirt, white T-shirt and high-heeled sandals, I tap-a-tapped down the stairs. A wolf whistle came from behind me followed by the clomping of heavy feet on wooden steps. "Nice."

I turned, giving David an icy stare. "Shut up."

He wore a black T-shirt emblazoned with a white cross and the words "It's about Him. It's not about me." His long black shorts sagged on his hips, and ratty black sandals completed his fashion statement.

The only church services I ever attended were Christmas Eve at the Episcopal Church with Nana. No one in that church would ever appear dressed in such an attire as this image appearing before me. I smirked. "You're wearing that to church?"

As we exited the front door, he pointed at me and mocked, "You're wearing that to church?"

I punched my cousin in the arm, stuck my tongue out at him, and giggled as I hurried ahead of him.

The fog had lifted, and the deep waters of the bay glistened beneath the Golden Gate Bridge as the morning sun welcomed a new day. The purr of the Mercedes broke through the morning quiet as Uncle Jim pulled out of the garage. David ushered me into the backseat and slid in beside me.

I could not resist the urge to tease him. "Aren't you the proper gentleman?"

"Don't get used to it."

We pulled up in front of a small restaurant with a sign in the window that read, "Best Pancakes on the Bay." Moments later, a stack of blueberry pancakes piled high with whipped cream teased my rumbling stomach. Sunbeams danced on our tabletop as the family talked and laughed through breakfast.

Then the moment shattered like a fractured mirror as I recalled my life with my family in Evergreen. A few days before the accident, we enjoyed a similar breakfast at a restaurant in Golden. The noise of clattering plates, the smoky smell of bacon, and the way the maple syrup pooled on my plate was too familiar.

Aunt Carol laid her hand on mine. "Brittany, are you okay?"

With a rumpled napkin, I wiped away an errant tear. "Sure. Yeah, I'm fine. Excuse me."

I hurried across the crowded restaurant and rushed into the restroom. Leaning against the cold metal door, I slipped the bolt. At the sink, I splashed water on my face and rubbed my cheeks with a rough paper towel.

Who was I kidding? I did not belong here with these people. I belonged nowhere.

Chapter 7

Inside the white stucco church with its stained-glass windows, dark woods, and brilliant red carpeting, Aunt Carol slipped her arm through mine. "You okay?"

"Sure."

I wanted to bolt at the first opportunity. But I swallowed my fear and smiled for my aunt's sake.

Two older women stood by the front doors handing out flyers, and two elderly men walked along the aisles placing books at the end of each row.

Aunt Carol leaned in and whispered. "I don't want you to be uncomfortable. I know Josh and Cali had their own ideas, and I respected their beliefs. I realize you didn't grow up in church."

She was so serious; I had to smile. My aunt cared more about me fitting in than I did. It seemed humor might be the best remedy to our situation and the urge to tease won out over reason. "They won't kick me out, will they?"

Aunt Carol's mouth formed an O. "Why would you think such a thing? Where did you get an idea like that?"

I'd caught her off guard, and her arched brows and wide-eyed expression were priceless. David chose that moment to step around my aunt and grab me by the hand. "It's okay, Mom. Dad said Britt could come to church with me."

The corners of Aunt Carol's mouth drooped into a pout. "I

was hoping—with this being her first time in our church—."

My cousin grinned. "Not on your life. You want to show her off to your church lady friends, and she doesn't need to go through that."

Her mouth scrunched into a deep frown. "Busted."

I did not understand where we were going, but I was certain wherever David was taking me would be better than sitting in church with Aunt Carol and Uncle Jim.

My cousin towed me along a hallway to the back of the church and opened a door into a sunlit garden. As we reached the other side, we entered a modern brick building where we stepped into an entrance decorated with large photos of kids at play.

Double doors to the left of the entry hall swung open. Two boys welcomed us as one exchanged playful punches with David. Groups of teenagers laughed and talked as band members tuned instruments on a stage.

The guys wore sagging jeans or well-worn khaki shorts. Sandals or canvas shoes with no laces complimented their fashion statement. Various designs and colors of T-shirts seemed to be the local favorite. The girls wore torn, faded jeans with crop tops or fitted T-shirts and flip-flops.

A tumble of confused thoughts and feelings overcame me. "David, I don't know."

He motioned for a petite, dark-haired girl to join us. "What don't you know?"

"This—is church?"

The girl snuggled up to David, and he dropped his arms across her shoulders. "Britt, meet Sara. Sara—Britt."

He patted Sara on the head and hurried toward the stage.

There I was in a room full of other kids, with a girl I met a few moments earlier, with no idea where I was to go or what I was to do.

Sara smiled up at me. "It's okay. You'll be fine."

"Is it that obvious?"

"Oh, yeah."

"So—you're dating David?"

A sheepish grin filled her face as her gaze followed David's movements to the front of the room. "Yeah, I guess."

"I've not seen you at Kennedy. What are your classes?"

"I don't go to Kennedy. I'm at Christian Academy."

"Where's that?"

"A few blocks from here."

Sara pointed toward two empty chairs. "Let's sit over there."

As the bass player strummed a loud chord, she introduced me to a red-haired girl sitting next to her. "Britt. This is Amy."

Amy smiled and wiggled her hand in a slight wave.

Everyone in the room stood and sang. Sara pointed to a large screen to the right of the stage that showed the lyrics to the song.

I was uncertain what I was doing, but it felt right. Everyone was smiling and singing, and I sang along to the words on a screen. The upbeat activity made me forget how uncomfortable I had been.

David was an amazing lead singer, and from time-to-time, my attention strayed from the words on the screen to watching his performance.

Sara grinned. "He's good. Isn't he?"

"I didn't know he could sing."

The third song opened with a drum solo, drawing my attention to the drummer, and I gasped when I realized it was David's friend, Kody.

At the end of the third song, a man, who looked to be in his early thirties, took the stage. "Great job, gang," he said as he clapped his hands, and the rest of us followed with applause.

"Please bow your heads for a moment of prayer," he said.

I bowed my head and listened as the man spoke, "Dear Lord, we thank You for bringing us to worship You and study Your word. We pray You will be with each one of us today and will open our hearts to what You have to teach us."

As I raised my head and opened my eyes, my heart sank as

I realized the band had left the stage.

We sat as the man took a seat on a tall stool. He introduced himself as Peter, the youth pastor. He laid his Bible on a table next to him and then clicked on a tablet.

Halfway through Peter's teaching, the sudden vibrancy of his voice caught me off guard when he said, "God loved the world so much He gave His only son to die for us." I couldn't help wondering if God loved me so much that he sacrificed his son for me, then why did He take my family.

Peter finished his teaching, and the band took the stage and played one more song. The youth pastor prayed again and then dismissed us.

As other members of the band filed from the stage and out a back door, David joined Sara and me. "So, Britt, what did you think?"

"You guys were amazing."

"Thanks, but what did you think of Peter's lesson?"

"Oh, that? Yeah, it was okay."

The truth was the message touched something deep inside me.

David returned to the stage where he and Kody wound up cords and packed instruments.

Sara tugged me through the entry hall and outside to the garden. "I had the most amazing thought," she blurted with an enthusiasm too insistent to ignore.

I stifled a chuckle at the expression created by her wide-open blue eyes and dark brows arched to her hairline. "Great. What is it?

"I'm spending the afternoon at Fisherman's Wharf with friends, and I thought you could go with us?"

I did not want to go. Despite my aunt, uncle, cousin and Millie doing all they could to make me comfortable, I still felt out of place. Now, here was this girl I met an hour ago asking me to join her and her friends for the afternoon. What if they hated me? "I don't know, Sara. Thanks for asking, but I—."

"Do you have plans?"

"Not that I know of. But I need to ask Aunt Carol."

Sara grabbed me by the hand and chatted nonstop as she led the way into the main church. "You'll have a great time. My friends are awesome. And I know they'll love you."

She released me from her grip as we reached the front lobby, and she bounded across the entry hall to where my aunt and uncle stood talking to a man I assumed was the preacher. She laid her hand on Aunt Carol's arm. "Excuse me, Pastor Kyle, but I need to talk to Mrs. Harper."

Aunt Carol turned and laid her hands upon Sara's shoulders. "Good morning to you, Sara. Why are you so excited?"

"Mrs. Harper, can Britt go with me and my friends to Fisherman's Wharf? We're going to have lunch and hang out along the pier."

Aunt Carol peeked around Sara, directing her gaze onto me. "Brittany?"

I shrugged.

"Do you want to go with Sara?"

I didn't want to go, but this girl's excitement was contagious. "Yeah, I guess."

"We don't have plans this afternoon." My aunt turned her attention to Sara. "Who is driving?"

"Mom can drop me off at your house, and we can walk to the pier from there, or we can go over a few blocks and catch a cable car."

"Sounds like a plan."

"I have to be home for supper around five or five-thirty, so I'll have her home before then."

My aunt tugged on my uncle's jacket sleeve. "I hate to interrupt you and Pastor Kyle, but we need to get going." She turned back to Sara. "You go find David and tell him to meet us at the car. What time should we expect you?"

Sara ran across the lobby, shouting back, "I'll be there in an hour."

*"Friendship is born at that moment when
one person says to another,
'What! You too?
I thought I was the only one!"*
-C.S. Lewis

Chapter 8

An hour later, I opened the door to find Sara standing on the porch brimming with excitement. "You ready?"

I was still uncertain about going, but I pasted on a smile, slung my denim bag over my shoulder, and joined her. "Let's go."

My earlier hesitation had diminished, but I held a measure of reluctance about hanging out with Sara's friends. We'd crossed over several blocks when steel tracks appeared in the street in front of us. A loud rattle-clatter and ringing bell startled me as a cable car swooped down from my right. It rattled past and continued down the hill toward the pier. I looked up to the top of the hill and then back to where the cable car had gone. "We will ride one of those?"

Sara laughed. "You've been in San Francisco for two weeks, and you haven't ridden a cable car?"

I shook my head. "No. Why?"

"Everyone does it when they come to San Francisco. They ride the cable car, visit Fisherman's Wharf, eat clam chowder and sourdough bread, eat chocolate at Ghirardelli's, and watch the sea lions."

"Ghirardelli chocolate? We buy that in Evergreen. What's the big deal?"

Her hands flew up to her cheeks as once again her eyes grew wide and her brows arched.

I soon learned this expression of amazement and excitement was common for Sara. She was a petite bundle of energy always on the edge of a new adventure. I had known the girl for only a few hours, but I couldn't help loving her. She tugged me across the street and stopped beneath a sign that read "Cable Car Stop."

"The big deal," she said, "is that the original Ghirardelli factory and flagship store are at the wharf. They closed this factory a few years back, but they have an amazing shop with every chocolate they make, and the ice cream sundaes are to die for."

"Is that what we're having for lunch?"

A whimsical grin crossed her lips. "Is that what you want for lunch?"

I shrugged and gave her a playful grin of my own. "Maybe."

"Do you like clam chowder?"

"I do."

"Ever had it with fresh clams caught the same day?"

"No." The only clam chowder I'd had was canned or frozen, but I didn't want my new friend to think I was a total hick.

"We're supposed to meet my friends at Scoma's Restaurant in about fifteen minutes. They have the best chowder on the wharf, and they serve the infamous Boudin's sourdough bread."

I pursed my lips into a teasing pout. "No chocolate sundaes?"

"We can stop at Ghirardelli's on the way home. Once you eat that sundae, you won't have room for one of Millie's fantastic dinners." Again, she assumed the *Sara expression* as her hands flew to her cheeks. "Oh wait. That's right. Millie went to her brother's today. The family will go out for dinner."

She knew an awful lot about the comings and goings of the Harper household. She was David's girlfriend, but I'd been living in that house for two weeks, and only today I learned that Millie goes to her brother's house on Sundays. "Don't worry, Sara. I can eat a lot. We can stop for ice cream, and I'll have room for dinner."

Moments later, we were on our way down the hill in true San Francisco tradition. I had to admit, it was a thrill to ride the steep incline toward the bay. My stomach quivered as I flew down the hill toward the wharf. As we climbed off the cable car, I looked up the hill. "That was fun. Can we go to the top again?"

"Maybe later. We need to hurry if we want to get to Scoma's before my friends think I've deserted them."

I hurried to keep up with Sara as she wove her way between souvenir shops and vendor booths. I had no problem with keeping pace, but my being unsure of where we were going gave her a distinct advantage. We entered the restaurant where white linen-covered tables led off in several directions.

A young waiter approached us. "Sara, it's great to see you. Your friends are waiting downstairs."

"Thanks, Charlie," Sara called back as she led me through a dark paneled dining room and down several steps. She held her hand next to her mouth and whispered back, "Charlie's two years ahead of me at CA. My friends say he's had a crush on me since my freshman year." She giggled. "He's just being nice."

Several girlish voices called out, "Over here, Sara."

We joined the other girls at a table in front of windows with a view of the docks. One girl commented that facing moored boats and boathouses was not the greatest view. I had to disagree. For a girl from a landlocked state, looking at colorful sailboats, rusting anchors, and nautical equipment was something new and interesting.

Amy, the red-haired girl from church, sat across from me. "Hey, Brittany."

Sara introduced me to a girl with dark blonde hair. "This is Krystian."

The girl smiled and offered a quick wave of her hand.

Sara pointed to the girl at the end of the table. "And that's Kelly."

With her glistening blonde hair, dark thick lashes, and flawless complexion, she could have stepped out of a fashion magazine. She looked me over, tilted her head to one side, and offered a chilly, "Hey."

The chowder and bread were the best. Sara and Amy carried the conversation through lunch while Krystian smiled and added a few comments whenever she could. Kelly said little and occasionally shot me a disgusting glare.

I had just met her. How could she dislike me?

After lunch, we walked to the far end of the pier and strolled barefoot along the shore in front of the Maritime Museum. Kelly slipped off by herself while the rest of us talked, laughed, and dipped our toes in the chilling surf.

A half-hour later, Krystian suggested we return to the other end of the wharf and shop.

Amy called out, "Kelly. We're heading back."

She kicked at the sand and trod with slow steps toward us but kept an obvious distance.

I leaned over and whispered to Sara, "What's with Kelly? Was it something I said?"

Sara stopped and looked back. "Hey Kelly. You okay?"

The girl shrugged.

I walked on with Amy and Krystian while Sara dropped back to walk with Kelly.

"You guys go on, Sara said. "We'll catch up with you at Captain Jack's."

"Don't worry about her," Amy said. "She gets like that."

Krystian huffed. "She's bummed because she's not the center of attention."

I shrugged, thinking it best to keep my thoughts to myself. I didn't want to say anything they might repeat to Kelly. It was obvious she didn't like my company. However, Krystian and Amy made me feel welcome, so I tried to overlook the negative.

We gathered at Captain Jack's Souvenir Shop, where I bought a bracelet and postcards to send back home. From there we visited a few shops selling various kinds of clothes, and then we spent an hour watching the sea lions at the end of the wharf.

Sara pushed back from the wooden railing. "I promised Britt we'd stop for sundaes at Ghirardelli's and ride the cable car before we head home. So, we need to get going."

While Kelly kept her attention riveted on the sea lions, the rest of us said our goodbyes. Sara and I headed for Ghirardelli's, my mouth salivating in anticipation.

"For one to fly, one needs only to take the reins."
-Melissa James

Chapter 9

My second week at Kennedy ended, and it had gone well. David and I shared an English class and a chemistry class. He helped me find my way around and introduced me to several classmates.

The high school was a quick drive through Golden Gate Park. I grew accustomed to David's Christian music blasting away as we cruised through the acreage of green, passing by museums and the botanical gardens.

One afternoon, as we exited the park, he slowed and turned left. "I've got something I want to show you."

We passed a directional sign to Golden Gate Park Stables. My nose picked up the faint smell of manure, and the white fence confirmed my suspicions. "Horses?"

He nodded.

A warm glow flowed through me. "There are stables in San Francisco? I didn't know you rode."

A muscle quivered at his jaw. "It's not my thing."

"I can't believe it—horses in San Francisco."

David pulled the car to a stop in the parking lot, and I bolted toward a training ring where a young man worked a black Arabian. As I drew closer, I recognized the trainer.

"Hey Kody," David called out.

Kody brought the Arabian to a halt. "I told the stable hand you'd be here soon. He should have the horses saddled and waiting for you at the barn. I'll meet you up there."

I spotted the barn behind a long row of stables. As I hurried in that direction, David shouted, "Britt, wait."

We entered the building where a large man wearing a dark blue jumpsuit approached us. "Hey David. It's been awhile. I saddled Jenny for you. She's a sweet baby. You shouldn't have any problems."

A chestnut mare and palomino gelding stood tethered about ten feet away. I assumed the mare was Jenny.

Stepping with care, I ran my fingers through the ivory mane of the gelding. "And what do they call you?"

The stable hand came up behind me. "That's Romeo."

I chuckled. "Romeo?"

"He likes the ladies." The man stroked the horse on his hindquarter. "Don't you, boy?"

With hesitant steps, David slipped around to the side of Jenny and grabbed the saddle horn. The man stepped up behind him. "Need a push?"

"No," he said in a grudging voice.

The man smiled at me. "I understand you know your way around horses."

My heartbeat quickened as I anticipated climbing in the saddle. "I have my horse in Colorado, and I grew up on a ranch."

Within seconds, with reins in hand, I settled into the saddle. "Where we headed?"

Kody appeared at the open barn door on the black Arabian. "Follow me."

It was a thrill to be riding again. We traveled along a pathway that wound through the park, and occasional saltwater breezes tickled my nose.

When we arrived at an open grassy overlook above the pounding surf, Kody dismounted. "Let's stop here."

He tethered the Arabian to a tree limb and stepped up next to David, who remained astride Jenny. "You want help."

"No."

I dismounted and Kody laid his arm across my shoulder, sending a tingle through my spine. "The last time David and I

36

went riding—let's say his dismount wasn't very graceful."

I stifled a chuckle as I visualized my cousin landing on his backside. One glance into Kody's deep brown eyes, my heart skipped a beat, and I stammered, "What's your horse's name?"

"Shahrazad, like in the *Arabian Nights*, but he's not mine. I take care of him."

This was the first time I'd been this close to Kody. With his mussed black hair, and coppery complexion—he was gorgeous. Watching him work the Arabian, his arm muscles bulging beneath his T-shirt, reminded me of a rock star.

David dismounted, landing on his feet with a thud. "So, are you ready for Sunday, Kody? We can get an hour or two of practice in tonight if you think we need it."

Working to hide my sudden preoccupation with Kody, I took a seat on a large boulder. The view of the ocean was amazing. As I sat and soaked in the warm afternoon sun, my thoughts shifted from Kody to my beautiful mare, Mariah. I held my tears in check as I recalled charging across the pasture, riding bareback through the forest, ducking under low hanging limbs, jumping the creek.

The sun sank lower on the horizon as footsteps crunched in the gravel. David laid his hand on my shoulder. "We need to get going. I promised Mom we'd be home by five." His cell phone sounded reveille, and he retrieved it from his jeans' pocket and punched a button. "Hey Sara."

I mounted Romeo and pulled up next to Kody. I swallowed hard as I worked at casual conversation. "Shaharazad is a beautiful animal. Do you have your own horse?"

"No. I work at the stables, and one bonus is I get to exercise the horses. The owners want me to ride."

With his horse in tow, David joined us. "Sara wants to know if you two want to come with us for a pizza and a movie."

Kody worked his bottom lip. "I don't know."

"Don't worry," David said. "I got it. Do you want to go?"

"Sure. I guess." Kody looked at me. "Are you going?"

Uncertain if Kody's hesitancy was because of me or something else, I didn't know what to say. "I guess."

David returned to his call. "Yeah Sara, they're in. When should we pick you up?" He paused for an answer. "See you then."

He clicked off the call. "We need to get home and clean up. We're picking Sara up at six."

Back in the barn, I unsaddled Romeo. As I brushed him down, I overheard Kody and David's voices in the stall next to me. Kody whispered, "Thanks for covering me tonight. I spent my last paycheck on a new jacket for Larry."

"It's not a problem. But you've got to stop spending your money on the others and take care of yourself."

"I know, but Larry's old, and he can't do much to make any money. I'll get by."

I leaned in closer to listen. I'd not seen this side of my cousin. I knew he cared about his friends, but for him to pay for Kody to go out with us was excessive, even for a bud.

And what about Kody? Why would a boy his age buy a coat for an old man?

"Love, free as air at sight of human ties,
spreads his light wings and in a moment flies."
-Alexander Pope

Chapter 10

David and I arrived home forty-five minutes before we were to pick up Sara and Kody. I flew up the stairs and into my room. I stripped away my clothes that reeked of the horse and then spent ten minutes in front of the closet deciding what to wear. Denim skirt and shirt? Jeans and T-shirt? Denim skirt and T-shirt? Jeans and tank? Cotton skirt and middy? I decided on my pink skirt and white middy with my denim jacket. Sandals? Tennis shoes? Boots? What was I going to wear on my first date with Kody?

David knocked at my door. "When will you be ready?"

I looked at my watch. It was five thirty.

Another knock. "Britt?"

Wrapped in my robe, I grabbed my clothes and sandals, opened the door, crossed the hall to the bathroom, and stopped for a second in front of David. "I need at least another thirty minutes."

He rolled his eyes and threw up his hands. "We don't have thirty minutes."

I closed the door. "Why don't you go pick them up and then come back and get me?"

His sandals clomped on the wooden steps as he began his descent. "You think you can be ready by then?"

I opened the bathroom door a crack. "I'll try."

My next decision was which soap and shampoo to use from the variety of fragrances Millie had stocked in my bathroom.

Deciding on the jasmine soap and scented shampoo, I hurried through my shower.

What to do with my hair? Up? Down? Pulled to the side? My heart fluttered, and I squealed as I smiled into the mirror and whispered to my reflection. "I've got a date with Kody."

I left my hair down, pushed behind my ears, and then I worked at my makeup. Not over done. Natural looking. Yeah. That's right. A little blush. Light pink lipstick.

"Britt? Are you ready?" David shouted from downstairs.

I grabbed my jacket, pulled my bag onto my shoulder, inhaled a deep breath, and hurried downstairs.

Sara met me halfway and looked up at me. Her standing several steps below stressed the height difference. "You look fantastic," she whispered and winked.

Kody's brown eyes glistened, and the glow of his smile warmed me from across the room. "Hey Britt."

I found it impossible not to return his disarming smile. "Hey Kody."

He took my jacket, wrapped it around me, and looked me over as if he was taking my picture with his eyes. "It's getting chilly. You'll need this."

I reached up to tug the jacket onto my left shoulder. His fingers felt warm and strong as his hand touched mine.

David and Sara waited on the front porch as Kody and I stood in the open doorway.

"You two coming, or are you going to stand there all night?" David teased.

The theater was only a short drive, but the time alone in the backseat with Kody was unnerving.

He stayed on his side of the car and drummed his fingers on the window, which he stared out of through most of the ride.

In front of the ticket counter, we debated for at least fifteen minutes before agreeing to see *Avengers: Infinity War*.

After the movie, we walked to the pizza place next door, and within seconds agreed on toppings and crust, whether it was because we all liked the same pizza or our stomachs were rumbling, I was uncertain. However, it was a great pizza.

It seemed we'd only been there a short while, when the manager approached our table and asked, "Will you folks be heading out soon? I hate to rush you, but my people need to go home."

A quick glance at my watch, and I gasped. "Oh my gosh. It's after midnight."

David handed the manager a wad of money. "I'm sorry. We didn't realize it was so late." He pulled out his cell phone and punched in a number. "Mom. Yeah. Sorry. We lost track of time." He nodded at her response. "I have to drop Sara and Kody off, and then we'll be home. Shouldn't be over thirty minutes." He paused again. "Yeah, sure." He clicked off his phone and looked at Sara.

She had her phone at her ear. "Yeah Mom. We're leaving the pizza place now. I'll be home soon. Sorry." She paused. "Yeah, he did."

She looked up at David. "She wanted to know if you called your mom."

David grinned. "Yeah, my mom asked if you called yours."

Sara clicked off her call to her mother.

I looked at Kody. "Need to call your folks?"

He hesitated and lowered his thick black lashes. "No. It's okay." He shot David an odd glance. "They're out of town."

There was a telltale tone in his reply, and I thought about questioning him about his parents. However, I did not want to spoil the evening by prying. I shrugged. "Whatever."

Chapter 11

The next morning, wrapped in my quilt, I snuggled in the corner of the window seat and checked my phone. There were several voicemail messages and a text. I had avoided friends and family from back home. Whenever I hung up after talking to them, the raw sores of my aching heart made me wish I had not taken their calls.

The text was from Uncle Scott. "All fine at the ranch. I miss you."

I punched back. "Miss you too."

Uncle Scott didn't reply, so I texted a friend in Evergreen. "What's up?"

No reply.

"Britt? You up?" David's voice bellowed through my closed door.

I clicked off my phone and tossed it on the bed.

"I'm awake. When do we need to leave?"

"Thirty minutes max."

Ten minutes later, I stood at the kitchen island eating a toaster pastry and drinking a glass of milk.

Millie shook her head. "You kids need a better breakfast. I can have omelets ready in a few minutes. You can't wait that long?"

David grabbed a pack of Pop Tarts and a can of juice and

headed out the back door. "Gotta run. We need to get to the church to load up for the barbecue."

I kissed Millie on the cheek as I hurried through the kitchen. I was growing fond of Millie. She reminded me of Nana, but in a louder more citified way.

The small parking lot at Bayside Community Church buzzed with activity. Uncle Jim and three other men loaded barbecue grills in the back of a pickup truck. A group of boys stacked folding tables and chairs into a church van. David and I entered the kitchen where several women loaded us with boxes of sandwich buns and bags of chips. They told us to put them in Mrs. Warren's car. However, I did not know who Mrs. Warren was or where she'd parked her vehicle, so I balanced my assigned load and followed David.

He slid his box into the back of a white SUV. "I've got to help get the stage and instruments loaded. Can you load this stuff?"

"Sure."

As I exited the building for the third time, I collided into Sara who carried a stack of empty cardboard boxes. Setting my load on the pavement, I helped her collect her cargo, now scattered across the sidewalk. "Sorry. Guess I wasn't paying attention to where I was going."

"I hoped I'd run into you." She grinned. "But not literally. Did you have fun last night?"

"Yeah, I did. That was great pizza. And the movie was awesome. I loved the special effects."

With an inquisitive grin she asked, "And what about Kody?"

"What about him?"

She peeked around the corner of one box. "Did he make another date?"

Unwelcomed warmth crept into my cheeks. "No. Why?"

Aunt Carol came through the doorway. "Brittany? Sara? Are you ready to go?"

"Give me a second to take these boxes inside," Sara said.

I picked up the last box of sandwich buns. "Let me put these in Mrs. Warren's car, and I'll be ready. But I thought we were riding with David and Kody."

Aunt Carol unlocked her Lexus. "Since David's relegated to driving the equipment van for the worship team, he asked me to give you two a lift."

We'd no more buckled up in the backseat of Aunt Carol's car, when Sara quirked a smile "So?"

"So—what?" I said.

"Are you going out with him?"

"No. I don't know. He didn't ask."

"I'll talk to David."

"No. Please don't do that." The volume of my voice elevated with each word.

"Is something wrong, Brittany?" Aunt Carol said.

"No, nothing's wrong." I turned back to Sara and whispered, "Please, promise me you won't do that."

"Calm down. I thought you liked him."

Thirty minutes later, Aunt Carol pulled into a parking spot in front of where David stood with several band members. Sara jumped out of the car and ran to my cousin, throwing her arms around his waist as if she had not seen him for months.

I exited my side of the car and caught up with Aunt Carol as she hurried across the road. My cheeks remained warm from my conversation with Sara. I did not want to face Kody. As we reached the others, he rounded the corner of the church van and slammed into me.

"Sorry." He grabbed my shoulders to steady me.

I stepped back, and he dropped his hands. "No problem." I worked to throttle the dizzying current racing through me.

In my haste to put distance between Kody and me, I ran smack into Uncle Jim. "Brittany, where are you going in such a hurry?"

"I need to help Aunt Carol unpack the food."

"Your face is flushed."

I ran my hands across my cheeks, pushing my hair back

from my face. "It's hot."

"Why don't you go sit and let the rest of us unload?"

I glanced to a shaded space where several men were setting up grills. A vacant picnic table looked like the perfect escape. "Okay." Folding my arms on the tabletop, I lowered my head to rest. Several moments later, someone plopped on the seat across from me. I raised my head and came face-to-face with Kody.

He smelled good. He looked good. A patchwork puzzle of frenzied emotion overtook me.

He reached a hand across the table and touched my forearm. "Are you avoiding me?"

"No. Why?"

"I like you, Britt. I like you a lot."

His touch sent ripples through my spine. "I like you too, Kody."

David and Sara ran up to us, laughing and out of breath.

"What's up?" Sara said.

Kody winked. "Nothing, I guess."

"Be strong and courageous.
Do not be afraid or terrified
because of them, for the Lord
your God goes with you; he
will never forsake you"
Deuteronomy 31:6

Chapter 12

At least two hundred guests came to the barbecue, and most of them were homeless people looking for a meal and conversation. Uncle Jim and three other men handled the grilling. Sara and I helped Aunt Carol set up tables and serve. The youth band entertained the crowd for several hours with Christian and popular tunes.

There beneath the canopy of green, I felt no fear or aversion as I had the first time I visited. David was right when he said we were the same. Three or four women shared their stories with me, and my heart broke for them. Others asked questions about Colorado and the mountains.

Many hands made light work of cleaning up and loading the trucks as the afternoon sun drifted toward the horizon. David and Kody left with the equipment van, and most of the volunteers headed back to town. A couple dozen homeless folks sat at picnic tables visiting and playing board games.

Aunt Carol and a friend went for a walk, and they had not yet returned. Uncle Jim rat-a-tapped his fingers on the table. "I can't imagine where they could have gone they're not back yet and she isn't answering her phone."

"Mrs. Harper said they were walking over to the shoreline," Sara said. "Britt and I can look for them."

Uncle Jim gripped his cell phone. "Thanks, Sara. You two go south, and I'll go north. Brittany, do you have your cell phone with you?"

I pulled it from my jeans pocket. "Yeah, sure."

"Call me if you find them, and I'll call you if I do." He rubbed at the late day stubble on his chin. "If you don't catch up to them in the next hour, meet back here."

"I know a shortcut," Sara said as she trudged ahead of me into a thicket of shrubbery.

"Are we going in the right direction? Uncle Jim said for us to go south."

"Yeah, I'm sure. I've gone this way lots of times. We are heading south, I think." Sara shot me a knowing grin. "So, what was that with you and Kody?"

I recalled his hand on mine, and his telling me he liked me. Warmth flooded my cheeks as I remembered telling him I liked him too. "Just talking."

"He was holding your hand."

I nudged her to move ahead. "We can talk about Kody at another time. We need to find Aunt Carol."

We emerged on a narrow trail, and there in front of us were Eric Preston and Jeremy Sherwood, the infamous bullies from my school. Eric stood at least six foot four and wore a long, black duster. Motorcycle boots, black jeans, and black T-shirts were his everyday attire. With his tattooed eyeliner and black nails, Jeremy was into the Goth thing. Shorter than Eric, what Jeremy lacked in height, he made up for in girth.

I resolved not to allow them to bully us, so I stepped around Sara and took the lead.

"What have we here?" Eric said as he blocked the path in front of us. "It's our new girl from Colorado."

He grabbed my arm. I lifted my chin to meet his icy gaze straight on and struggled to free myself. "Keep your hands off me, Eric."

"Oh, did you hear what she said, Jeremy? She knows my name." He tightened his grip and pulled me closer.

Jeremy grabbed hold of Sara. She struggled to get loose. With her blue eyes blazing, she faced him with fury. Screaming and clawing like a wild woman, she at last succumbed to his strength as he pulled her with him to the ground.

Her cries for help unleashed something within me. With my free hand, I worked to grab my cell phone from my back pocket. Eric tightened his grip and reached for my other arm. I bit his hand. He screamed obscenities and shoved me, sending my phone flying into undergrowth and me sprawling on the gravel path.

"You got yourself a wild one there, Eric," Jeremy said.

I feared Sara was unconscious as her body lay crushed beneath Jeremy's bulk.

Eric flopped on top of me. "So, you want to fight, huh? I'll give you a fight."

His mouth covered mine as he forced my arms against the sharp stones. Mounting rage seethed within me as I struggled against him.

My phone rang and stopped. Seconds later, it rang again and stopped.

Was that Uncle Jim? How could I let them know we were in trouble?

Sara's weak screams for help grew stronger until her pleading cries reverberated through the air. Jeremy held his hand over her mouth and then swore as he jerked away a bloody palm. She screamed, "Help."

I pushed against Eric's prone body to shove him from me and then clawed at his neck. I shouted, "Help us. Please help us."

Quick footsteps in gravel stomped in the distance. I screamed, and Eric smacked me. The metallic taste of blood flooded my mouth.

Jeremy rose to his feet, leaving Sara curled up in a ball on the ground. "Let's get out of here. Somebody's coming."

As they ran between a clump of trees, Jeremy shouted, "This isn't over. We'll get both of you."

From a short distance, Eric's threat came back loud and clear. "And if you tell anyone—we'll make you sorry."

Two young men I had seen at the barbecue came to our rescue. One started toward our attackers. The other man kneeled by my side and shouted, "Come on back. You'll never catch them."

Sara rocked back and forth and sobbed as the rescuer who'd started after Eric and Jeremy worked to calm her.

Pointing to the dense weeds with one hand, I touched my swollen lip with the other. "My phone is over there somewhere."

My rescuer found it and placed it in my hand.

I was on my feet, shaky, but standing. Punching in Uncle Jim's number, I swallowed hard and forced my voice to calm. "Uncle Jim. It's Brittany."

"Brittany," his voice broke. "Are you okay? I tried to call, but it went to your voicemail."

"Yes, we're fine." I fought against the tears. "Did you find Aunt Carol?"

"They were on their way back. We're waiting for you at the table where we stacked our things."

"We'll be right there." I clicked off my phone and turned to thank the two men, but they'd left. "Where did they go?"

Sara ran her hand over scratches on her cheek. "I bent over to pick up my phone, and when I stood up, they'd disappeared."

What were we going to tell Uncle Jim and Aunt Carol? There was no hiding this busted lip and Sara's scrapes, but we could not tell them the truth.

"13 Therefore put on the full armor of God, so that
when the day of evil comes, you may be able to
stand your ground, and after you have done
everything, to stand. 14 Stand firm then, with the
belt of truth buckled around your waist,
with the breastplate of righteousness in place,
15 and with your feet fitted with the readiness
that comes from the gospel of peace.
16 In addition to all this, take up the shield of faith,
with which you can extinguish all
the flaming arrows of the evil one.
17 Take the helmet of salvation and the sword of the Spirit,
which is the word of God."
Ephesians 6:13-17

Chapter 13

During the drive to school on Monday morning, something
rotten held my heart.

How was I going to avoid Eric and Jeremy? I'd seen them
at lunch a few times, so I knew they had the same lunch break I
had.

"You okay?" David asked as we passed the botanical
gardens.

I jerked in surprise as he pulled me from my thoughts.
"Yeah. Fine."

"You're awful quiet."

"Just tired."

He laughed. "You napped most of yesterday afternoon.
Since you left your bedroom door open, I checked on you a
couple times. I figured you were asleep."

"I'm fine."

"Your lip looks better today." He glanced over and then back to the road. "Yep, it's hardly noticeable."

I huffed with impatience at his concern. "I'm not worried about my lip."

He cranked up his music and gripped the steering wheel.

"Okay. Got it. You don't want to talk."

"I'm sorry. I didn't mean to bark."

He lowered the music volume. "I get it. You're tired." He smiled. "It's okay."

When we arrived at the school parking lot, I tried hard to dredge up a smile for David. He was trying to be extra nice, and I was being a drag. As he hurried to catch up with two other friends, he waved at me.

I shuffled through the hall to my first period class feeling as if I walked through a hostile valley. Eric and Jeremy could be anywhere. Other kids chatted and hurried passed. Morning sunlight filtered through the high-set windows casting sunbeams onto the shiny tile floor.

I breathed a sigh of relief as I took my seat, and my English teacher closed the door. There was no way I could absorb any of her lecture on Hemingway while my mind still blazed with the memory of Saturday. I couldn't let them do this. It wasn't fair. What was it Peter said? It was something about a helmet, sword, and shield, and how God would protect me.

I jumped in my seat as the period bell rang. Now I needed to get to my locker and then to calculus class without running into them. The outdoor route across campus circumvented the hallways.

Safe in my calculus class, I relaxed when the teacher closed the door. The memory still lingered on the edges of my mind, and it was difficult to focus on the lesson. A jumble of fear and anger occupied my thoughts. I had to talk to Sara.

One more period before lunch. Someone could go with me to the coffee shop on the corner. I'd be off campus and around lots of people.

Chemistry was two rooms away from my calculus class. I

scanned the hall before exiting, and then with a crazy mixture of hope and fear, I hurried to class.

I passed through the door and from behind heard, "Boo." Panic rioted within me. I scurried into the classroom, took my seat, and looked up to see David standing in the doorway.

He sat next to me. "Hey, Britt. I'm sorry. I didn't mean to scare you."

Tears welled up, and I swiped at them.

He leaned on my desk. "You okay?" He hesitated and looked around the room. "You look sick. You should go home."

I nodded and sniffed. "That might be a good idea."

"Call Mom. She'll come and get you."

Twenty minutes later, I settled on a bench in front of the school. I felt safer sitting where anyone who passed saw me. Within a few minutes, Aunt Carol pulled up to the curb, and I hurried to the car.

Her soothing voice probed, "What is it, Brittany? What's wrong? You said you weren't feeling well. Do you think it's from your fall on Saturday?"

I whispered, "I need to lie down."

"If I call the doctor now, they might get you in today—or at least tomorrow."

I shook my head. "I'm just tired."

Aunt Carol seemed to know when I needed time and space to work through something. So, she asked no more questions the rest of the way home. We pulled into the garage, and before my aunt turned off the ignition, I hurried from the car and into the house.

Snuggled in my quilt on the window seat, I texted Sara, "Need 2 talk."

She came back. "Me 2."

"Come here?"

"B there by 4."

"K."

I curled up on the bed. Aunt Carol called in a soft voice

from the hall, "Brittany? Can I come in?"

"Sure."

She sat on the edge of my bed, running her hand along my hip. "I thought maybe it's your time of the month, and you were having cramps. My cramps were horrid when I was your age. And I'd get sick to my stomach. I have pills that could help."

"No. It's not that."

She laid her hand on my forehead. "No fever. That's good."

"I'll be fine."

As she stepped toward the open doorway, I remembered. "Sara's coming over around four. Send her to my room, please?"

She offered me a reassuring smile and nodded.

The next few hours dragged as I waited for Sara. No matter the situation, she could make me laugh.

At four o'clock on the dot, Sara bounded into my room. "Hey girl." She plopped on the bed next to me. Her glistening, blue eyes held a sadness to which I could relate.

"What are we going to do?" I said.

She shrugged. "I don't know. What do you think they'll do if we tell?"

"Who can we tell?"

"If I tell my folks, my dad will hunt them down and shoot them before the cops get called."

I chuckled at the image of Mr. Alexander searching the streets of San Francisco in camouflage, carrying a shotgun. "Uncle Jim would have the authorities on it right now, and he'd call in all kinds of favors from his friends in the mayor's office."

"It would be our word against theirs. You know they'd deny it happened."

Tides of weariness and despair engulfed my body. "I wish they weren't at school. At least, I would feel safe when I'm there. But with them on campus, I know I could run into them."

Sara wrapped her arms around me and pulled me close.

"I'm sorry."

"Why are you sorry?"

"That you have to deal with them at school, and I don't."

Fear and rage transformed into a determined sense of vengeance. I rallied to my knees, my feet beneath my bottom. "I know how to stop them."

Sara assumed her wide-eyed expression. "How?"

"A Taser. Yeah. I'll buy a Taser. Then if they get close, I'll let them have it."

Sara grinned. "So—where do we shop for a Taser?"

*"Anger is a legitimate feeling, one
often designed for self-protection."*
— Kimberlee Roth

Chapter 14

Saturday morning, Sara and I canvassed the streets of the city
to find a shop that sold Tasers. In front of a rundown
storefront, Sara asked a guy in a black hoodie and ratty jeans,
"Hey buddy, do you know where we can get a Taser?"

I stifled a giggle at her tough-girl routine.

The guy let out a howl of laughter. "Oh, you're priceless.
Yes, princess, I do."

He led the way to the corner of Haight and Ashbury, where
through a few inquiries of street people, we learned since I was
over sixteen, I could purchase a nonlethal stun gun, but I would
need a consent form signed by my parents.

Discouraged and ready to head back up the hill, our
newfound friend flagged down a bald guy. "Hey Gus."

Gus offered a half-toothless grin. "Hey man, ain't seen you
for a while. Where you been?"

"Around. You still hang with that guy that sells stuff'

Gus eyed Sara and me. "Who are your little ladies? Looks
like you're movin' up in the world."

Our new friend chuckled, "I took pity on them."

"What are you lookin' to buy?"

"They're wantin' a Taser."

Gus laughed. "Yeah. I'm sure." He coughed then lit up a
cigarette. "He's workin' legit now. Got a shop over there on
the corner. He can hook 'em up."

I whispered to Sara, "I'm not sure about this. It sounds like we're breaking the law. Maybe we should forget about it."

Too late. Sara was in the middle of an adventure, and she was not ready to let it go. "Are you crazy? This is awesome. Come on. Did Eric or Jeremy stop because they were breaking the law?"

Since her argument held logic, I nodded. We followed the men to the store on the corner and entered a dark, moldy-smelling room. An old man with several days' beard growth stood behind the counter. "Gus, you bringin' me customers off the street now? Next you'll want me to pay you for advertisin'."

Gus coughed and took a drag on his cigarette. "These little ladies are lookin' to buy a Taser. Can you help 'em?"

The man chuckled. "Come on up, and I'll show you what I got. Can't sell you a Taser. I'd put myself in a world of hurt doin' that. But I have some stun guns I can sell you, and I can misplace the paperwork with your parents signin'."

Sara hurried ahead of me then returned and dragged me to the dirty glass case.

"I got this here lipstick stunner. I can sell it to you for fifty bucks. You tryin' to hurt somebody bad or you wantin' them to leave you alone?"

I cleared my throat. "We want them to leave us alone."

"This should do the trick."

He opened the box and lay what looked like a tube of lipstick on the counter, except I had never had a lipstick with a wrist strap. He pulled off the lid and clicked a button. It appeared to be an LED flashlight.

I had my doubts about this being a stun gun. "What's that going to do?"

He clicked it again and tapped it on Gus's arm. I heard the zap, then Gus's arm jerked, and he howled in pain.

The man grinned. "That's what it does."

Gus supported himself on the cabinet and rubbed at his arm. The man behind the counter smiled with more gaps than teeth, reminding me of a jack-o'-lantern.

With the lipstick tube in my bag, Sara and I hurried to a cable car stop and rode the clattering vehicle up the hill.

David and Kody had practice with the worship team that morning, and we were to meet them at the house around noon to go riding. It was a quarter to twelve when we burst through the front door.

Sara giggled as we ran up the stairs. "That was fun."

"I guess, but I'm glad to be out of there. I wasn't sure about those guys."

She popped a piece of gum in her mouth. "They were different."

David appeared in the doorway to the living room. "What was fun and what guys?"

Sara chomped on her gum and rolled her eyes showing I needed to get us out of this one.

"We were walking around the city. It is interesting, the different neighborhoods and all. You know. There are those cruddy places down in Haight-Ashbury, then you've got those painted lady houses over by the park. We met some interesting people."

Kody came in. "What were you two doing down in the Haight?"

I shrugged then grabbed Sara by the hand and advanced up the staircase. "We need to get changed to go riding. See you in a minute."

By the time we reached my room, David and Kody were at the foot of the steps. "The man asked you a question," David called.

*"I followed my heart
and it led me to the beach."*
-Anonymous

Chapter 15

The last weeks of school passed without incident. I carried the stunner with me wherever I went, but Eric and Jeremy seemed to have disappeared. Rumor was they got in some trouble and their folks took them out of school saying they were taking vacation early. Some students said they heard Eric and Jeremy were spending their summer vacation in the juvenile detention center. I didn't care where they were as long as they were far away from me.

The Friday before Memorial Day, we packed Aunt Carol's SUV tight with groceries and luggage.

"You sure you have everything?" Uncle Jim teased.

My aunt pulled out a checklist and ran her finger down the side. "Yep, got it all."

Millie settled into the backseat behind Uncle Jim, while David, Kody, Sara, and I piled into David's convertible. "We've got a little room in the trunk if you've got anything else," David said.

"Let's get this show on the road," Uncle Jim shouted as he started the engine. "Dillon Beach, here we come."

The memory of the beautiful house, the wild ocean, crashing waves, and white beaches brewed an excitement within me. "I can't wait." I nudged Kody. "Have you been there?"

"A few times."

"Sara?"

"A few times, but my folks wouldn't let me come without them. The only reason they agreed this time was because you were going."

"What difference does that make?"

She sighed. "It wouldn't look proper for me to go alone with David."

"Aunt Carol, Uncle Jim, and Millie will be there too."

"Who knows?" She turned to face me. "I'm just glad they're letting me go."

Until now, I'd not realized Sara's parents were so strict. I'd never met them, but Sara seemed to go wherever she wanted whenever she wanted.

I changed the subject. "Who else is coming to this Memorial Day shindig?"

"Some of Mom and Dad's friends from the club and church."

"Are they staying all weekend too?"

"They won't stay with us. Some of them have houses on the beach. Some rent places. I guess they'll be staying close by."

"Will there be other kids besides us?"

"Yeah. There will be kids our age. But most are younger."

We crossed over the Golden Gate Bridge with its bright orange girders as the roadway clunk-a-clunked beneath us. Under a cloudless sky, wind surfers, boats, and barges drifted along. Joggers, bikers, and tourists filled the walkways on either side.

"Busy place," I said.

David sighed. "Yep, it's official. Tourist season has begun. Check out all the new T-shirts."

I stared at the people walking across the bridge to my right. "New T-shirts?"

"That's how you spot a tourist. New T-shirts, kids carrying bags of junk. It's great for the economy, but it's crazy for those of us who live here."

"I'm glad your folks let us come along," Kody said.

"Yeah, I'm a little surprised they agreed. It's kind of like Sara said, it's because of Britt."

I still didn't understand why my presence mattered. "Me?"

"They let Kody come with me a couple times last year. Mom and Dad expect me to leave my city friends behind and reconnect with kids at the beach. Those kids are okay, but it's not the same as hangin' with you guys."

"So, what does my going to the beach house have to do with them letting Sara and Kody come?"

"They want to make sure you have a good time."

I smiled at Kody and shrugged. He dropped his arm across my shoulders and grinned.

*"The loss of young first love is so painful
that it borders on the ludicrous."*
-Maya Angelou

Chapter 16

Saturday and Sunday were peaceful. Sara and I took walks along the beach, painted our nails, and recorded crazy videos. David and Kody spent most of their time playing video games or surfing.

Late Sunday afternoon, I sat on the deck with my feet propped up on a chair to dry my toenails. David and Kody, dressed neck-to-toes in wet suits, came running around the corner of the house.

"That water's freezing today," Kody said.

David propped his board against the deck rail and peeled away his outer layer. "Oh, that sun feels good! You're right, dude. I don't know why, but it was a lot colder today."

Sara entered from the back door carrying a tray with two glasses and a pitcher of lemonade. "Oh, you're back."

"Too cold," David said.

She set the tray on a round table in the seating area. "I didn't expect you back for hours. Your mom offered to drive Britt and me into town to shop."

I leaned over the rail to talk to Kody. Hanging with Sara was fun, but I'd missed having Kody around. Bracing my hands on his shoulders, I whispered. "I'm glad you're back."

Sara huffed. "So, I guess this means you don't want to go shopping."

"If you don't mind, I'd rather hang with Kody."

"No. Not at all." She turned on her heel. "I'll tell Mrs. Harper we don't want to go."

David caught Sara by the shoulder. "What's wrong?"

"Nothing."

It was obvious something was wrong, but I'd noticed Sara copped an attitude whenever David and Kody were around. She and my cousin disappeared inside, and Kody took a seat next to me. "What's up with her?"

I shrugged, "No idea."

****

On Memorial Day morning, the beach house filled with activity. Uncle Jim and some other men set up a pig roaster in the backyard and worked to get the hog installed and basted. Aunt Carol scurried about the house straightening and fussing. In the kitchen, Millie prepared large bowls and trays of food.

Entering Millie's domain, I surveyed the controlled chaos before me. "Can I help?"

Millie looked up. "Sure, but don't you want breakfast first?"

"Do we have any cereal?"

She scrunched her brow. "I think we do." She opened a cupboard door. "Sugar Pops, Corn Flakes, Rice Krispies?"

"Sugar Pops."

She handed me a bowl, plopped down a small box of cereal, and handed me a spoon. "The milk is on the counter."

Sara took a seat at the table. Still in her flannel pants and tank, she stretched and yawned, then ruffled her bed-head with both hands. "What's for breakfast, Millie?"

I set my bowl of cereal in front of her. "Sugar Pops. Eat up. Millie's busy."

Sara scrunched her nose. "You've got to be kidding."

Grabbing another box of cereal, a bowl, and a spoon, I sat across the table from my friend. "No. Millie has enough to do with getting ready for the party without her cooking breakfast. I'm sure, if we'd gotten up earlier, we could have eaten with Aunt Carol and Uncle Jim, but since we slept in, we'll eat cold

62

cereal."

David and Kody padded in on bare feet. "Wow, cereal. We haven't had cereal in forever," David said. "Do we have any Count Chocula?"

Millie returned to the cupboard and pulled out an unopened, full-size box of Count Chocula. She set out two more bowls and spoons then returned to her preparation of party food.

David ripped open the box like a little kid then filled his bowl to the top. "Mom doesn't let me have this stuff. She says its junk food. But sometimes Millie lets me have it."

Sara eyed David with a look of disgust. "You're kidding, right?"

"No. I love it."

Kody poured himself some cereal and took a seat. When he smiled at me and winked, the realization hit me. I was still wearing my flannel pants and tank, no bra, my robe hanging open, no make-up, and my hair had to be a mess. I jumped up from the table. "Excuse me."

Around noon, the guests arrived. Aunt Carol scheduled dinner for six o'clock, but Millie kept everyone fed with all kinds of snacks. A large container in the backyard held iced soft drinks and bottled water. The volleyball net was set up on one side of the yard and a croquet course on the other.

Every time I turned around, Sara was behind or next to me. I dropped my arm across her shoulders, "Don't you want to hang out with David?"

She grinned. "Trying to get rid of me?"

"No, but I'd think you'd rather be with him than with me."

"Would you rather be with Kody?"

I wasn't sure what she was getting at, but she'd been acting strange for the last two days. "What's with you?"

"David doesn't treat me like Kody treats you."

"What?"

"Kody's always making google eyes at you, and every time you're together, he either has his arm around you, or he's holding your hand. David doesn't do that. He treats me like a little kid."

"I hadn't noticed."

She shrugged. "Maybe its nothing. We've been together for a long time."

"How long?"

"Since I was in sixth grade and he was in eighth. Our dads are in the same office and work on many of the same projects. Our families hung out together more often back then. David and I would do our own thing. Maybe he's tired of me."

I pulled her closer. "I think no one could tire of you. You and David are so much alike. You laugh and joke around. I never know what kind of adventure one of you will come up with. Life is never dull with you two around."

She wrinkled her nose. "Maybe you're right."

"Why don't you go spend time with him? He's playing volleyball."

She grabbed two Dews from the ice barrel and ran in the direction I'd sent her. I hoped I was right. I'd hate to see either of them get their heart broken.

"And my God will meet all your needs
according to the riches
of His glory in Christ Jesus."
Philippians 4:19

Chapter 17

A few weeks later, as the early morning sun warmed the room, David and I sat at the kitchen table eating breakfast. Millie shuffled about humming the song "Mariah."

I sang along, and Millie turned to face me. "I'm surprised someone your age knows such an old song."

"It's the first one Mom taught me on the guitar. Nana used to hum it when she worked around the house."

"I've seen the guitar in your room, but I've never heard you play."

The song brought back too many memories I didn't want to recall. "It's more like I play *at* it."

Millie's eyes twinkled, and she seemed to fight back a grin as she yanked away my breakfast dishes.

"You in a hurry?" I teased.

"If you are sorting clothes for the shelter, you need to get over to the church."

David gulped down the rest of his juice and headed toward the back door. "Come on, Britt. We need to pick up Sara and get over there."

"I didn't realize we were on such a tight schedule."

"We like to get there early and hang out with the other kids. Besides, it's a great way to spend the morning and maybe the afternoon."

"I didn't realize sorting through stacks of old clothes could be so entertaining." I rubbed my palms together in jest. "Gee whiz. I can't wait."

David acted strange, and so did Millie.

"You wait and see. When you work with everyone talking and laughing, the time flies by. And think of the good you're doing by helping others."

I nodded. "Right. We're doing it to help others. That is why we will spend the entire day sorting through old clothes. It has nothing to do with you spending time with Sara."

He had no rebuttal but hurried out the door. His relationship with Sara was a mystery. Were they a couple, or weren't they? Neither dated anyone else.

Two hours after getting to the church, it seemed the piles of clothing were no smaller. Sara peeked over a stack in front of me and I jumped. She handed me a sports drink. "Thirsty?"

I accepted her offering and unscrewed the cap. "How long does this take?"

"It depends on how many people show up to help. Since the church women have something going on today, it's pretty much us kids."

David and Kody carried in more boxes and stacked them against the wall then disappeared leaving Sara and me with four other girls to do the work.

I folded a child-size T-shirt. There seemed to be an awful lot of clothing in those piles. "We will never get through all this today."

"We'll do what we can."

"Not quite the way I planned to spend my birthday."

Sara's thick-lashed eyes opened wide. "Today's your birthday? Does David know?"

"I guess. When I was in Colorado, Aunt Carol and Uncle Jim always sent me a birthday gift, but no one has said anything this year. Maybe they forgot."

David and Kody reappeared around noon, carrying pizzas

and soft drinks. David sported a wide grin. "You're doing a great job."

I planted my fists on my hips, trying to look stern. "Where have you two been all morning?"

David shoved a piece of pizza in his mouth, and Kody did likewise.

"Answer me. Where have you been?" I threw a girl's dress at David. "And quit stalling."

Kody's mouth twitched into a grin. "We went to the airport."

David's jaw tightened. "Kody."

"The airport?" I took a slice of pizza. "Did Uncle Jim go someplace?"

David gulped down the rest his drink before answering. "No—it was two friends of his—yeah, that's who it was. It was Dad's friends."

Kody scrunched his nose at David. "But we didn't . . ."

Sara wiped pizza sauce from her mouth with a paper napkin. "Did you guys know today is Britt's birthday?"

Kody pulled me into a hug. "It's your birthday?" He faced David with a creased brow and squinty eyes. "Why didn't you tell me?"

David smacked his forehead with the palm of his hand. "Wow, Britt. I'm sorry. I guess I forgot. Mom said something about it last week."

I shrugged. "It's okay. No big deal."

Back home in Evergreen, Mom always made a big deal about our birthdays. We'd start with our favorite breakfast, pick our favorite activity for the day, and she'd make our favorite meal for supper.

My cousin grinned. "We're just fooling with you. Mom ordered a cake, and I'm sure Millie is whipping up something special for dinner."

David grabbed Kody by the arm. "Come on, we need to make that run to the bakery for Mom."

A niggling suspicion flitted across my mind that perhaps

they were planning something for my birthday. If they wanted to keep that a secret, I would not spoil it for them—or for me. "So, you won't be helping us sort clothes?" I plopped a folded dress on an empty table. "Gee, David, you said this would be so much fun. You were so looking forward to sorting clothes, and now you're taking off and leaving us here to do the work."

David called back as he hurried out the door. "We'll be back in an hour to help. We'll pack up the folded clothes in boxes and put them away."

I squinted at Sara, "What are they up to?"

She avoided my question and turned to talk with one of the other girls. Still wondering what they were planning, I returned to folding clothes.

****

Less than an hour later, as promised, Kody and David returned to pack up the clothes and take them to the storage closet.

I joined Kody in the backseat of David's convertible and Sara slid into the passenger seat. As we left the church, we traveled in a different direction than we normally took to go home. "Where are we going?"

"Kody needs to stop by the stables and feed the horses," David said. "If we all pitch in and help, he'll get done sooner."

I nudged the back of his seat. "Will we have time to ride while we're there?"

"Doubt it." His answer was sharp.

"Is something wrong?"

"Nope."

David grew quiet. Kody drummed his fingers in silence. Sara chattered something about her cat.

When we reached parking area, it was filled to near capacity. "What's going on?"

"Don't know." David pulled into a space near the barn. "Let's go check it out."

David and Sara bolted from the car. They were at least

thirty feet ahead of Kody and me when I called out to them, "Wait up."

They picked up their pace, laughing as they ran through the front doors of the activity center. I kept a slow pace alongside Kody. "Do you know what's going on in there?"

As if on the edge of laughter, the corners of his mouth curled. "Looks like some kind of party."

My suspicions from earlier arose again. I searched the parking lot but recognized none of the cars. "We're crashing a private party?"

"Guess so."

He held the door open and motioned for me to go in ahead of him. The large room overflowed with people—people I knew from church, from school, and—it couldn't be. "Happy Birthday, Brittany," came a chorus of voices.

Two sets of strong arms embraced me and tears flowed. "Uncle Scott? Nana?" Wrapped in a silken cocoon of euphoria, if this was a dream, I did not want to wake up.

"It's us," Nana said, her gray eyes filled with joyous tears. "Oh sweetie, we've missed you so much."

Uncle Jim and Aunt Carol joined in and formed a group hug. "I hate to interrupt this beautiful moment, but the ladies have dinner laid out for us, and it's getting cold," Aunt Carol said through her sniffles. "Scott and your Nana will be here all week, and we're looking forward to getting better acquainted."

Sara joined me as I walked to the dining table. "And you thought they forgot."

"You knew?"

"Sure. We all did."

I couldn't believe they'd kept it a secret. "Even Kody?"

"It was his idea. He mentioned it to David, who took it to your aunt and uncle, and they made it happen."

I grabbed my friend into a loving hug. "You guys are the best."

Stepping up behind me, with tender fingers, Kody brushed the hair from my neck. "The best is yet to come."

Uncle Scott sat next to me through dinner, quizzing me on my life in San Francisco and filling me in on what was happening at the Bar K. A lady wearing an apron took his empty plate and silverware away, and he pushed back from the table, stood and stretched. He loomed above most of the other guests and his blue eyes sparkled with mischief. "There must be over fifty people here. You have wasted no time making new friends."

"It's been hard getting used to a new home, a new family, a new school. I miss you so much—you, Nana, my friends—Mariah."

I forced back tears of yearning for home.

With a strong gentleness, he took my face in his work-worn hands. "This is your seventeenth birthday. It's only another year, and it doesn't seem to be that horrible. Look at the new friends you've made. Do Carol and Jim beat you?"

I giggled. "No. They're great."

"What about David? Does he pick on you?"

"No. He's great too."

"Sara and Kody seem nice. Do you spend a lot of time together?"

Heat enveloped my neck as I thought of Kody.

An easy smile played at the corners of his mouth. "Brittany, you're blushing. It's Kody isn't it?"

Aunt Carol came to my rescue. "Brittany, it's time to open your gifts. Come up to the front, so everyone can watch."

My face grew even hotter. I didn't know which was worse, fending off my feelings for Kody with Uncle Scott or being the center of attention.

I took the lone seat behind the pile of gifts on the floor. As I unwrapped the presents, Aunt Carol wrote the names of the givers and the gifts so I could send thank-you notes. I got CDs, a journal from Uncle Jim, a Coach bag from Aunt Carol, and a hand-carved plaque that read in large script font "Wind Rider" from David. Nana Masters crocheted me a beautiful sweater and hat. Millie gave me a CD of the *Paint your Wagon* movie soundtrack that included the song "Mariah." I also got over $300 in gift cards. Overwhelmed with everyone's generosity, I offered a weak, "Thanks."

Uncle Scott carried a worn bridle that looked like the one I used for Mariah. "You may need this."

My thoughts spun. Why would he bring Mariah's bridle here? Unless—no I couldn't hope—was it possible?

Uncle Jim joined us. "You need to come with us."

Followed by a parade of people, we headed out the door. When we reached the stables, Uncle Scott tied a scarf over my eyes. "Don't peek."

My heart pounded with hope and fear of disappointment as my uncle guided me in front of him. I breathed in the sweet smell of hay and horses as we took slow steps forward. There was the unmistakable sound of a latch on a stall door opening. Uncle Scott released the scarf. "Happy Birthday, sweetie."

Hot tears trickled down my cheeks as the familiar scent of my beloved horse filled me with overwhelming joy. My arms encircled her chestnut neck, and I nuzzled my face in her ebony mane. I whispered into her twitching ear, "My Mariah. How I've missed you."

*"Blessed are those who mourn
for they will be comforted."*
Matthew 5:4

Chapter 17

The days flew by much too fast toward the next weekend when
Uncle Scott and Nana would return to Evergreen. My two
uncles spent many hours behind closed doors in the home
office, but today they sat in the living room laughing and
talking about the 49ers and the Broncos.

Nana had gone up to my bedroom for a nap and asked me
to wake her in an hour.

I tapped on the bedroom door and opened it a crack. She sat
on the window seat, the silver streaks in her dark hair
glistening in the afternoon sunlight.

I smiled. "It looks like you're already awake."

She patted the space next to her. "Come join me."

I curled up in the corner and rested my head on my knees.

"What's on your mind?" Nana asked. "You look sad."

"I don't want you to leave."

She patted my foot. "Maybe we can come back for
Christmas—or maybe Carol and Jim will bring you and David
to the ranch."

I wrapped my arms around her. "Oh Nana, do you think we
could?"

"Why not? You and David will be out of school. I can't
make any promises, but I'll talk to Carol before we leave."

Aunt Carol entered the room. "You'll talk about what?"

"I was telling Brittany maybe you and Jim could bring her

and David and join us at the ranch for Christmas."

"That's a wonderful idea, Deborah. Jim and I will discuss the details, and we'll let you know."

I danced around the room. "We're going to Colorado!"

David and Uncle Jim stood in the open doorway.

"What's going on in here?" Uncle Jim said. "We heard you downstairs. Are you ladies having a party?"

David leaned on the doorframe. "If they are, I don't think we're invited."

Grabbing David's hands, I danced around the room pulling him along. "We're going to Colorado!"

"Yeah, right," he said. "Did you forget we have a date to go riding with Sara and Kody?"

I stopped with an abrupt halt, sending David tumbling onto my bed. "Oh, I forgot."

Scrambling on all fours, I pulled my boots out from under the bed, jerked them on, and ran out of the room. I called back as I hurried down the stairs, "Come on. What are you waiting for?"

Uncle Scott stood in the kitchen talking to Millie. David and I bolted through the room. "Slow down. Where's the fire?"

I pecked him on the cheek. "We have a date with Sara and Kody to go riding, and we're late."

He slipped his arm through mine and pulled me to him. "Can I go?"

"You?"

"I know how to ride, you know."

"I know. It's—"

Millie's laughter rippled through the air.

Uncle Scott's eyebrows arched. "Something funny, Millie?"

"No, nothing at all," she said as she opened the refrigerator.

David stood at the back door. "Sure Scott, we'd love to have you. Wouldn't we, Britt?"

My thoughts swirled. I would be with Kody. What would Uncle Scott say? Would he embarrass me? Would he say something about my feelings for Kody?

I couldn't believe David invited my uncle to join us, but I pasted on a smile and responded through gritted teeth, "Sure that's fine.

"Can I drive your convertible?" Uncle Scott said. "I've wanted to get my hands on that baby ever since we got here."

David tossed him the keys. "Let's go."

On the way to pick up Sara, I offered little prayers that Uncle Scott would not embarrass me in front of Kody.

When we arrived at Sara's house, she climbed in the backseat and sat next to me. She nodded her head toward my uncle and shot me a questioning glance. "Nice to see you again, Mr. Masters. I didn't know you were going with us."

"Great to see you again, Sara. You can call me Scott. I'm not old enough to be Mr. Masters."

Kody had our horses saddled and tethered outside the barn when we arrived. "Hey guys, it's about time."

He flashed me a devastating grin then straightened with a look of surprise as Uncle Scott climbed out of the car. "Mr. Masters—I didn't know you were going with us."

"It's Scott and have you got a horse for me?"

"This way." Kody led my uncle down the center aisle of the barn.

I tugged at David and lowered my voice to a whisper. "Why did you tell him he could come?"

"It seemed the right thing to do."

Sara mounted Romeo. "It will be okay, Britt. What's your problem? Your uncle's a great guy."

"Oh yeah? How would you feel if your dad tagged along with you and David?"

She giggled as she turned toward the trailhead. "Oh, I see."

Uncle Scott and Kody reappeared with my uncle leading a roan mare. They laughed and talked as if they'd known each other for years.

"Thanks, Kody," Uncle Scott said as he swung into the saddle. "I believe this one will be fine. You've got good stock in there."

As we headed down the riding trail, my uncle pulled up alongside Kody. "So how long have you worked here?"

"About four years."

"Do you go to school with David and Brittany?"

"No."

"Are you at the Christian school where Sara goes?"

Kody didn't like to talk about school. The one time the subject came up, he grew quiet, and later David told me not to bring it up again. He said Kody had to quit school, and it embarrassed him.

Determined to end my uncle's interrogation, I led Mariah around to bring me up alongside Uncle Scott. "What's happening with the new stock you bought last spring?"

He reined in his horse. "If I didn't know better, I'd think you were changing the subject. But since you asked, they are perfect. We're using several at the equestrian center for dressage classes, but the others need a little more work before we turn the students loose on them."

"You own an equestrian center?" Kody said.

"It's on the ranch. We built the building about ten years ago, and we have folks from across the county using it. It's been a good investment."

"You must have a big spread."

Uncle Scott rubbed his chin. "With the acreage we purchased last year, the Bar K covers about a thousand acres."

Kody cast me a quick glance then spurred his horse into a trot.

Uncle Scott shrugged. "Was it something I said?"

****

That night the family gathered in the living room for one last time before Nana and Uncle Scott flew out in the morning. Uncle Scott leaned against the fireplace mantel with a near frown crossing his lips as he began. "Brittany, we need to speak with you about something important."

Uncle Jim nodded. "We didn't want to bring it up earlier, because we wanted you to enjoy your visit with your uncle and your grandmother. But we can't put it off any longer."

I grew frightened. "Is something wrong? Are one of you sick?"

Nana took my hand in hers. "No, sweetie. This isn't bad news, but you need to understand what your uncles have to tell you."

I shrugged. "Okay."

Uncle Scott rubbed his brow. "Jim and I have spent a lot of time this week going over all the legal documents for Josh and Cali's estate. We didn't want to talk to you until we understood everything. Many years ago, when the ranch was first started, your great-great-grandfather stipulated the oldest child of each generation of Masters would inherit the property."

We were all so happy, and these were our final hours together before my Colorado family left to return home. Thoughts of Mom and Dad being gone only brought thoughts of sorrow. "I don't want to talk about this."

Nana pulled me down to the couch. "You have to, Brittany. You must understand what has happened, and how it affects your future—the future of all of us."

Uncle Jim offered a reassuring smile. "You are young to have this put on your shoulders, but we'll be here to help you whenever you need us."

"The ranch belongs to you, Brittany," Uncle Scott said.

Swallowing the sob that rose in my throat, I looked up at him. "No—you're my dad's brother, so the ranch is yours. I don't deserve it."

Uncle Jim straightened in his chair. "Brittany, I don't think you understand. The Bar K belongs to you. What do you mean you don't deserve it?"

Covering my face with my hands, I gave vent to the agony swelling within me. "You don't understand. None of you understand." I sobbed. "It's my fault they're dead. I killed them. How can I make you understand? The accident was my fault."

Nana wrapped her arm around my shoulders and stroked my arm with her other hand. "Honey, the accident was no one's fault. It happened. Because you were driving doesn't make it your fault."

I stood trembling and shouted through my tears, "My cell phone rang. I lost control. It was my fault."

No one in the room spoke. The accusing silence was deafening.

"I don't blame you if you hate me!"

Uncle Jim drew me into a warm embrace and stroked my hair. "No one hates you. It could have happened to any of us."

"You can give without loving
but you cannot love without giving."
-Amy Carmichael

Chapter 19

The next morning, after taking Uncle Scott and Nana to the airport, Uncle Jim announced that I needed a change of scenery. He drove my aunt and me to the house at Dillon Beach where we would be staying for a few days.

David, Kody, and Sara arrived a few minutes before sunset.

We all retreated to the back deck. David and Sara sat in one of the wicker loveseats, and Kody and I took the other. My aunt and uncle settled into their lounge chairs. The flames in the fire pit popped and crackled as the sweet smell of burning wood filled the air.

Sometime later, Aunt Carol slipped her hand over Uncle Jim's shoulder and yawned. "Come on, honey. It's past our bedtime."

As they reached the French doors, Uncle Jim turned to face us. "You kids, come in soon, you hear?"

David stretched, dropping one arm behind Sara. "Yeah Dad. We'll be in soon."

Through the smoky shadows, I watched Sara snuggle closer to David.

Kody dropped his arm around my shoulder. He brushed his lips across my cheek. "You shuddered. Are you cold?"

My heart turned over in response. "No. I'm not cold."

"Am I out of line?"

"No."

"I don't want to do anything that makes you uncomfortable."

"I don't know how I feel. When I'm with you, I never want to leave you. My stomach gets squishy."

He whispered, "I don't see the problem."

He kissed my ear and my heart fluttered.

I stood and offered my hand. "Let's take a walk."

Clouds of fog swirled about us as we strolled down the street toward the beach. "You're quiet."

"A lot of things have happened that have set me to thinking about my future."

"I hope I'm in those thoughts."

Knowing I would return to the Bar K to run the ranch and—who knew what else—I wasn't sure how to answer. Everything was uncertain. Falling in love was not part of the plan. A relationship with Kody was perilous. I longed for his embrace and of him loving and protecting me. I wanted it, but how could we ever be together?

When we arrived at the beach, I took off my sandals and we walked hand in hand.

An uneasy tension cut through his voice. "Is it the ranch?"

"You know?"

"David told me." He hesitated then turned me to face him. "I have something to tell you."

His warm arms pulled me tight to his chest, and he buried his face in my hair. "Please don't hate me, Britt. I've been afraid to tell you, afraid you wouldn't want anything to do with me."

I raised my chin then he lowered his head and our lips met. His mouth throbbed with a passionate message as my heart hammered within my ribs.

He dropped to the sand on his knees and pulled me down with him. We leaned against an outcropping of rocks, and his fingers trembled. "I love you, but there is something about me that you don't know—something I must tell you."

"I love you too, Kody, and there isn't anything you can tell me that will change that."

"You're rich, and smart and pretty—and you own a ranch. I must be crazy to think this will last. I'm crazy to think you'll be here for a long time and you'll love me, but I love you, Britt. Despite everything, I love you with all my heart."

"What does my owning the Bar K have to do with me loving you or if you love me. I'm still the same person. It doesn't matter."

He brought his nose to touch mine. "That's one reason I love you."

"Why?"

"Because you're so naïve."

"I don't know what you're talking about."

"That's it. You have no idea."

Misty raindrops rolled down my cheeks, and I nuzzled my face in his shirt. "Let's go back to the house before we get soaked."

"I'm homeless."

I couldn't believe I heard him right. "What?"

"I live in the park—the one where we had the barbecue."

"Where are your parents?"

"They died."

This was impossible. How could Kody be living in a park? He wasn't like those other people—there I went again, thinking they were different. "I don't understand. You and David are together all the time. How could he not know?"

"He knows. I met David two years ago when the church held their annual barbecue. Over the next few weeks, we became good friends. He came to the park to hang with me several times a week. I went to church and then I got involved in the youth worship team. David gave me clothes and food and sometimes a little money."

"How did you keep it from Aunt Carol and Uncle Jim? I mean two years is a long time. Besides, you know they'd help you if they knew."

"After my folks died, and I had no family to take me in,

Children's Services placed me in foster care. No one wants a ten-year-old kid. For four years, they bounced me from one foster home to another. I ran away from the last one three years ago, and I want nothing to do with Children's Services. If Mr. and Mrs. Harper knew, they'd have to get the authorities involved."

I wrapped my arms around his neck and pulled him close. "I know you wouldn't keep something like this from me if you didn't think you had to."

He caressed my back. "I love you, Britt."

I knew I loved Kody, and I always would.

"Can I ask how your parents died?"

He pulled me closer and whispered in my ear, "It was a car accident. I was ten and my little brother was eight. I was the only one who survived."

Chapter 20

Despite the astounding news of Kody's revelation and the thrill of hearing him say he loved me, the sound of rushing waves lulled me into a sound sleep. But the night was far too short as a rap came on the bedroom door.

Sara moaned. "Go away. I'm not awake."

David shouted. "Come on, sleepyhead. The Pacific is calling, and it's a great day to learn to surf."

I rolled over and pulled the covers over my head. "You've got to be nuts to do this."

She yanked back my blankets. "I'm not doing it alone. You're going with me."

Fifteen minutes later, she forced me to my feet and into my clothes before leading the way to the kitchen where Millie had breakfast waiting.

Aunt Carol and Uncle Jim sat on the deck reading the morning paper and drinking coffee.

I inhaled the sweet smell of pancakes and bacon. "Smells great," I said. "Where are Kody and David?"

Millie wiped her hands with a dishtowel. "David said they were going into town to pick something up and they'd be back soon. He wore that silly grin that tells me he's up to no good."

Millie left the kitchen and Sara whispered. "Last time he

came back carrying a surfboard with a teddy bear painted on the bottom and my name written on his belly."

I grinned at her. "You didn't like it?"

"It was nice, but I don't surf." She slumped in a chair, a smile tugging at the corner of her mouth. "I will kill him. He knew all along he'd get me on that surfboard."

I laughed until tears threatened. "He knows you can't turn down a dare. He was waiting for the perfect moment." I gathered my fork and plate. "I'll take my breakfast outside, Millie."

Sara picked up her laden plate. "Me too."

Millie was back at the sink washing up the griddle. "Go on you two. It's a beautiful morning. I'lll soak up some of those rays myself when I finish in here."

Millie's blueberry pancakes were delicious. They needed no maple syrup, but I made sure puddles of the yummy stuff oozed around on my plate as I crunched the hickory smoked bacon and savored the pancakes.

"These are superb," Sara said through a full mouth.

"For sure," I garbled out.

Down on the beach, waves lapped at the sandy shoreline where the morning tide left behind piles of shells and seaweed.

"I'm going for a walk," I said as I returned my dishes to the kitchen. "Are you coming?"

Sara set her dirty dishes on the counter. "Sure."

We carried plastic buckets to gather any treasure the sea gave up during the night. On the far horizon, the crystal blue sky and deep green ocean met. As we walked along the road, I tossed my empty bucket into the air and caught it several times. Sara hadn't said a word all the way to the beach. "Something on your mind?"

She ran her finger along the handle of her bucket. "You're the best friend I've ever had."

I came to a halt, surprised with her declaration. "And you're my best friend, but why does that make you sad?"

"You're like my big sister. I know you're only two years

older, but I look up to you."

Holding back a smirk, because Sara looked up to everyone, I stopped and curled my toes in the sand. "So, what's the problem?"

"Next year you're going back to Colorado."

"That's the plan."

"And we'll never see each other again."

"Now you sound like Kody." I picked up a shell and dropped it in my bucket. "It's taken me so long to get used to living here, and the only way I got through those early days was telling myself it would only be for a year and a half. I admit I gave no thought to the people I'll leave behind when I go back."

Tears streaked down Sara's face. "So you don't care about us?"

"Stop it, Sara. I don't want to think about it. It's a year away. Things happen. People change and people move away." I slipped my hand around hers. "You're the best friend I've ever had, and no matter what, I'll never be so far away we can't see each other. We can text or Face Time—we'll keep in touch always. I promise I'll always be there for you."

David and Kody ran up the beach with David carrying a florescent yellow surfboard under his arm.

Sara wiped away her tears and grinned. "Looks like we have a more immediate problem."

The yellow surfboard David carried turned out to be for me. He knew that was my favorite color, and on the bottom of the board was a mural of a mountain with horses and a hazy "Wind Rider" drifting across the peaks. It took his teasing and dares for over an hour before I agreed to go along.

****

As the waves broke across the front of my board, I had serious doubts this was a good idea. I snorted water out of my nose. "I can't believe you convinced me to do this."

84

"Nice board," Sara teased.

"Yeah, I guess. My cousin is dangerous, you know. He finds the weak spot then goes for the jugular."

David paddled in closer. "I'm only thinking of you girls. Believe me, after your first ride in, you'll be begging to go again."

Kody paddled up between Sara and me and winked. "You'll be fine. Don't worry."

I scanned the water beyond the breakers. "And what if we're lunch for some great white?"

David paddled ahead of us. "Guess it won't matter. I won't have to listen to you complain. You don't have to worry about the sharks. The riptide will take you down before a shark gets you."

Riptides? Sharks? Great.

Kody was the first to catch a wave, and he made it look so easy I had to try. "Tell me what to do, David. I want the next one. It can't differ much from snowboarding, right?"

"I wouldn't know. I've never seen snow much less gone snowboarding." He slipped alongside me. "If you know you will fall, jump away from your board. Jump toward or over the wave. Never jump in front of the board. It's best if you can jump straight off the back. And if you fall, always use one hand to push the board away so it doesn't hit you."

Water splashed me in the face, and I swiped at it as I wiggled on the board. "You're assuming I will fall off?"

"You will."

"Great vote of confidence. What else should I know?"

"Jump shallow. Assume you only have two or three feet of water below you. So jump shallow and jump butt first. Never dive head first."

Sara paddled around to the other side of me. "Giving you a speed lesson?"

"Yeah," I said. "I guess you've heard all of this?"

"Why do you think I haven't stood up yet?"

David interrupted and grew serious. "This is no joke, you

two. Do what I'm telling you or you could get hurt."

"Go on," I said. "I'm listening."

"Jump shallow. Always cover your head with your arms when you're spinning under water and don't fight the wave. Sometimes it may tumble you around but go with it. The water is always calmer along the floor, so let yourself sink and you'll pass under the wave."

A flicker of apprehension coursed through me. "I don't know about this, David. Jumping, sinking, you have said nothing about coming up for air."

"When you come up, do it slow, and always keep one arm extended in front of you. You never know what, or who, is above you. As soon as you come up, try to get back on your board."

"And if I don't come up?"

"You'll come up. It might feel like you're being held under, but relax, go with it and at some point, you'll pop up."

A wave came under us. David called out, "Paddle with the whitewater as it breaks. When you feel the wave surge, get in a squatting position with both feet perpendicular to the board. Let go of the sides and stand in a crouch until you fall off."

"You're hilarious!" I called back as I caught the wave.

For over an hour, I fell off several times, but on my fourth attempt, I did it. "Wind Rider," I shouted as I glided atop the wave on the florescent yellow board.

David was right. The thrill of flying along on the top of the waves was awesome. I rode into shore and paddled back until my arms couldn't take anymore. It was the next best feeling to riding Mariah bareback across an open pasture, riding the wind.

Several hours later, the four of us gathered on the beach, exhausted but excited. "Didn't I tell you it would be great?" David said.

Kody laid his hand on my bare back, sending a tingle up my spine. "And you didn't get nibbled on by a great white."

I was about to poke him when a scream came from down

86

the beach.

"Shark," a man screamed. Then several people pointed and shouted, "Shark. Shark."

People on the beach stood shading their eyes and pointing in the direction where we'd been surfing.

Two surfers caught a wave and rode into the path of the dark fin. My pounding heart from Kody's hand on my back now did a sluggish thud as my stomach churned. "We've got to stop them."

Sara gripped my hand as we watched. The surfers drew closer, and the dark fin circled in the water. The surfer to the far right fell from his board, and the fin disappeared beneath the surface.

"No!" I screamed.

In a few ticks of time, our joyous outing had crumbled into one of horror. The surfer who'd remained upright reached the shoreline, turned his board around and paddled toward his friend.

Sara gripped my hand. "Is he crazy?"

The huge fin reappeared further out then dove under.

The beach grew silent as we watched and waited. Both surfers disappeared beneath the waves. Sara gripped my hand tighter. She was praying. I bowed my head and offered my petition. I begged the Lord to save those surfers.

An eerie silence enveloped the shoreline as we watched and waited. Each second seemed like hours. Then a cheer waved down the beach as both surfers fell onto the sand. They knelt, catching their breath, but they were unharmed.

I shivered, thrilled the surfers were okay but terrified of ever going back in the water.

"Maturity doesn't mean age.
It means sensitivity, manners
and how you react."
-Anonymous

Chapter 21

The next morning, Uncle Jim tossed his briefcase in the backseat of David's convertible, "Sorry to run out on you gang, but duty calls."

Sara slipped into the passenger seat, a serious pout and tear-streaked cheeks revealing her disappointment. "I don't see why I have to go back just because you're leaving."

"When your dad called to say they needed me at the office, he asked me to bring you home. That's all I know, honey."

Leaning against a fencepost, David revealed a pale blue lightening of amusement between his lashes. "The rest of us are heading back this afternoon. I don't get why you're so upset."

Sara replied in a clipped voice. "I'm tired of everyone treating me like a child."

David shrugged and headed into the house, brushing past me as he went. "Maybe they wouldn't if she'd stop acting like one."

I followed behind and caught up with him on the back deck. "You and Sara having problems?"

"No. Why?"

"Just wondered."

I had enough to deal with sorting out my relationship with

Kody. Sara and David could work their problems out themselves.

Millie pulled drinks from the refrigerator and wiped down the inside. I leaned against the counter. "Need any help?"

She smacked her head on the edge as she stepped back holding two plastic bottles of Diet Pepsi. Her usual lively eyes revealed a weariness as she set the bottles down and rubbed the injury. "Ms. Brittany, you are something else."

"What do you mean?"

"The way you jump in and want to help. I've never seen the like."

"You work so hard taking care of all of us. You look tired. Why don't you give me something to do?"

She took me by the shoulders, turned me around, and patted my behind. "You get on into your bedroom and pack up your things. I'll take care of the kitchen." She paused in front of the open refrigerator. "But thanks for offering."

Packing my belongings and tidying up the bedroom, I came across Sara's diary lying on the floor under her bed. I looked in the hall. No one was there. I knew I shouldn't read it, so I laid it on the nightstand and continued cleaning up.

David came in. "Kody and I thought we'd take in a few waves before heading home. You want to come?"

I glanced at the nightstand then back to him. "No. Thanks anyway."

He'd caught my eye movement and picked up the diary. "This is Sara's, isn't it?"

A twinge of guilt ran through me as I recalled my first thoughts. "Yeah."

He fluttered through the pages, and I grabbed it from him. "David Harper, you wouldn't."

"You didn't think about it?"

I stammered out, "No. Never. Those are her personal thoughts. I wouldn't—"

"Right." He chuckled as he left the room. "You wouldn't."

After slipping the diary in the mesh pocket in the top of my suitcase, I grabbed my cell phone and texted Sara, "Got your diary. It's safe."

A few seconds later she texted back, "Thanks. C U 2 nite."

"I'll get it 2 U then."

As I finished cleaning up and packing, a gnawing feeling tugged at me. If I read it, I might understand what was going on with her. However, I wouldn't like it if someone read my diary. I didn't keep one, so I didn't have to worry about that. Most of my thoughts I kept to myself.

*"Do not forsake wisdom, and she
will protect you; love her, and she
will watch over you."*
Proverbs 4:6

Chapter 22

Back home in Evergreen, when July 4th came around, we'd
pack up for an overnight trip, load up the horses, and go riding
in the high country. Before dark, we'd build a campfire and
wait to watch the fireworks go off in the towns and villages
below. Pitching tents on either side of the fire, one for Tiff and
me and one for Mom and Dad, we'd hunker down in our
sleeping bags then share made-up stories about bears, mountain
lions, and creepy forest creatures until we fell asleep. Dad
always told the best stories.

I sat there in the family room, immersed in my thoughts of
home and trying to push down the grief. The TV turned off,
and I looked up and there was David with the remote in hand.

"I hope you weren't watching that."

I swam in a haze of memories. "Huh?"

He bent down and stared. "Earth to Britt."

"Sorry. What did you want?"

He flopped into a leather recliner. "Sara and I are going to
the Marin County Fair this afternoon, and we thought you and
Kody might want to go with us."

I leaned my head back and considered his offer.

He pushed. "Do you?"

"Did you ask Kody?"

"Not yet. I wanted to check with you first."

"You know how he is about doing things he can't afford."

Kody's ring jangled on my phone, and I grabbed it from the end table. "Yeah."

"Hey Britt. What you doin'?"

"Watching TV."

David mouthed, "Is that Kody?"

I nodded with a grimace and motioned for my cousin to go away.

Kody's voice drew my attention back to his call. "You want to hang out at the stables? I've got to work until three, but then we can ride and maybe catch fireworks."

"Sounds great. I'll come out around three."

David ran his hand through his hair. "Let me talk to him?"

I clamped the phone between my hands. "No."

As I put the phone back to my ear, the sound of a horse whinnying came from Kody's end. He laughed. "Gerty is getting impatient for her hay."

I smiled at the thought of old Gerty with her swayed back and cantankerous attitude. "I'll pack sandwiches."

"Okay. I'll spring for drinks out of the vending machine."

David reached for my phone and shouted, "Let me talk to him."

"Is that David?" Kody said.

"Yes."

Relinquishing my phone, I stuck my tongue out at my cousin.

"Hey Kody. Yeah, she didn't want me to talk to you."

I grabbed at the phone, but David spun around and pushed my hand away. "Sara and I are going to the fair this afternoon, and we thought you guys might want to go."

My cousin offered a smug grin. "Yeah, we had a great time last year. Do you want go?"

He handed me my phone. "He wants to talk to you."

I took my phone and through gritted teeth I said, "Yeah."

Kody chuckled then cleared his throat. "Sounds like you

and David aren't getting along so well today. Do you want to go?"

"If you do."

"Yeah. It's a good time."

"Okay."

I passed the phone back to David. "You guys figure it out and tell me when to be ready."

****

We picked Kody up at three thirty and headed north along Highway 101. Sara and David laughed and talked in the front seat. I couldn't hear with the top down and the wind blowing, but I didn't care what they were saying. I was glad they were getting along. The tension last month was unbearable.

Kody wove the fingers of his left hand through mine and tap-a-tapped a rhythm on the armrest with his other hand. Occasionally, he passed me an enticing glance or a wink.

Did all drummers do that tap-a-tap thing on solid objects?

Speeding along the highway, I once again felt like a Wind Rider as sea breezes whipped through my hair, and David opened wide the power of his muscle car. For miles, we flew along claiming the highway for our own. It surprised me when we didn't run into more traffic that time of day, but that all changed as we reached the San Rafael city limits. We came to an abrupt halt, creeping forward every few minutes then stopping again. Leaning up next to David's ear, I asked, "What's happening? Do you think there was an accident?" I glanced behind us to see lines of cars. Up ahead were more cars. Occasionally, they inched forward then came to a full stop. "There weren't any sirens."

He chuckled. "The traffic gets crazier every year. You may as well sit back and relax. It will be a good hour before we get to the fairgrounds entrance."

"Are all these people going to the fair?"

"Probably. If they weren't, they'd take another route.

Everyone knows 101 backs up during the fair."

I slumped in my seat. "How big is this place?"

Kody leaned toward me. "Huge. And very crowded."

****

An hour later we entered the gates of the fairgrounds and spent another thirty minutes finding a place to park. We then walked for what seemed like a mile to the entrance and ticket stand.

The entry fee was $16, and it included all the rides, exhibits, and a concert. I slipped Kody a twenty.

He pushed it back into my hand. "I've got it."

I whispered in his ear. "Please take it. I'll enjoy myself more knowing I paid my way."

His lips brushed against mine, sending the pit of my stomach into a wild swirl like riding a spinning amusement park ride.

Sara ran past shouting, "Hurry. We've got to get in line for the Zipper."

I suppressed a chuckle at her first selection of rides, seeing how my stomach continued to spin and dip from Kody's kiss.

From the Zipper, she dragged us to the Ring of Fire then to the Energy Storm that flipped us upside down and spun us in every direction. I asked if we could ride the Giant Wheel. The poster touted the ride as being one hundred feet high and seeing how there was no line, I couldn't wait to climb in one of the swinging seats and ride to the top.

Kody gripped my fingers tighter. "You sure you want to ride that?"

David and Sara craned their necks to look up at the ride. David bent toward me. "Yeah, are you sure?"

I taunted them. "You guys afraid of heights?"

Kody shook his head. "No, I'm not afraid."

Taking Sara by the hand, David turned away from the Giant Wheel and walked in the other direction. "You guys go

94

ahead. We'll catch up with you at the concert. It starts in thirty minutes so you'd better hurry."

The ride in the sky was amazing. Looking down on all the people, the wind blowing and rocking the gondolas, took me back to riding above the ski slopes. "Isn't it great?"

Kody gripped my fingers until they tingled. "Yeah. Great."

A group called The Temptations performed at the concert, and recognition dawned on me when the tune "Papa Was a Rolling Stone" reverberated through the sound system. "I know that song."

Kody led the way through the Pavilion as we scanned up and down the rows of people who clapped, sang, and danced in the aisles. His head tilted back, he raised his hand to shield his eyes from the glare of a stage light. "Yeah?"

"Nana plays it on her guitar."

His distraction was clear through his quipped replies. "Great." Kody's gaze meandered up and down rows of spectators. "They've got to be here someplace."

The concert was half over before we found Sara and David. "Kody. Britt. Up here," David shouted from several rows above us.

There were two empty seats in the row where we stood. Kody waved to David then pointed to the seats. Kody whispered in my ear, "Now we can be alone."

Glancing around at the people crowding in, I laughed.

****

The concert ended about an hour before the fireworks were to start. Most people filed out fast, leaving many empty seats, so David and Sara were able to regroup with us. Sara nudged me, "I need to use the ladies' room. Will you go with me?"

With Kody gripping my hand, he and David escorted us girls outside the Pavilion. I kissed Kody on the cheek then tugged free of his grasp. "Don't worry."

A shadow of concern passed over his expression as he took

my hand in his and kissed my fingers. "It's my job to worry. It's getting dark, and I've got a bad feeling about you two going off by yourselves."

Sara grabbed my hand. "I've got to go"

I grinned at Kody. "Stop worrying. We're only going to the restroom."

We waited over fifteen minutes in line before getting inside. Sara stepped close and whispered in my ear. "Do you have the stunner?"

I peered through the crowd. There were a few hard-looking women in line ahead of us, but they didn't seem at all threatening. "Yeah. In my pocket. Why?"

"I have a bad feeling."

I sighed. "Not you too."

"Maybe it's all these people crowding around. I don't know. I'm being silly."

We finished our business and made our way through the line to the exit, coming out on the opposite side from where we'd gone in. People pushed and crowded all around us, and then I lost Sara.

"Sara." I waited a few seconds and called out again, "Sara."

She screamed. "Britt. Help!"

Pulling the stunner from my pocket, I pushed my way toward Sara's cries.

"Sara!"

The mass of bodies between us pushed and shoved to get a better view of the fireworks, and the booming of gunpowder drowned out my shouts.

"Sara!"

I removed the lid from the stunner and pushed the button for the flashlight.

Between booms, I heard Sara's cries for help.

A rough hand grabbed my left wrist. Instructions for using my weapon ran through my mind. *Press the button. Hold the stunner against the assailant's shoulder or hip for several seconds.* The instructions did not include, 'Go.' I spun around

96

to see the face that haunted my dreams for months. He pulled me to him. I raised my hand and pushed the Taser as hard as I could into his shoulder. Eric screeched and dropped to the ground.

I couldn't move fast or far in the crowd, but I caught sight of Sara and Jeremy as he gripped her wrist and she struggled to get away. Everyone watched the sky. No one cared what Jeremy did to Sara. I slipped between several large men and came up behind Jeremy. I pressed the stunner into his shoulder and shouted at Sara, "Go. Now."

She escaped and I followed, leaving Jeremy, just like Eric, writhing on the ground. We pushed through the crowd past the restrooms and back to the Pavilion.

Sara stopped to catch her breath and grabbed my arm. "That was awesome." She laughed. "That was awesome."

I panted then cleared my throat. "Are you crazy? It was awful. Do you know what I did to them? Did you see Jeremy on the ground?"

"Them? Who else did you stun?" Sara's eyes opened wide. "Eric?"

I nodded. "He grabbed me when I was trying to get to you."

Kody and David pushed through the crowed and Kody pulled me into an embrace. "Where were you? We've been crazy thinking something happened to you."

Sara said something to David that included the mention of a tazer. The noise in the crowd was so loud I was uncertain if he heard her but I shot her a glare and shook my head. "We're fine. We got caught up in the crowd and had trouble finding our way back."

David grabbed the wrist string of the stunner. "What's this?"

I yanked it back. The last thing I needed was for the thing to jolt him. I flicked the button. "See. Just a flashlight."

*"The prettiest smiles hide the deepest secrets.
The prettiest eyes have cried the most tears,
and the kindest hearts have felt the most pain."*
-Anonymous

Chapter 23

The day we celebrated David's seventeenth birthday at Dillon Beach, the summer was nearing its end. I should have been excited for him, but my dread of school starting and the probability of encountering Eric overshadowed everything else. David asked Aunt Carol not to make a big deal about his special day. All he wanted was to spend the weekend surfing with Kody.

With a folding picnic table and deck chairs, Aunt Carol set up on the beach for a small private birthday party. Soon after we arrived, a scruffy-looking surfer dude exited a van carrying a large bundle. "One of you guys David?"

My cousin flashed a grin. "That'd be me."

"My instructions are to teach you kiteboarding. You ready?"

David jumped and shouted like a small child getting a pony, "You bet. Let's go."

My aunt and uncle, Millie, Sara, Kody, and I took seats along the beach and awaited our entertainment. David grabbed the board from the surfer dude and ran to the water's edge.

Surfer dude dropped a bicycle pump on the sand and spread out a cobalt blue kite that looked like bat wings. He said something to David, and my cousin ran to Aunt Carol. "I need my lifejacket."

"It's in the car. I'll get it."

Uncle Jim chuckled. "He should have known she'd have everything covered."

Aunt Carol returned to the beach and gave the lifejacket to David.

By now, the surfer dude had the kite inflated and a harness and cables attached. In no time, the wind caught the kite and pulled it high into the air. David hooked another harness around his waist then the surfer dude hooked the kite and cables onto the front. He made David walk up and down the beach for a while. We watched the blue kite sail back and forth with David's movements.

Soon David was on the board, surfing away from shore, and then swooping back and forth over the waves.

Sara squirmed in her chair. "That looks like so much fun. Don't you think, Britt? Wouldn't you like to do that?"

"I've done it on a snowboard."

"You're kidding?"

"A couple years ago my dad taught me. I prefer the snow. At least I know nothing will jump out of the snow and make a lunch of me."

Aunt Carol laid her hand on Kody's arm. "Would you like to try?"

He was on his feet in seconds. "Sure."

Aunt Carol talked to the surfer dude, and when David returned to shore, the guy went through the same routine with Kody he'd done with David.

Sara pouted as Kody skimmed over the waves. She looked over to Aunt Carol. "Can I try?"

"Call your mom first. If she says it's okay, we'll let you try."

Sara huffed. "Forget it. She'd never agree to that."

"Sorry, honey. I can't let you do it without her saying you can. You know how she feels about you coming up here with us. I don't want you to get hurt."

Sara stomped away, kicking sand as she went. Aunt Carol's

gaze followed. "It's hard for her."

"Why are her folks so strict?"

"They worry because of what happened to her brother."

"I didn't know she had a brother. I thought she was an only child."

"He was seven years older than Sara."

"He died."

"It was a surfing accident. He suffered severe head injuries and a broken neck."

"She said nothing about it."

"Sara avoids talking about things that upset her. If she can't make a joke about it and move on, she won't talk about it."

"So that's why her parents are so strict with her?"

"I don't think they could handle anything happening to Sara. It devastated them when her brother died."

I didn't mention Sara surfing with us. This explained much of what I didn't understand about Sara. Maybe she wasn't the happy-go-lucky girl I thought she was. Maybe, like me, she let everyone think she was okay while her real feelings brewed beneath the surface.

"An honest witness tells the truth
but a false witness tells lies."
Proverbs 12:17

Chapter 24

Monday afternoon Aunt Carol took David and I school
shopping at the Stonestown Mall. I couldn't recall the last time
I'd been in a mall. Mom did most of our shopping online, or
we picked up what we needed at the Wal-Mart on the outskirts
of Evergreen.

Uninspired at spending the afternoon shopping, David
slumped in the backseat of the Lexus, popped in his earbuds,
and brooded. His expression was almost comical with his arms
crossed, lip stuck out, and eyes squinting.

Aunt Carol carried the conversation, telling me all about
the wonderful stores at the mall and what great clothes I'd find
there. I would have been content with a new pair of jeans and
two new T-shirts. It sounded like she planned to buy an entire
new wardrobe.

Entering Nordstrom's, my aunt turned to David. "You've
got your card, and I'm sure you don't want to look at ladies'
things with Brittany and me. Meet us at Subway at five
o'clock."

With his earbuds still in, he nodded. "Okay."

I stood alone with my aunt in the junior department. She
sorted through a pile of bikini briefs and thongs. "I don't know
how you girls stand these things, but I understand from Millie
this is the style you wear, so why don't you pick out a dozen

pair you like."

Millie and Aunt Carol discussed my underwear? My cheeks grew warm, and I knew they had to be flaming red. My aunt laughed, "Oh dear Brittany, we're both women. I want you to get what you need."

Working to regain my composure, I picked at the underwear.

Aunt Carol set her purse on the edge of the display table and dug. "Uncle Jim got you a credit card. I know it's in here somewhere." She dug deeper, laying her cell phone, address book, lipstick, and a dozen other objects on the table. "Here it is."

She plopped the piece of plastic in my hand, and I dropped it like a hot iron. "No. I don't need that. I've got money from my birthday."

She picked it up. "You need it. Don't be silly."

"Mom wouldn't want me to have that."

"We paid cash for everything or used a debit card. They always taught me if I didn't have the money to pay for something, I didn't get it."

She set the card aside while she picked up her belongings from the table and plunked them back in her purse. She offered the card to me again. "I understand. Please let us do this for you. We haven't bought you any new clothes or shoes and carrying the card is safer than carrying cash."

"I don't need that much. I still have money from my birthday. I don't need new underwear right now. Is there another store in this mall that isn't so expensive? I never paid $10 for a pair for underwear. That's crazy."

We headed to Macy's where I bought a pair of jeans and two T-shirts. Then we hurried to Subway where we found David lounging in a booth toward the back of the store, his head bouncing to the rhythm of whatever tune was playing. No shopping bags were in sight. Aunt Carol slid onto the seat across from him, jerking out an earbud. "Where are the things you bought?"

"I don't need anything."

"The shorts and T-shirts you've worn all summer are ratty. And those sandals!" She pointed under the table to his feet. "Those are going in the trash."

"Mom."

"David Harper. You have one hour after we eat to buy two pairs of shorts, two T-shirts, and a pair of sandals or sneakers."

"Nobody wears sneakers anymore."

She scooted over on the bench to give me a space to sit down. "You heard me. One hour."

He plugged in his earbud. "Okay. One hour. Got it."

I pulled my phone from my purse, and my stunner fell out onto the table. Aunt Carol picked it up. "Is this a new brand of lipstick? I've not seen it before." She ran her fingers along the wrist strap. "I've never seen lipstick with a wrist strap. Where did you get it?"

David grabbed it out of her hand and popped off the cap. My heartbeat quickened.

He pressed the top button and lit the flashlight. "It's not lipstick. It's a flashlight. See."

I tried to grab it back, but he was too quick. "What's this other button for?"

"Is this high beam?"

I squealed, "Don't."

He pressed the button. The stunner buzzed a jolt and David dropped it, sending it rolling to rest in front of me. "What the heck?"

Aunt Carol's heavy lashes flew up, and she pushed back from the table. I grabbed the stun gun, replaced the cap, and shoved it into my purse. I stammered. "It's for protection. Remember, David, they had that class at school where they talked about how we girls might want to carry pepper spray or a stunner."

My aunt's gaze riveted on my purse. "Pepper spray? Stunners? Are they crazy? You could get hurt with that stuff. Why do you need protection? Where are you going that you'd need something like that? And where did you buy it?"

I had to think fast. I couldn't tell her about Eric and Jeremy. Not until I was sure they wouldn't retaliate.

"Life is a fight, but not everyone's a fighter.
Otherwise, bullies would be an endangered species."
-Anonymous

Chapter 25

Two weeks into the school term and I'd had no problems with Eric and Jeremy. I could only hope the incident at the fair taught them to steer clear. The period bell rang, and I hurried down the deserted hallway to my locker.

Eric and Jeremy called out. I flinched at the sound of their voices, and when I didn't answer, hot breath blew on the back of my neck.

"Look here what we got, Jeremy," Eric said. "It's little Miss Colorado, and she's all alone."

Eric grabbed my bag, tossed it to Jeremy, and shoved my face into the lockers. The locker handle pushed into my chest, and my face pressed hard against the cold metal. His breath reeked of rancid beer.

Eric spun me around and jerked my arms above my head, holding my wrists with one hand. I tried to call out for help, but his mouth covered mine, his teeth drawing blood from my lips. I fought the tears. They wouldn't see me cry. My legs withered like limp stems beneath me.

He yanked me away from the locker. Jeremy gripped my arms behind my back while Eric ran a hand under my shirt.

"What? No scream?" Eric whispered in my ear. "You think a little zapper will stop us?" He squeezed my right breast. "Think again, sweetheart."

I lifted my chin and spit in his face. "Get your hands off

me!"

He wiped away my spittle with one hand and struck my face with the other. "So you want to play rough? I'll play rough."

Jeremy's grip on my arms pulled tighter, and Eric squeezed my face between his fingers, shaking my head from side to side. If Jeremy had not held me from behind, I would have collapsed to the floor. My legs were so weak. Even if I could break free, I couldn't run.

The clock tick—tick—ticked on the wall as moments that seemed like hours passed. The sudden echo of voices came from down the hall, and Eric jerked back, his dark eyes staring in the sound's direction. He turned to me, his gaze penetrating mine. With a quick brush along my jaw, he threatened, "This isn't over."

Jeremy released my arms, and I collapsed to the floor, my breath coming with ragged efforts while my stomach whirled. They disappeared into the shadows.

"Britt?" The familiar voice set me trembling as I struggled to pick up my books. "Britt? Are you okay?" David knelt beside me. "What happened?"

I stared down the empty hallway, breathed deep and exhaled, but I couldn't stop shaking. Tears wet my face—the tears I swore no one would see.

My neck and cheeks grew hot as I brushed away the dampness with the back of my hand. I swallowed hard. "You'd…you'd better get to class. I don't want to get you in trouble."

David brushed wet hair from my face. "I'm not going anywhere until you tell me what happened."

I held his gaze for a heartbeat then turned away and began gathering my papers that had scattered across the floor.

David reached for some of them. "Let me help you pick these up."

When we finished gathering them up, David helped me to my feet. "Did someone hurt you, Britt?"

"Don't worry about it. I'm fine now."

With my belongings in my arms, I walked ahead of him, glancing over my shoulder every few steps.

****

After school, David caught up with me as I hurried to his car in the parking lot. "So are you going to tell me what happened this afternoon?"

He wouldn't stop until I gave it to him straight, and I didn't want to talk about it at home where someone might overhear. I swallowed hard, trying not to reveal my humiliation and anger. "If I tell you what happened, you can't tell anyone else. Do you promise?"

His features contorted with rage. "Tell me what happened."

I told him Eric pushed me against the lockers and forced a kiss on me.

"You're not telling me everything." David slid into the driver's seat and slapped the steering wheel. "You wouldn't be this upset if that's all he did. You'd be mad as a wet cat. It takes a lot to make you cry, and you were freaking out. Is this the first time they've bullied you?"

I sat next to him in the passenger's seat. "No."

"How long has this been going on?"

I'd tried so hard to force the memory of the previous attacks from my mind. Sara and I agreed we would tell no one. It would be our word against Eric and Jeremy's, and no one could stop them from doing it again.

"The first time was last summer." I wished I could pull the words back. "It was nothing."

We rode several blocks in silence before he swung the convertible into a parking space in front of the library, slammed the gearshift into park, and yanked out the key. "Tell me everything or I'm going to Mom and Dad with this."

I met his gaze and told him all that Eric and Jeremy had done at school, the details of the attack on Sara and me after

107

the barbecue.

As I told him each detail, something inside me broke—something I'd only felt once before in my life, and again I was helpless to change the outcome.

David slumped and stared straight ahead. In the tense silence, I sat gripping my hands, aware of my every breath.

"Who were the two guys who came to help you and Sara?"

"I don't know. I remember seeing them at the barbecue, but I didn't meet them."

"What did they look like?"

Why was he so concerned about them? This was about Eric and Jeremy. It was not about the guys who rescued us.

My lips puckered with annoyance. "Thirties maybe—maybe late twenties—average height. They wore white ball caps. I didn't get a good look at their faces."

"If they were from our church, Sara would have known them, so they must have been with the other people. I'll ask Sara."

"No David. Please don't tell anyone about this."

As he placed one leg out of the car, he turned and faced me. "I will talk to Sara about this and ask her why she didn't tell me."

I ran after him as he thundered toward the library entrance. "You can't tell Kody. Okay, I understand you wanting to talk to Sara, but please don't tell Kody. I know him. He'll do something stupid."

David spun around. "I'm sorry, Britt. You're in danger—maybe Sara too. For now, I won't tell Mom and Dad. You're right. It would only make things worse at school. But I'm going to tell Kody and have a long talk with Sara." His mouth twitched. "Is that how you busted your lip and Sara scraped her face?"

Kody stepped through the glass doors of the library. His glowing smile shadowed as he stepped in front of us. "What's up?" He looked at David. "You look mad enough to chew nails." He switched a stack of books to under his other arm and

108

pulled me to him. "And you, beautiful, you're not your usual cheerful self."

David stormed through the doors. "We'll talk about it later. I need to do research for a history paper. We will be here for a while."

The library was a respite of quiet, cool air. I took a seat at a small table where I laid out my English book and tablet.

Kody whispered, "Are you going to tell me what's going on?"

"Not now. I've got to finish this English paper."

He slid his stack of books onto the other side of the table and sat across from me. "Something's wrong. Are you mad at me?"

If I told him what had happened, he would go after Eric and Jeremy. I laid my hand on his, finding a reassuring comfort in his presence.

I fingered the stack of books he'd checked out. *Acing the GED exams, GED Social Studies, GED Basics, GED Mathematics, Master GED Science,* and on the bottom, *Veterinary Medical School Admission Requirements.* "I'm impressed. I didn't know you were studying to take your GED. You never told me you wanted to be a vet."

He pulled the books to him and hung his head. "Yeah. It's no big deal."

"I will be a vet someday."

"Yeah, you told me that."

"Kody, look at me."

He raised his head but kept his eyes averted. I leaned over the table and took his face in my hands. "It's wonderful."

His eyes met mine. "I guess."

"I knew you spent most of your time in the library when you weren't working at the stables, but I didn't know you were studying."

He slumped. "What did you think I was doing here?"

"I heard homeless people hang out in the library because it's safe, and no one will chase them off as long as they bother no one."

Standing erect, he slammed his hand on the stack of books. "Is that what you think of me? Do you feel sorry for the homeless boy that hangs out at the library? Geez, Britt. You've been with me for months now. I'd think you'd know better."

The librarian stood in front of us with her eyeglasses perched on her nose. "If you two can't keep your voices down, I will have to ask you to leave."

Kody took his seat. "Yes, ma'am. It won't happen again."

"I hope not. You are here every day, and I've never had to reprimand you. I would hate to make you leave."

Kody's mouth drew into a tight line, and he nodded as the librarian hurried away.

I reached across the table, but he jerked back. "Kody, I don't feel sorry for you. I love you. I, of all people, understand much of what you've dealt with. But I can't imagine being on my own and not having my family to care for me."

He stood, lifted his stack of books to under his arm, and stretched his other hand out to me. "Let's go outside where we can talk."

We sat on the grass in front of David's car. "I'm sorry, Britt. I get defensive about being homeless. When most people look at me, and they know where I live, they don't see me as a normal person but as a homeless person."

"I don't see you that way. And David doesn't."

He lay back looking up at the sky. "Next year I can take my GED, and then I can apply for scholarships and grants. I hope to move to Ohio and get a decent paying job to help with my school expenses."

I straightened in surprise. "Why Ohio?"

"Ohio State University has one of the best veterinary schools in the country, and I will go there."

I'd known I wanted to be an equine vet since I was twelve years old, and I would go to Colorado State after I finished high school. Kody wanted to be a vet too. He had it all planned out. While I was in my classes at Kennedy, he was studying to

110

take his GED. A sense of shame overwhelmed me. But this conversation wasn't about me. It was about Kody, and I didn't want to make him feel bad because he had to work so hard for something I took for granted.

"That's great, Kody. And I know you'll do it."

Tires squealed at the corner, and I looked up. Eric and Jeremy pulled into McDonald's drive-thru. David hurried down the library steps, staring in their direction. "Get in the car."

Kody slipped in next to me and buckled his seat belt. "What was that about?"

David put the car in drive and pulled out of the parking lot. "You want to tell him or should I?"

As we passed McDonald's, Eric's black pickup pulled out of the exit and fell into traffic behind us. I sunk low in my seat. "Can we wait until Sara is with us?"

Kody glanced behind us. "Will someone please tell me what's going on?"

Several blocks from the library, David pulled into Sara's drive and jumped out of the car. The black pickup turned the corner and moved on down the street. David's engine idled as Kody and I waited. Kody leaned against his door and drummed his fingers on the armrest.

I knew he would have the same reaction as David, and I didn't want them getting involved—or getting hurt because of me.

"Hey gang," Sara said as she slipped into the passenger's seat. "Oops. Did I interrupt an argument?"

David buckled in and drove in silence for some time.

Sara turned toward the backseat. "What's going on?"

A lump formed in my throat. "David knows what happened at the barbecue."

"You told him?"

"I had to."

"We said we would not tell anyone!"

David inhaled a sharp breath. "Our resident bullies made Britt their target of the day."

Sara turned to face me again. "Why didn't you text me?"

Kody jerked off his seat belt and slid next to me. "What's going on?"

"I'm fine."

David slammed his hands on the steering wheel. "She may be fine now, but I'm not. Those two need to keep their hands off our girls."

Kody moved in closer. "What did they do to you?"

I repeated everything I'd told David.

Kody's knuckles grew white as he balled his hands into fists. "Who are these guys, David? Why are they going after Britt?"

David stopped in the church parking lot. "I don't know, but I intend to find out."

David unlocked the back door of the Youth Center and led the way in as Kody came up behind me. He never even held my hand when we were at the church, but now he gripped my waist and held me close to his side.

As the door closed, I watched the black pickup glide by on the side street. I gasped and Kody halted in his step. "What is it?" He pushed the door open and looked out. "What did you see?"

"It was them."

Kody stepped outside. "Eric and Jeremy?"

I gripped his hand. "Why are they are following us?"

Holding the door open, David looked one direction then the other. "They're gone now. I wouldn't think they'd hang around here for three hours until we're done. We shouldn't need to worry about them anymore tonight."

David and Kody joined the others in the youth band and set up for worship while Sara and I went to the kitchen.

"Is this the first time they've bothered you at school?" Sara asked as she took paper plates from a cupboard.

I motioned for Sara to follow me into the storage room. "No, it's not the first time. But it's the first time they touched me at school. Before they only taunted with obscene gestures and foul language. Sometimes they talked about what happened after the barbecue and made lewd comments about how they didn't get to finish what they started."

Sara took my hand. "Why didn't you tell me? You know you can tell me anything."

"I didn't want to worry you, especially after the deal at the fair. I never thought they'd go through with it. It was obvious they were both drunk that day at the barbecue and at the fair. Today I smelled beer on Eric, but he wasn't drunk. He knew what he was doing, and so did Jeremy. I'm scared of what they might do next, but I don't want Kody and David getting hurt."

"We've got to tell Mr. and Mrs. Harper. They'll know what to do. They'll get the police involved and make them stop."

"Are you crazy? That will make it worse. We have no proof. It's our word against theirs. At the most, they'll get their fingers smacked and told to stay away from us. It will make them more determined to prove they're above authority."

"What about those two guys that helped us? They saw part of what happened."

"They didn't see Eric and Jeremy's faces. Besides, we don't know who they were."

Sara replied in a small voice. "You're right. I didn't recognize them, and I haven't seen them since."

Voices echoed from the kitchen, and the smell of hot pizza seeped into the storage room.

"Sara? Britt? Are you in there?" The girl's youth pastor opened the door. "Are you two hiding in here?"

"To fear the Lord is to hate evil;
I hate pride and arrogance, evil
behavior, and perverse speech."
Proverbs. 8:13

Chapter 26

After the midweek worship service, Sara and I left the clean-up crew to finish in the kitchen. On our way out, we passed the stage. The band members shuffled about packing up their instruments. Kody remained seated behind the drums as he and David talked in hushed tones.

"I bet I know what they're talking about," Sara said.

I rested my back against the stage. "No mystery there. I don't know how we can keep them from doing something stupid. They're no match for Eric and Jeremy."

"Do they carry weapons?"

"I've heard they do."

"How long have they been at Kennedy?"

"I'm not sure. They were new to the school last year, and they hung out together right away. I guess two of a kind, birds of a feather, and all that."

A hand clasped my shoulder, and I looked up to see Kody standing over me. "Want to take a walk?"

"Sure. Where to?"

"I'm thinking the courtyard would be the safest place, and I'd like to talk to you about this in private."

A dense fog rolled in the cool night air, casting foreboding shadows from overhanging branches of the decorative trees. The otherwise beautiful flowering shrubbery formed odd shapes in the darkness.

A chill, black silence surrounded us as we walked along the winding pathway. We sat on the bench farthest from the Youth Center and out of the glow of the security lights. Kody raised my chin, his kiss offering a safe place for my tired soul to rest. He gazed into my eyes. "I'm so sorry this happened to you. If I could have stopped it, I would have."

My mind relived the velvet warmth of his kiss. "I know." I caressed his cheek. "But you can't protect me twenty-four hours a day." A sudden icy fear twisted around my heart. "Kody, promise me you won't go after them."

"I can't promise you that."

"You don't know them. Those two are plain evil. I'd never forgive myself if they hurt you because of me."

"Oh, isn't that sweet? 'I'd never forgive myself if they hurt you because of me.'" It was Eric's taunting voice. I stood to run but he grabbed me and clamped his hand over my mouth. I bit at his hand and tasted blood but he didn't react. He had to be drunk or high or both. I squirmed and kicked but he was too strong for me to get away. He dragged me down the path between flowerbeds and shrubbery. The fog enveloped us, and I lost my bearings.

Where was Kody?

Through the dense silence came a loud grunt and a heavy crashing. Eric was on top of me ripping at my shirt. His putrid mouth covered mine. Smothered by the cruel ravishment of his mouth, I couldn't scream. His rough hands grabbed at me, and something sharp pricked my neck. Warm liquid trickled down my bare chest. "Scream and I'll kill you," he said.

"Kody? Britt?" The muffled sound of David's voice echoed in the distance. "Are you two out here?"

I prayed a silent prayer. *Lord, don't let them come out here. Please Lord. Stop this now.*

"David, it's Eric and Jeremy. They parked across the street. I called the police." Sara's voice echoed through the night.

Sirens, flashing lights, loud voices, pounding feet, a punch to my jaw, and everything went black.

A muffled voice spoke, "Britt? It's Sara. Can you hear me?"

Someone lifted me from the ground onto a gurney and a hand grasped hold of mine. I was moving and voices grew loud then muffled. My jaw throbbed in pain and unseen fingers probed at my neck.

A man at my head called out. "Her vitals look good. She took quite a belt to her jaw, and she's got a cut on her neck that may need a few stitches. How's the boy?"

After a long silence, a stranger's voice broke through. "Not so good. He took quite a beating, and it looks like they stabbed him, but I can't say for sure with all that blood. He's got a slight pulse."

The agonizing thought of losing Kody tore at my insides.

The gurney beneath me bounced along. Blinding lights. A sharp stick to my arm. I was in an ambulance. I worked to force my eyes to open, and my thoughts went back to the day of the accident. "Mom? Dad?" The words seemed loud and clear, but no one answered. A siren blared. Then blackness engulfed me once more.

*"Is anyone among you sick? Let them
call the elders of the church to pray
over them and anoint them with oil
in the name of the Lord."*
James 5:14

Chapter 27

"Lord, bring our girl back to us. Please Lord. Be with Kody
and wrap your loving arms around them both. Brittany's been
through so much. Please bring her back. Please." Aunt Carol's
pleading voice penetrated the darkness. "Let her know she's
not alone. Reach into that dark place where she is and bring her
back. Only you can bring her back to us."

My head and face throbbed with a dull ache. My entire
body hurt. I forced my eyes open. The light was blinding at
first but then dimmed.

"Kody?" I mumbled.

"No dear, it's Aunt Carol and Uncle Jim."

"Where's Kody?" My eyes focused on my aunt and uncle
hovering above me. "Where's Kody? Is he okay?"

Uncle Jim laid his hand on my arm. "Calm yourself,
sweetie. We'll go check on Kody as soon as we know you're
okay."

I worked to sit up, but a hand pushed me back down. "You
lay still for now." A nurse stood next to my bed. "You took a
bad bump on the head, and you've got quite a shiner there, but
you will be okay."

My hand went to my throat where a bandage stuck to my
neck. The nurse pulled my fingers away from the injury. "Just
a few stitches." She fussed with the sheets then left the room.

I grabbed Uncle Jim's hand. "Please check on Kody. You heard the nurse. I will be fine. Please check on him and come back and let me know how he is."

Aunt Carol nodded. "Go ahead, Jim. I'll stay with her."

He disappeared into the darkened hallway, and Aunt Carol sat on the edge of my bed. "Do you remember what happened, honey? David said boys bullied you at school. He thinks one of them attacked you at the church. Did you see his face?"

I closed my eyes and recalled the attack. "It was Eric Preston and Jeremy Sherwood. I heard their voices at the church." I tried to get up. "Someone said Kody had a pulse, and he was alive."

Aunt Carol laid her arm across me and forced me back down. "Relax. I'm sure the hospital has reached his parents, and they're with him. Uncle Jim will let us know as soon as he hears something."

With dazed exasperation, I tried to explain, "You don't understand. Kody doesn't have parents."

"Yes, he does. You're confused. It must be the sedative. David and Kody have been friends for years now, and I'm sure we would have known if Kody was an orphan."

David spoke from the hallway. "She's not confused, Mom." With stealth-like movements, he went to stand on the opposite side of my bed from Aunt Carol. "She's right. Kody's homeless. He has no parents."

"What do you mean?" Aunt Carol stepped around the bed and wrapped David in her arms. "Honey, that can't be. You told me his parents traveled a lot, and we assumed someone stayed with him when they left."

David pushed back from his mother's embrace. "We always told you they were out of town."

"David William Harper, are you telling me you've been lying to us?"

"I didn't lie."

"Then what would you call it?"

"We said they were out of town—and they were—they are.

They're in heaven. Kody's parents and his little brother died in a car accident when he was ten." David sobbed. "He was in the foster care system until he was fourteen. He ran away, and the homeless people in the park took him in. Mom, he's alone, and he's dying."

A gasp tore at my throat as I rose in my bed. Tears burst like a torrent, and I screamed, "No! Kody can't be dying. No!"

Aunt Carol tried to force me to lie down. She pressed the call button, and a nurse came running. "What's going on?"

I struggled against my aunt's arm. The nurse pressed the intercom button. "Get another sedative in here now."

Moments later, everything around me grew fuzzy. Kody was dying—and it was my fault.

****

The hospital released me the following day. I thought I would lose my mind during that first week after the attack. Kody remained unconscious. The doctor said it was a good sign he'd made it that long. All I wanted was for him to wake up healed.

Jeremy had broken his right arm in two places and his right leg above his knee. A fractured skull, severe concussion, cracked ribs, and a collapsed lung from knife wounds had the doctors worried. He'd lost a lot of blood. They couldn't say when, or if, he would wake up. Infection was high on their list of concerns. I watched him day after day and pleaded with God to save him, to help him—to do something.

Uncle Jim and Aunt Carol received temporary guardianship. They covered Kody's medical expenses for the best surgeons and doctors. He had a private room in Critical Care where I spent every day from early morning until late at night.

Exhaustion overcame me, but when I closed my eyes, I'd see Eric's face above mine and jerk awake. The doctors said I needed counseling and medication, but I refused. I would not

119

leave Kody's side, and I would not let them drug me into a stupor.

David stood in the doorway. A tall, thin man stood in the shadows behind him. David entered with hesitant steps and joined me at Kody's bedside. When the man came into the light, I almost didn't recognize him. It was obvious David had a hand in this transformation. Our friend carried a Giant's ball cap and wore a button-down collar shirt and dress pants. I couldn't believe this was the same man I'd met only months earlier.

I rose from my chair and reached out my hand. "Larry?"

The old man's eyes welled with tears as he came closer. "Ms. Brittany. Came to see our boy." He stepped to the side of the bed. Gawking at the beeping monitors and wheezing respirator, his eyes came to rest on Kody's face. "Oh, my boy—my dear sweet boy. What did they do to you?"

Watching the old man standing, trembling with unabashed tears streaming down his face, tears filled my own eyes, magnifying and distorting the scene into a hazy blur. I motioned for Larry to sit in the chair. "Would you like time alone with him?"

He nodded and pulled tissues from the box on the bed stand. "That'd be really nice if you don't mind. I'd like to talk to my boy."

David and I left Larry and Kody to their private moment. In the hall, David rested against the wall. "Do you think Kody hears us?"

"I have to believe he does."

"You look beat."

What could I say? The will to fight had gone out of me. How could I explain the melancholy of my soul that deepened with each passing hour? I offered a forlorn nod.

"The entire church is praying for him. They've set up around-the-clock prayer vigils and are asking people who can't come to pray on their own. God has to hear our prayers, Britt."

"I tried that."

"Praying?"

I wiped away a straggling tear. "Yeah. The first few days I prayed constantly."

"And now?"

"I don't understand. It's as if God disappeared. Where is He? Where's God in all this? Why doesn't Kody wake up?" A spasm of sobbing overtook me. "It's all my fault."

David pulled me into a hug, letting me soak his T-shirt. He said nothing. He stood there and held me. It seemed he knew what I needed. Sniffing back tears and wiping at my cheeks, I stepped back and gazed into his clear blue eyes, brimming with his own tears.

Larry stepped into the hall. "Ms. Brittany? He needs you."

From the old man's words, I thought Kody was asking for me. My heart burst with joy. "He's awake?"

Larry laid his hand on my shoulder. "Oh no, missy. He ain't awake. Not yet."

Hurrying past him, I reached Kody's bedside. "Then how do you know he needs me?"

"He loves you and needs you. That I know for certain."

I sat on the side of the bed with David standing beside me. Larry sat in the chair, and we were silent for several minutes.

The old man cleared his throat. "I'll never forget the day that boy came into my life. It was a blessing, you know. All he had was the clothes on his back and some books in a tattered old backpack."

On the far side of the bed, David slumped into the leather recliner. "He told me you were the only one who'd talk to him that day."

"Yep. We're a family, you know. And families stick together, but they ain't all that quick to let outsiders in till they get to know 'em. We ain't like those folks in the park and around the city. We're family."

Curiosity got the best of me. "What do you mean, Larry? Are you saying the people living in the Recreation Area differ from other homeless people in the city?"

"I said we're family. That's how we're different. We take care of each other."

"Are you related?"

A smile tugged at the corner of his lips. "You might say that. The good part is in our family we get to pick our relation."

I held down a chuckle at his retort. "And the other homeless people? The people in the park and other places? They aren't family?"

He chuckled. "No, ma'am. They sure ain't. Oh, some of them hang together for a time, but then they move on. They sure can't trust each other. Never know when one of the others might steal from them. We ain't got much, but what we got is ours."

He rested his hand on Kody's casted arm. "But this boy here—he's somethin' special. He's goin' places. And thanks to David, he's on the right path and gettin' the help he needs to get there."

I thought of David differently than before. He helped these homeless people in so many ways. "Yeah, David's special."

My cousin blushed then hung his head.

Larry plunked his cap on his head. "David?"

He looked up. "Yeah."

"It's time for you to take me home and for us to leave this little lady here to work her magic on our boy." He took me by the hand. "Love is magic, you know. Keep lovin' him and keep prayin'. You're doin' a fine job."

"No one ever told me that
grief felt so like fear."
-C.S. Lewis

Chapter 28

Late the next morning, a woman's scream echoed from the room next door. "No, no. She can't be dead."

In the hall, several people sobbed.

A pastor wearing a black suit and collar hurried toward the room.

They'd brought someone in that morning, but I'd not paid much attention. With my every thought on Kody, the rest of the world faded in and out.

A female janitor entered Kody's room.

"Did someone die?" I said.

She nodded. "I'm afraid so."

"What happened?"

She looked toward the door then back at me. "I guess I can tell you but tell no one I told you this."

She swiped away a tear. "She had her whole life ahead of her. I wish I understood why she did it."

"What did she do?"

"She jumped off the bridge." The woman shuddered. "She was only fifteen. What makes someone so young think life isn't worth living?"

Aunt Carol appeared in the doorway. The janitor hurried past her, wiping a tear as she went.

"She looked upset," Aunt Carol said.

"The girl in the next room died. That lady said she jumped

from the bridge."

Aunt Carol stepped to Kody's bedside and stroked his hand. "No change?"

"No."

She took a seat in the recliner. "I'm sorry to hear about the girl."

"I heard voices late this morning, but I didn't pay a lot of attention."

"Jumps from the bridge happen so often it's no longer big news. The suicide prevention people say broadcasting the jumps only encourages more people to do it. Few survive."

"You make it sound like people jump from the Golden Gate every day."

Aunt Carol's blue eyes misted. "At least one every two weeks, and it's been happening for years. How can someone that young be in such darkness they feel their only option is to take their own life."

I understood that kind of hurt—that feeling of being lost. I'd thought about killing myself. Over these past few days, those thoughts crept in again.

"But enough of that." Aunt Carol let out an audible breath. "I was hoping to talk you into having lunch with me today."

"I don't want to leave Kody."

"Honey, there's a nurse in here every ten minutes. He'll be fine."

I shook my head. "No. I won't leave him until they force me out of here."

"What if I bring something in?"

"I'm not starving."

A man dressed in a business suit, accompanied by a uniformed police officer, appeared in the open doorway. The man stepped inside. His eyes showed little trace of emotion. "Ms. Masters?"

"Yes."

"I'm Detective Jenkins and this is Officer Mills. Could we have a few moments of your time, please?"

124

"More questions? This past week I've answered more police officers than I can count. I told them everything I knew."

The detective glanced across the room then returned his attention. "It's about your assault, Ms. Masters. It should only take a moment."

My gaze returned to Kody lying in the bed. His pale cheeks and the faint sheen of perspiration coating his upper lip told of the physical battle he fought.

Why can't he wake up? Why can't this nightmare be over?

Aunt Carol came to my side and placed a reassuring arm around my waist. "What is it you need, Detective? She's been through so much, and I thought we answered your questions."

"This won't take long. Are you Mrs. Harper?"

"Yes, and if you must talk to Brittany, I insist on being with her."

"No problem. Follow me, please."

With a heavy heart, I left Kody's room, looking back over my shoulder. Detective Jenkins led us to a private meeting area down the hall.

I sat in a plastic chair across from the two officers. "Can we please make it quick?"

Detective Jenkins nodded. "I understand your concern, but the nurses will keep a close eye on him."

I glanced to the open doorway then back to the detective. "What do you want to know?"

"We understand Sherwood and Preston have been bullying you for some time, and last summer they accosted you and your friend. Is that true?"

"Yes."

"And before this last attack they bullied you and assaulted you at school?"

"Yes. I told the lady officer all this yesterday. Why do we have to rehash it again?"

"Ms. Masters—Brittany—are you prepared to testify against Eric Preston in court?"

Aunt Carol patted my hand.

The detective continued. "We understand it will be hard for you, but without your testimony we won't have much of a case. You don't have to answer today. Take time and think about it."

A sudden strength enveloped my body. I stood and slammed my palms on the table. "I don't have to think about it. You put that garbage behind bars where they can't hurt anyone else. They need to pay for what they've done. I will testify, and I will sign anything you need to put Eric Preston and Jeremy Sherwood in jail for a long time."

Trembling, I turned away to gather my composure then steeled my emotions. "Will you need Kody's testimony to put Jeremy in jail?"

"We have a warrant for both. We are charging Preston and Sherwood with sexual assault and also charging Sherwood with aggravated assault for his attack on Kody."

Officer Mills's cell phone vibrated on the table. "If you'll excuse me, I need to take this."

She took her call out of the room and spoke in hushed tones. While Aunt Carol spoke with Detective Jenkins, I stepped into the doorway and listened in on Officer Mills's conversation.

"That is good news. Thanks for letting me know. I'm sure the news will relieve her and her family." Officer Mills clicked off her phone.

"Relieved about what?"

"They've apprehended Eric Preston," Officer Mills said. "He's in custody at the county jail."

"And Jeremy?"

"We should have him soon. Preston's lawyer will encourage him to flip on Sherwood to get a lighter sentence."

"Are you telling me Eric could be let go if he leads you to Jeremy?"

Officer Mills's eyes closed to narrow slits. "Possibly. But that's for the District Attorney to decide."

Jeremy off the hook? That wouldn't be justice. I stormed to

my seat and let out a heavy sigh.

Detective Jenkins spoke in hushed tones. "We'll do everything we can to keep them locked up for as long as we can. However, I know they will be out on bail within a few days. They are not to come near you, and if they do, you call us."

Sudden chaos erupted in the hall, drawing us out of the room. Two doctors and a nurse pushed a bed toward the elevators. Multiple IV bags swung from poles at the head of the bed. Alarms sounded from a portable heart monitor.

I ran to the elevator bank. Kody lay on the bed, his skin ashen gray against the white sheets.

A nurse grabbed my arm. "Stand back."

"What happened?"

"Are you family?"

"I'm his girlfriend."

Aunt Carol stepped between the nurse and me. "My husband and I are his legal guardians."

"You can come with us, and I suggest you call your husband right away."

Aunt Carol slipped onto the elevator. The nurse held her hand out stopping me from entering. Sheer black fright swept through me. I reached out grabbing her arm. "Tell me what's happening. Where are you taking him?"

The nurse jerked from my grip and joined the others on the elevator. "I'm sorry, but privacy considerations don't permit me to tell you anything. Now please step back."

The doors closed. A muted reflection of my disheveled self revealed disbelief. I grabbed my cell phone from my jeans pocket and speed dialed Uncle Jim.

He answered on the first ring. "The hospital already called me, and I have your aunt on hold. I'm on my way. As soon as we know anything, we'll let you know. Wait in Kody's room. Millie and David will be with you soon."

Less than ten minutes later, Sara grabbed me and clung tight. Her damp hair and hot cheek pressed against my neck.

She held me and sobbed, "Oh Britt, I'm so sorry."

"What? Why are you sorry? What happened? Is he dead?"

Millie embraced us both. "No. Kody is not dead. He's in surgery, and he may be there for a few hours." The anxious look on her face revealed more than she was telling. She brushed the back of my head with a gentle stroke. David paced in the hall as the three of us stood in a solemn embrace. "Where are Aunt Carol and Uncle Jim?"

Millie took me by the hand. "They're in the surgical waiting room. They asked me to bring you there."

I trudged with Millie, David, and Sara to the elevators. I flashed back to the day I learned Mom, Dad, and Tiff were dead. A sharp pain stabbed my soul then vanished and left me with a misery so acute it was a physical ache. Old feelings resurfaced, bringing with them intensified grief. The elevator doors swished shut and enveloped us in a vacuum of sterile walls and harsh lighting

When the doors opened on the surgical floor, the only sound was the beeping of monitors. No nurses scuttled about. In the dim light, shadowy images of furniture formed at the end of the hall.

My aunt and uncle kneeled in the center of the waiting room. Uncle Jim prayed aloud and reached out a hand as we entered. I dropped to my knees next to him while David kneeled on my other side. Sara and Millie kneeled between him and Aunt Carol.

I bowed my head, offering a silent prayer. *God? Can you hear me? Please God, don't take Kody. I'll do anything for you. I'll give up anything you ask. Please don't take Kody.*

As Uncle Jim, Aunt Carol, and David took turns praying aloud, I pleaded with God to save Kody.

Wednesday night and early Thursday morning hours passed slowly as we prayed and waited. The nauseating sinking of despair assailed me as time crept by, drowning me in a sea of hopelessness and helplessness.

How could I go on without him? Just like before, it was my

fault. If he died, I had no one to blame but myself.

Hours later, they allowed us a few moments in the recovery room. Had I not known it was my beloved Kody lying in that hospital bed, I wouldn't have recognized him. Monitors beeped and tubes weaved in and out of his body. His face was paler than I thought possible for a living human. A ventilator tube ran into his mouth, and they'd applied new bandages to his head. His arm and leg casts created prominent bumps beneath the bed covers.

I kissed his cheek then caressed it. Bending down, I whispered in his ear, "I love you. Please don't leave me."

With the all tubes and wires weaving around his body, I couldn't take his hand in mine, so I gripped the rails on the side of the bed and prayed. Only two of us could be in the room at any one time, so Aunt Carol and I had to leave before David and Uncle Jim could come in.

A nurse stepped into the room, "It's been ten minutes, ladies. I must ask you to leave for a while."

I bent down and kissed Kody's forehead. His skin was cold to the touch. A tear slipped from my cheek to his and I brushed it away. Swallowing the sob that rose in my throat, I left the room.

Sara waited in the hall. She embraced me, unleashing a low tortured sob.

I wept aloud, "I told him I loved him."

I pulled away from Sara and sank to the floor, my back against the cold tile wall. I bent my knees beneath my chin and wrapped myself in a cocoon of anguish.

The long steady wail of a monitor flat lining emanated from Kody's room, and a flurry of doctors and nurses raced in, forcing Uncle Jim and David into the hall.

A nurse stepped from behind the nurse's station and directed us to return to the waiting room. "The doctor will be out to talk to you as soon as possible. Please wait here."

Uncle Jim took my hand, grief breaking through his fragile control. "I'm so sorry, honey."

He didn't ask to pray with me. No one asked to pray. We sat in numbed silence waiting—just waiting—waiting for a doctor to confirm what we already knew. It seemed so pointless.

Kody died, and that was all that mattered.

I slipped my hand from Uncle Jim's grasp. "I'll be in the ladies' room."

Aunt Carol's gaze clouded with tears. "Let me come with you, honey."

"I'd like to be alone."

Exiting the waiting room, I headed to the main lobby, out the front doors, and hailed a taxi.

The driver asked, "Where to?"

I opened my mouth to speak, but nothing came out.

"Where to, miss?"

Racked with the pain of losing Kody, my body trembled.

"I got other people waitin' if you can't decide. For the last time, where to?"

I swallowed hard. "The Golden Gate Bridge."

Chapter 29

I paid the driver and exited the taxi. My steps were slow, yet determined, as I climbed the steep walkway winding past flowering shrubs and green-carpeted lawns at the Visitors' Center. Grounds people busied themselves clipping and tending the foliage with care. Tour buses, cars, and taxis filled the parking lot. Beyond the large windows, inside the Golden Gate Restaurant, servers scurried about serving hot coffee and breakfast to anxious customers. The world moved on.

A female police officer on a bicycle passed. Two bridge workers dressed in splattered painters' pants chatted as they stepped around me. No one noticed I was there. No one had any idea what I was about to do. No one cared.

Since I'd come to San Francisco, we'd driven across the bridge many times, every trip to Dillon Beach, every trip to the park to visit the homeless. I chatted with Sara or laughed at David's antics. The only time I noticed any details of the bridge was when Uncle Jim pointed out the enormous towers topped with their Art Deco designs or the massive cables supporting the roadway. He once told us, "The Golden Gate is renowned as the most beautiful bridge in the world, and it is the symbol of San Francisco."

Today I wasn't chatting or laughing. Today the bridge was a means to an end. It was an end to the guilt and grief that haunted my every waking hour.

Through the morning fog, I passed a concrete wall then a wide section of chain-link fence topped with razor wire. I found no beauty in this structure. No amazement filled my heart as I forced myself to look down. Shrouded in foggy fingers, the parking lot and rocky shoreline peeked through diamond-shaped sections of fence.

I walked on, sliding my hand along the cold metal railing. Above me the first tower, pushed through a wispy patch of fog. Like a judgment bench, it loomed overhead.

Joggers and bikers hurried past as the suspended road of steel twisted and groaned beneath the rush of morning traffic. I looked down into the swirling waters of San Francisco Bay.

From somewhere in the distance, a faint voice called. "End it. End it now."

I passed by phone booths mounted beneath signs offering crisis hotline phone numbers, encouraging people to call if they needed help. However, those calls would not go to God, and He was the only one who could help me now.

God wouldn't help me. Of that, I was certain. For over a week, I'd prayed for Him to heal Kody. But He wasn't listening—or He didn't care. My family and the only boy I'd ever love were dead. I had nothing to live for.

God didn't care if the anguish and guilt in my heart grew greater each day, greater than any physical pain I'd ever endured. I killed my family. Kody was dead, and it was my fault. God would never forgive me for that. My prayers didn't matter to Him.

Midway between the towers, I leaned far out over the railing gripping one of the thick steel cables. Strong breezes assaulted me, heavy with pungent odors of the sea. Gone was the amazing fresh air of Dillon Beach. Here in the city the bay smelled of rotting seaweed, dead fish, and offerings of food vendors from Fisherman's Wharf.

The bridge vibrated with the weight of passing cars as I stepped onto the lower edge of the railing and leaned out farther. The sound of a ship's horn startled me as a cruise liner glided between the concrete supports beneath me. Pulling my weight upward, I swung my right leg, then my left, over the railing and dropped to the wide outer edge. I gripped the cold steel cable with both hands as I stepped out and around it. Only inches of steel girder now supported me above the swirling, beckoning waters. The twisted steel cable bit into my hands. I trembled as my gaze fell on Alcatraz Island.

I heard there is a thin wall that separates sanity from madness. Was I mad? Would a sane person be standing where I was?

The bay winds blew, their force taunting with the despair and loss of those who had stood here before.

Was I to be like the others? Would the current sweep me out to sea like a piece of trash?

My hair blew back from my face with the force of a thousand tiny fingers.

Would I land in the water and go straight down? Would the strong crosswinds blow me into the side of the bridge?

The sun broke through the morning fog, creating a hazy, golden light above the prison. My mother's voice reached out of my soul. "We love you, Brittany. Don't do this. Please don't do this."

Startled by the clarity of Mom's voice, my right foot slipped away beneath me. I grabbed at the cables with both hands. At that moment, I knew I did not want to die. Supporting my weight on the few inches beneath my left foot, I worked my right foot back up. The cables were wet with morning dampness. I lost my grip. Both feet slipped from the beam.

My body plummeted then seemed to drift on the breeze. My life did not pass before me. Time did not stand still. My heart did not stop. The pain of my feet slamming into the swirling, frigid water reverberated up my legs sending a shock wave through my entire body. Deeper and deeper I sank.

More terrifying than the silent ride down was the clawing, cold, beckoning darkness beneath the surface of the bay.

My mind went blank. My senses numbed. Seconds passed as I drifted into the depths below.

What happened?

I changed my mind.

I want to live.

Fear alerted my senses. Breaking out of the numbness the realization hit me. Something went wrong.

I reached for the cable.

I pulled myself up.

What happened?

Drifting deeper, the terrifying greenish-bluish-gray of the water turned darker as the piercing cold permeated my body.

Under water, I panicked and opened my mouth to scream, but frigid water flowed in, choking me.

Panic increased as seconds passed.

I struggled, waving, and beating my hands and legs in every direction.

Nothing happened.

The only thing I could touch was water. It passed from under my hands as I touched it.

Shaking my head in a panic-driven frenzy, I looked in every direction. All around me was the ominous dark color, growing darker as I sank deeper.

I tried breathing again through my nose.

I closed my eyes. I couldn't wake from this nightmare. This couldn't be happening.

I knew how to swim. This couldn't be happening.

I prayed. *God help me*.

My lungs ached as if my chest would burst. The air inside screamed to escape. But I didn't want to let it go.

With renewed panic, I opened my eyes and looked up. Something drifted above me. A large shadowy form drifted away then circled back.

My mind raced. Why was this happening? How did I get myself into this? Why did I sign my own death warrant?

Calming, I gave in to the realization. My body tired from pain and lack of air. The cold water numbed me. Sadness overcame me as I thought of my family. What would this do to them? I'd never see them again.

Seconds passed.

The water in my stomach rushed out. I puked in the water. I tasted the disgusting liquid as it came out. It mixed with the surrounding water.

I closed my eyes and shook my head working to escape the sour pool of regurgitation.

I grew frustrated. Angry. Where was the air?

I struggled to right myself. Which way was up?

A clear, calm voice came. "Don't believe the lie, Brittany. I love you. Don't believe the lie."

Battered and disoriented, I swallowed hard and worked to swim.

"Don't believe the lie. I love you. Don't believe the lie."

I could hold my breath no longer and was about to draw a fatal breath of water when a hand grasped my wrist and tugged. Surging through the frigid bay, I at last broke through the surface, sucking in life-giving breaths of air. An agonizing stab penetrated my chest. Every breath and every throb of my pulse racked my body.

I slipped from the grip of my rescuer. Water was everywhere. Above me. Below me. In my eyes, my mouth, my nose. It was salty.

Gasping for more air, all I got was water. When was it going to end?

A ghostly image of Mom, Dad, and Tiff floated in front of me. Kody, Uncle Jim, Aunt Carol, David, Sara. The images appeared then disappeared. Nana, Uncle Scott, Lisa. They drifted in and then away. I told them I loved them. I told them I was sorry.

Dear God, please save me. I'm sorry.

A strong but gentle arm surrounded me and pulled me to the surface. Time sped up to warp speed as I struggled against the pain. Someone lifted me from the water then laid me on a bed of sand and seaweed.

Opening my eyes, I recognized my rescuer as the man who'd helped me that day after the barbecue. I'd never seen his face, and if anyone asked, I couldn't describe him. But I knew it was him. He laid his hand on my cheek then brushed away debris. "Lie still. I called for help."

The realization of what I'd done flooded me with a terrible sense of guilt. My head throbbed, my vision blurred then cleared, then blurred again. Through a sludgy semi-consciousness, tears of agony and shame slipped down my cheeks.

*"Jesus looked at them and said, 'With
man this is impossible, but with God
all things are possible.'"*
Matthew 19:26

Chapter 30

Bright lights and anxious voices surrounded me. A blanket cocooned my body. Stabbing pain in my chest and sides imprisoned each breath. Both legs throbbed with pain.

Voices echoed around me.

"Do we know who she is?"

"No."

"I can't believe she survived."

Screams of frustration stuck in the back of my throat. What was happening? They were talking as though I couldn't hear them, as though I couldn't respond. I worked to form words, but nothing came out.

"She's one of the lucky ones."

"It's a miracle."

"She's coming around."

My gaze focused on a small woman with blonde hair and penetrating blue eyes. "Don't talk, whisper. What's your name?"

"Brittany," I squeaked out beneath the mask. "Can't breathe."

"I'm Dr. Kemper. I'll take good care of you."

A young man interrupted the doctor. "A cab driver found her purse in the backseat." He handed something to the doctor. "Here's her information."

She pushed the oxygen mask back in place. "I'm giving you something for pain."

She inserted a needle into my IV line and a peaceful darkness overtook me.

****

My vision cleared to see a nurse standing over me, her hands resting on my shoulders. A tube filled my mouth, and a machine that sounded like a sleeping giant wheezed next to me.

"Don't try to talk," the nurse cautioned. "Nod or move your head from side to side."

I felt no pain, but drifted cocooned in a blissful, beautiful calm. Then fear wrapped its cold tentacles around my heart. Was I dying? What was happening?

The nurse offered a reassuring grin. "I know you're scared. Surgery took several hours, and the machine is helping you breathe. You broke your right ankle, left leg, cracked several ribs and swallowed a lot of water. Do you understand?"

I nodded.

"Are you woozy?"

I nodded again.

"Your pain medication is causing that. You shouldn't have any pain. Do you?"

I shook my head, and she smiled.

Where were Uncle Jim and Aunt Carol? Why weren't they here? I wouldn't blame them if they never came. What I tried to do was unforgivable.

A woman with short brown hair and a friendly smile came through the door. "Good morning. Good to see you're awake."

She acted as if she knew me, but I'd never seen her before.

"You don't know me, although I've been in to see you several times over the past few days. My name is Mary Payne. I'm a social worker with the hospital."

A social worker? Do they think I'm an orphan? Maybe they couldn't find Aunt Carol and Uncle Jim. Oh, how I wish I could talk. I could tell them.

"Your family's worried about you."

If they were so worried why weren't they there?

Mary pulled a computer tablet from her briefcase, tapped it a few times, and put it in my hand. "For now, you can communicate with this." A grin tugged at the corner of her mouth. "Do you know how to use a tablet?"

I nodded and typed, "Where are my aunt and uncle?"

"At home."

"Are they angry with me?"

"No, they're not. They're concerned and relieved you survived. I'll let them know you're awake."

Dropping the tablet to my lap, I cradled my face in trembling hands as the shame overcame me. With a reassuring squeeze, she took my right hand in hers. "It's okay, Brittany. Take a few moments. Don't fight the machine. Let it breathe for you."

I settled my head against my pillow and closed my eyes. Regaining my composure, I picked up the tablet. "When can I see them?"

"Maybe tomorrow. Other than your doctors and nurses, you'll only see me today. We've been keeping a close eye on you. It's hospital policy for accidents such as yours. They don't allow visitors for the first seventy-two hours."

****

The next morning, I awoke to find Aunt Carol sitting in a chair next to my bed.

"Jim, she's awake."

My uncle stood on the other side of my bed and took my hand in his. "Good morning."

They had been through so much. I couldn't believe I'd done this to them. I picked up the tablet and typed, "I'm sorry."

Uncle Jim sat next to me on the bed where he could watch me type on the screen. He'd aged so much since the attack on

Kody and me. He squeezed my shoulder. "It's okay, honey." His voice trembled. "We should have insisted you get help."

He looked at my aunt. "She said she's sorry."

Aunt Carol looked worn and much older than before all this happened. "It's not your fault. None of this is your fault."

They were wrong. It was my fault. Mom, Dad, Tiff, and Kody—they were dead, and it was my fault. And I was the one who decided to end it all.

Aunt Carol rubbed at her forehead then her chin as if she didn't know what to do with her hands. Uncle Jim ran his fingers through his hair then picked at his stubble of beard. It was obvious they were uncomfortable talking. Who could blame them?

"Are David and Sara here?" I typed and turned the tablet to where my aunt could see it.

She leaned forward in her chair. "They were here earlier. You were sleeping. They're with Kody."

I fought the cobwebs of a drug-induced stupor. Sinking my head into my pillow, I closed my eyes. My breathing quickened, fighting the machine and causing a sharp pain in my ribs. I grabbed the tablet and typed with a trembling hand, "Kody?" I turned the screen to face her.

Aunt Carol's mouth dropped open. "I thought Ms. Payne told you." She looked at Uncle Jim then back at me. "It's been a miraculous week. They resuscitated him, and he breathed on his own. We looked everywhere for you. The doctors said it was a true miracle he came back to us, and they say he will make a full recovery." Unchecked tears flowed down her cheeks. "It seems God's been working overtime for our family. First Kody and then you. It's a miracle you survived."

Uncle Jim squeezed my hand. "There's no doubt God blessed us."

Girding myself with a resolve to get to Kody, I struggled against my covers, the tubes and cords. The pain was excruciating. Aunt Carol held me down. "Where do you think you're going?"

A sharp pain shot through my chest, and I clenched my jaw to kill the sob in my throat. I typed, "Does Kody know what I did?"

My aunt's intense gaze shifted to my uncle. Uncle Jim drew himself up. "No, we haven't told him. We didn't want to upset him. However, he's been asking for you. He feared you were dead. We told him you received minor injuries in the attack, and you slept a lot." He hung his head. "We hated lying to him, but we felt you should be the one to tell him."

Regret and shame hung like steel weights as a hot tear rolled down my cheek. I was to be the one to tell Kody.

*"And without faith it is impossible to please God,
because anyone who comes to him must
believe he exists and that
he rewards those who earnestly seek him."*
Hebrews 11:6

Chapter 31

After over a week in the hospital, knowing Kody lay only a short distance away drove me nuts.

That morning, Dr. Kemper checked my chart then grinned. "It looks like you're being a model patient. We'll take you off the respirator later today and give you a little freedom to move around and talk."

My heart swelled with tremendous anticipation, like a four-year-old on Christmas morning. I grabbed my tablet and typed, "Can I see Kody?"

"Maybe tomorrow. For today, I want to keep a check on your oxygen levels without the respirator. How's your pain?"

They'd reduced my pain medication, and it hurt when I moved the wrong way, but nothing like the devastating pain when they admitted me. "Not bad," I typed then laid the tablet aside.

"Okay then. I'll be back to check on you this afternoon."

I retrieved my tablet, and she returned to my bed. "Was there something else?"

With the index finger of each hand I typed, "I'd like to speak with my aunt."

"I'll be glad to call her."

What seemed like hours later, Aunt Carol appeared in the doorway carrying my tablet case, some books, and an overnight bag. "We thought you might want your own clothes, toiletries, books, and things."

I typed, "Thank you. Can we talk about what happened?"

A nurse entered the room. "Dr. Kemper said we could take you off the respirator. Would you like that?"

My aunt looked at me and grinned. "I think she'd like that very much."

After removing the machine and winding the cords and tubes up next to the bed, the nurse set a glass and a pitcher of water on the bed table. "You'll want this." She scooted the over-the-bed table in front of me. "You'll find it difficult to speak for a while. Don't overtax your voice."

I nodded and waited for her to leave before speaking. As warned, my words came out weak and raspy. "I have questions I need answered. Some things happened I don't understand."

"What do you want to know, honey?"

"When I was standing on the bridge, a glowing light sparkled over Alcatraz Island. I swear I heard Mom say, 'Don't do it Brittany.'" I took a sip of water. "The voice startled me, and then I heard it again. I didn't want to jump. I wanted to live."

She nodded.

"I did, Aunt Carol. I wanted to live. My foot slip, and I fell." Tears trickled down my cheeks. "You all think I tried to kill myself. I guess you're right—sort of."

"This is something you need discuss with Ms. Payne, Brittany. Have you told her?"

I nodded. "We've talked about it." I took another sip of water. "I needed to talk to you. Something else happened— kind of like hearing Mom's voice." It was getting harder to talk, so I took a long drink of water and waited a few minutes before going on. "I heard God."

Aunt Carol smiled. "That's possible."

"You believe me?"

She pushed the table out of the way and drew me to her chest in a gentle hug. "Yes, I believe you. And I believe you changed your mind." She leaned back and held my hands in hers. "So tell me—what did God say?"

"He said, 'I love you. Don't believe the lie.' That's what he said. 'I love you. Don't believe the lie.'" I took a drink and stared out the window. "Do you think it was God?"

She smiled. "I'm sure it was. The bigger question is; do you believe it was Him?"

"I'm not sure what He meant. 'Don't believe the lie.'" It was frustrating to stop talking and drink water. "Pastor Peter said the devil tells us lies. I didn't know if I believed in the devil, or God, or Jesus, or the Holy Spirit."

"And now?"

My tears flowed, and sweet warmth radiated in my chest. "Yes."

She handed me a gift-wrapped package. "You will find the answers you're looking for in here."

I opened the package to find a brand-new Bible with my name embossed on the bottom right corner. Inside Aunt Carol had written a personal message. "All you need, all you look for; you will find here."

I fluttered through the pages. "I don't know where to begin."

She took the Bible and opened it to the book of John. "Start here. If you have questions, I'll try to answer them. If I can't, I'll find someone who can."

I read, and she stood to leave. "I'll leave you with that while I go peek in on Kody." She sat down again and laid her hand on the Bible. "We had to tell him what happened."

The thought Kody knew tore at my insides. "What did he say?"

"It upset him, but he loves you very much, and he will be fine. We told him you were getting better every day, and it wouldn't be long before he could see you."

"Will the Bible tell me how I can feel better about what I did?"

She patted my leg as she turned to go. "Yes, dear. It's in there. You only have to look."

"Hope is being able to see that there
is light despite all the darkness."
-Anonymous

Chapter 32

It was late the next morning, and I'd had a restless night filled with hellish dreams.

Uncle Scott and Lisa sat in chairs on either side of me. Nana sat on my bed and I rested against her as she brushed my tear-soaked hair from my face.

"Shh," she said. "You've got to calm down, Brittany. If you don't, they'll sedate you and put you back on that machine. I know you don't want that."

I sobbed. "You all should hate me. I'm a terrible person. I've done terrible things."

Nana wiped my face with a cold wet cloth.

Uncle Scott handed me a glass of water. "Drink this." He gripped my hand in his. "No one hates you."

Lisa's brown eyes reached the depths of my soul as she took my face in her hands. "We all love you very much."

Ms. Payne entered the room. "What's this? My model client is having a pity party?"

Nana assumed a protective stance next to my bed. "Pity party? She's upset. She's been through more tragedy in this past year than most of us experience in a lifetime."

I gripped my grandmother's hand and sniffled. "It's okay, Nana. She's right. I'm feeling sorry for myself."

Nana huffed and scurried past Mary to the open door, muttering as she went, "I never."

Lisa and Uncle Scott excused themselves.

"Rough morning?" Mary said.

I straightened in bed. "More like a rough night."

"The dreams again?"

"Yeah."

She pulled a packet of papers from her briefcase. "I believe I've found something that might put an end to some of those nightmares."

I swung my legs around to sit on the side of the bed and wiped a tissue under my nose. "What?"

"Has anyone ever talked to you about what caused the accident?"

"I told you. I glanced over at my cell phone in the console and lost control of the car."

"But that didn't cause the accident." She pulled a pair of jeans and a tank top from the drawer and laid them on the bed. "Get dressed, and I'll be back in a few minutes."

What did she mean? What was in those papers?

I'd dressed and settled in the recliner in the corner of my room when a tap came at my door. "Come in."

Mary returned with my family trailing behind. The hospital didn't let this many people in my room and a slight tremor of fear ran through me. "Did something happen to Kody?"

Mary sat on the edge of my bed then reached over and patted my hand. "Kody's fine and I understand he may come to see you soon."

A bold smile crossed my lips. "I can't wait!"

She pulled a file from her brief case and laid it on my lap. "According to the accident report, the power steering belt on the car broke. That would make it very difficult to turn the car. For an inexperienced driver, such as you, it would have been almost impossible. The police attribute your accident to power steering malfunction. It was not your fault. There was nothing you could have done."

Offering a melancholy smile, Uncle Scott laid his hand on my shoulder. "We're so sorry we didn't discuss this with you in more detail. That night in Jim's living room was the first time we realized the level of guilt you carried and how you much you blamed yourself."

Uncle Jim spoke up. "To be honest, none of us ever read the report. We filed it away with the other papers."

My thoughts spun in confusion. I wasn't certain of anything. Nothing I'd believed was true. The Lord tried to tell me. He told me it was a lie. I was still trying to understand what He meant by that, and here it was right in front of me. He knew all the time. Hearing the accident could not have been my fault, but the power steering malfunctioned, brought a long-needed peace to my heart.

****

That afternoon, a tap came on my open door, and Dr. Kemper stood next to a wheelchair occupied by Kody. "This young man said he would not wait any longer to see you."

He wheeled over to the recliner and took my hand in his. A smile tipped the corners of his mouth. "Brittany." His hand trembled in mine as he whispered, "I thought they killed you."

A cry of relief broke from my lips and tears flowed. "I thought you died."

Dr. Kemper stood in the doorway and swiped at her cheek. "I'll give you some time alone, but then Kody needs to go back to his room, and you need to rest."

Kody nodded, "I'll make sure she stays quiet."

She called back as she disappeared in the hall, "And I don't want you trying to get out of that contraption by yourself. Ring for a nurse when you get back to your room and let her help you."

Kody sighed. "Yes, ma'am."

I inhaled a deep breath. "If only I could go back and change what happened. Aunt Carol told me you know what I did."

"Yeah, they told me. Do you want to talk about it?"

"I thought you died, and it was my fault—like I thought the

accident with my family was my fault. I didn't want to live."

"Britt, none of this was your fault. It was Eric and Jeremy. They did this to us."

Shame and fear screamed from inside. Tears streaked my cheeks. "I hope you'll understand. Please don't hate me. The monitor flat lined."

He reached for my hand. "I'm okay."

"I went to the bridge because I thought you were dead, and I didn't want to live without you."

His dark eyes showed the tortured dullness of disbelief. "Oh Britt, how could you?"

Misery weighed in my heart like a sinking anchor. I pleaded, hoping I could convince him. "I changed my mind. Please believe me. My foot slipped, and I fell."

"It's okay. We'll get through this. We're both going to be okay. I promise."

"Take the first step in faith. You don't
have to see the whole staircase,
just take the first step."
– Martin Luther King, Jr.

Chapter 33

Monday morning, they released Kody and me from the hospital. We were quite a sight as we hobbled into the house with our crutches. Uncle Jim assisted Kody and Uncle Scott picked me up and carried me up the front steps.

In the entry hall, my eyes followed the winding staircase to the top then back down. Aunt Carol came close to my ear and whispered, "I've redecorated the bedroom at the back of the house for Kody, and we can help you up to your room."

"I can make it on my own."

"You're sure the steps won't be too much?"

"I'll take them slow but I need to do it myself."

Millie held out a plate of chocolate chip cookies. "Welcome home."

I started toward her when Uncle Jim stepped in front of me, and with a quick gentle movement he lifted me off the floor. "You and Kody are going to your rooms to rest."

As my uncle carried me up the steps, I looked back over his shoulder at my family gathered below. God was so good. Only a few weeks ago, I thought I'd lost Kody, and for a foolish moment, I'd almost lost my own life. Now Kody and I were healing, and I had my entire life ahead of me.

I thought about how Pastor Peter talked about God having a plan for each of us, and how He only let us know a little at a time. He showed us what we could handle now, but not so much as to overwhelm us. But God knew my past, my present, and my future. That was difficult to accept and to understand, but I had to try. The only way I could move forward and put the past behind me was to believe He had everything under control.

David scurried up the steps. "Don't get too used to that. I'm not carrying you around when he goes to work."

****

An hour later, Uncle Scott, Lisa, and Nana joined me in my room as I savored a plate of cookies and milk. Nana sat next to me on the bed. "We have to leave soon to catch our flight, and we want a few minutes with you before we go."

"I know, Nana. It's okay. I'm fine."

Uncle Scott and Lisa sat at the foot of my bed, and he laid his hand on my leg. "We know you're in good hands."

Lisa grinned. "Call us if you need anything. I don't care what time of day it is. Call even if it's only to talk."

They still didn't believe I'd changed my mind. It was obvious they thought I tried to kill myself, and they walked on eggs so as not to upset me. But I was too tired to persuade them otherwise.

"Jesus is with me. He's my protector, and He always will be."

David appeared at the door. "You guys ready to go?"

Uncle Scott grinned. "Are you our chauffer?"

My cousin offered a comical bow. "At your service, sir. We aim to please."

"I'm counting on you to keep our little girl safe."

I swung my legs over the side of my bed and struggled to stand. "Let's get something straight. David is not responsible for me."

David cleared his throat. "It's okay, Britt."

"No, it's not okay. No one needs to feel like I'm their

150

responsibility, as if it's up to them to keep me from getting hurt or doing something stupid. I'm an adult, and I'm responsible for me."

"Your uncle didn't mean you can't take care of yourself. Cut him a break. He's just worried."

Uncle Scott pulled me into an embrace then released me. Tears welled in his eyes. "We love you so much. It's hard being so far away when things happen, and you need us."

A moment of shame pulsed through me, and I hugged him back. "I'm sorry. I shouldn't have barked at you."

Nana interrupted. "You're tired, and you need to rest."

She sounded like she did when I was a little girl and she'd say I was getting crabby and needed a nap. Resisting the urge to defend myself, I hugged her. "That's right, Nana. I need another nap. Call me when you get home."

****

The following morning, Kody and I sat at the kitchen table enjoying Millie's pancake breakfast. Kody downed three pancakes and four sausages and worked on a second helping. Between mouthfuls, he praised Millie. "This breakfast is the best I've ever had." He swallowed a gulp of milk. "I've never tasted pancakes this good."

Millie laughed. "You've been eating hospital food for so long you forgot what home cooking tasted like."

"That's for sure. Hospital food can't compare to your cooking."

The front doorbell rang, and Millie crossed the kitchen, glancing at her watch. "My goodness, who could that be so early? It's not even eight o'clock."

Moments later, she returned to the kitchen. "It's Ms. Chatham. She said she's here to tutor you."

Kody stopped chewing and swallowed. "Who's she here to tutor?"

Millie shrugged. "It sounds like both of you."

Leaving Kody at the table, I went to meet with the counselor. Ms. Chatham paced around the entry hall, running her finger over a marble table then sniffing the flowers arranged in a cut crystal vase.

"Ms. Chatham, why are you here?"

"Now that you and your friend Kody are on the mend, Mrs. Harper hired me to tutor you until you're ready to come back to school."

Panic gripped my heart as I recalled David saying Kody didn't want to go to school because that would get Social Services involved, and they'd put him back in foster care until he was eighteen. Knowing my aunt and uncle were now his guardians didn't ease my fears. "Kody?"

"I understand he's been out of school for some time and he's studying to take his GED. What an ambitious young man." Her soft giggle seemed out of place for an adult. "Homeless and desperate. No family to speak of. On his own, he studies for his GED. I can't wait to meet him."

"You don't have to wait any longer. I'm right here." Kody's voice held an edge of resentment as he stood in the doorway. "And I don't consider myself all that amazing, although you may be right about my being desperate. A few weeks ago I was homeless, but not anymore. I don't need your help."

He left the room when Aunt Carol appeared at the top of the stairs. She hurried down. "I am so sorry. I lost track of time this morning, and with all the activity getting Brittany and Kody settled in yesterday, I didn't talk to them about you tutoring them." She directed Ms. Chatham to Uncle Jim's office. "You'll be undisturbed in here. Why don't you get started with Brittany, and I'll talk to Kody."

I'd been in Uncle Jim's office once, and it was only for a few minutes. An antique table and chairs sat in front of the bay window. Floor to ceiling bookshelves lined two walls. Several pieces of Renaissance artwork caught my attention. I sat at the table and surveyed the beauty and serenity my aunt created for

152

my uncle.

Ms. Chatham sat in a chair across from me. "You've already missed four weeks of school this year, and your aunt and uncle feel you should not return until after winter break. Which is why I'm suggesting you use the online homeschool program. I'll check in with you two or three days a week."

"Online homeschooling?"

"Are you familiar with it?"

"I've seen ads on TV, but I don't know how it works."

She slid a booklet and file folder across the table. "These are the assignments you've missed, and the brochure explains how to get set up and continue on with your classes."

"And I won't return to regular classes until January?"

"That is the plan. You'll return after the winter vacation break. By then, between your online classes and with my help, you should be on track for graduation in June. You already have enough credits, and you only need to take one more of the required classes."

What were my classmates saying about me? I'm sure the rumor mill was grinding out all kinds of horrific tales. Maybe I'd ask David. But, then again, it was best I didn't know. Thinking back, the only kids that came to see me in the hospital were friends from church. None of the kids I hung out with at school came by or called. I didn't remember getting cards or flowers, other than those from some of my teachers and Ms. Chatham. "Would I be able to do the online classes all the way through and not return to my regular classes?"

"I suppose."

"I don't want to go back."

"Why don't we take this one step at a time? For now, we'll get you set up with the online classes, and I'll tutor you. Before winter break, you can decide if you want to come back. I'd hate for you to miss your senior year and hanging out with your friends."

What friends? Other than my family, Sara, and Kody, no one wanted to hang out with me. They thought I was the crazy

girl who jumped off the bridge. "I'll think about it." Then I
remembered my study group for the ACTs and SATs. "What
about college tests?"

"I can arrange that when you're ready."

The door opened and Millie stuck her head in. "I hate to
interrupt, but Ms. Payne is here for Ms. Brittany. She says they
scheduled an appointment for eight thirty."

Ms. Chatham gathered her portfolio and purse. "That's it
for today. Please tell Mrs. Harper to call me when Kody is
ready for tutoring."

I escorted Ms. Chatham to the front door. I introduced her
to Mary, and we said our goodbyes.

Ms. Payne grinned. "So that's Ms. Chatham."

"I've mentioned her to you?"

"No. But I've heard her name before."

"From whom?"

"I can't say. Patient confidentiality. Are you up to a short
walk? It's a warm, clear day, and I could use the fresh air."

"Sure. Let me grab my jacket."

We walked at a slow pace for several blocks, admiring the
colorful Victorian homes. Mary checked her phone then turned
it off and slipped it in her pocket. "You're deep in thought."

My lips puckered with annoyance. "Everyone still thinks I
tried to kill myself, and I can't convince them I changed my
mind."

"Tell me about the car accident."

"We've been through that. I'm fine now."

"Humor me. I have a point to this."

My voice grew hoarse as I once again recounted the
accident. "We were coming back from Sunday lunch at Little
Bear, and it snowed. Dad was teaching me to drive in snow,
and he thought it was an opportunity for me to get practice. We
were a mile from home when we came around a curve in the
road, and the rear of the car slid on the ice. I tried to turn the
wheel and work the brakes as he taught me, but the wheel
stuck. My cell phone rang in the console, and I glanced away

from the road. As the rear of the car slipped over the drop-off, Dad grabbed the steering wheel. I remember little after that."

"And you still blame yourself?"

"Yeah—sometimes. I know the power steering malfunctioned, but I was driving."

"Tell me, Brittany, if your dad had been driving, and you were the only one who survived, would you blame him?"

"No."

"And do you think your parents and little sister blame you?"

"No."

"Brittany, you have many people who love you very much. Suicide hurts those people you leave behind."

"But I changed my mind. I didn't mean to do it. How can I make you understand I changed my mind?"

She caressed my arm. "Would you have gone out on the bridge if you didn't intend to jump?"

I inhaled a deep breath and shook my head.

"What hurts them is thinking there may have been something they could have done to stop you."

My frustration collapsed into dull shame. "Do they think it's their fault."

"They believe they should have known how you felt and stopped you."

"My best friend and cousin pretend everything is fine, but they don't treat me the same. Are you saying they think they could have stopped me?"

She quirked an eyebrow. "Misplaced guilt?"

"I know what you want me to understand."

"What's that?"

Mary always saw through my mask. It did no good to pretend with her, but I didn't want to accept what she meant. "You're saying my guilt about the accident and their guilt about me going out on the bridge is the same."

"What do you think?"

A tight knot within me begged for release. "I don't know."

A familiar voice called out from across the park, "Hey Eric. Wait."

I trembled.

Mary gripped my arm, took my crutches and lowered me to a park bench. "What is it?"

I craned my neck to scan the park. I knew it was them. They must have seen us.

"Are you okay? You went pale for a minute."

"I heard Eric's voice."

She looked across the park. "No one is there."

I clasped my hands together to stop them from shaking. "I know it was him."

"Maybe we should head back."

"You believe me, don't you? I wasn't hearing things. I swear I heard him."

She patted my hand. "Yes, I believe you, and we should head back to the house."

"However unpleasant the truth
may be, it is better to face it once
for all, to get used to it and to
proceed to build your life in
accordance with it."
-Bertrand Russell

Chapter 34

Several weeks later in the early afternoon, Aunt Carol called through my bedroom door. "Brittany, the lady from the DA's office is here. Could you come down, please?"

I shuffled downstairs where merriment echoed from the living room. A shapely, blonde woman in a short navy skirt and fitted jacket laughed with Kody. His face was red, and he gasped a breath. "Britt."

The woman offered her hand. "Frances Deering, Ms. Masters."

I shook her hand then dropped into a soft leather chair. "What's so funny?"

"Kody was telling me a story about a friend of his." She looked at Kody. "Larry? Right?"

He chuckled. "Right."

A strange emotion kicked me in the gut. She called him Kody but me Ms. Masters. He had told her something about Larry he'd never told me. He doesn't trust people this fast. What's with her? "I don't think I've heard the story."

Ms. Deering inhaled to stop laughing. "It may be the telling and not the story that was so funny. Some people have the innate ability to tell stories that make you laugh."

"I didn't realize Kody was such a comedian." I glanced over at him. "This is a side of you I've not seen. Have you been hiding your light under a bushel?"

Kody shrugged.

Ms. Deering's mouth drew into a firm line, and she assumed a professional posture. "I apologize." She looked at her watch. "We have several items we plan to present in court, and I need to go over a few things with you to clarify what we know."

She shuffled through a file of papers, running her finger down the pages. "Your friend?"

"Sara."

"Yes. Ms. Alexander." She folded back pages and pointed to something on the page in front of her. "Mr. Sherwood and Mr. Preston assaulted you and Ms. Alexander last April. Is that correct?"

"Yes."

"And what were the circumstances that led up to the attack? Was this the first time they'd harassed you? Were you talking to them when they attacked you, or were you taken by surprise?"

"All of that is in the police reports. Haven't you read them?"

She huffed. "Yes."

She clicked on a recorder and asked if she had my permission to record my interview. I agreed and spent the next thirty minutes telling the story of Eric and Jeremy's harassment attacks.

Kody gasped and grabbed my arm. "What happened at the fair?"

I realized my mistake. Only Sara and I knew about that night at the fairgrounds. We hadn't told the police nor David or Kody.

Ms. Deering searched her reports with fervor. "There's nothing in here about them attacking you at a fair."

I hesitated. The stunner was illegal because I didn't have my aunt or uncle's signature. They'd want to know where I got it. "It was when we went to the restroom."

Kody's jaw tightened. "I knew something happened to you two. You both acted weird when you came back."

"Do you still have the stunner?" Ms. Deering said.

"Yes."

"Please speak up, Ms. Masters."

I shouted, "Yes."

"Would you get it for me, please?"

I retrieved the stunner from my room and shuffled back downstairs and handed it to Ms. Deering. "Is this what you wanted?"

She grinned. "For the record, what Ms. Masters has is a nonlethal stun gun." She removed the lid and pressed the top button. "It is a red lipstick tube with a black wrist strap attached. It is also an LED flashlight. One button works the light; the other button works the stunner." She met my eyes with hers. "Is that correct, Ms. Masters?"

I resumed my seat, my head hung in fear of what might happen next. "Are you going to put me in jail?"

She laughed. "Why would we put you in jail?"

"I bought it without my aunt or uncle's consent, and they told me that was illegal, but the man said he'd misplace the paperwork."

Kody chuckled. "They won't put you in jail, Britt. Will they, Ms. Deering?"

"No. The man selling it to you broke the law by not getting the consent form. Unlike a Taser, this device causes muscle contractions and pain, and that might cause the person to drop to their knees."

I exhaled. "So I did nothing wrong?"

"Our only problem may be if Mr. Sherwood and Mr. Preston's attorneys raise the issue that you attacked them unprovoked. We'll deal with that if it happens."

She clicked off the recorder. "I'm glad you told me about this. It could have been an ugly surprise if the defense were to use it in court."

"Will you be the one talking to Sara?"

"No. One of my coworkers is interviewing her as we speak. I'll call him when I leave, so he knows to ask for her statement about the incident at the fair."

Ms. Deering turned to Kody. "What do you remember about your attack? Can you identify Mr. Sherwood as your attacker?"

Kody shook his head. "It was dark, and he came at me from behind. He stank of beer and cigarettes. He hit me over the head with something heavy. I fell to the ground about the same time something crashed next to me. I tried to get up, to get to Britt, but he kept pounding me. Something sharp cut through my side. That's the last thing I remember."

"According to the police report, someone struck you with a statue. They found it shattered and identified your blood on it, but there were no fingerprints or any other DNA evidence."

Kody averted his eyes. "So you have no evidence to prove Sherwood attacked me?"

She sighed. "No. Even if Sara can identify him as her attacker that will carry no weight in proving he attacked you."

I stood, my blood pounding in my temples. "Don't you have any of those things we see on TV? I mean, weren't there any hair samples, fibers or DNA? Anything? What about the knife?"

Ms. Deering smirked. "I wish all those futuristic tools were available to us. The truth is most police departments can't afford them. I'm sure you're aware of the financial problems facing the state right now. We can process DNA and fingerprints, but we don't have all the gizmos and gadgets you see on television."

I plopped back into my seat. "What about the knife?"

"They never found it."

"So Jeremy will walk?"

"The DA's office is doing all we can to build cases against these two. However, it gets complicated with the different attacks at different times involving different victims. In addition, Mr. Preston's father is a powerful attorney with one of the most respected law offices in California. I'm sure Eric will have the best defense money can buy."

"And Jeremy?"

"His mother works in the same office." Ms. Deering gathered her things and stood to leave. "Don't lose heart. We'll have your testimony. That will carry a lot of weight with the judge."

"Juvenile court, right?" I said.

"No. They're both eighteen."

I sighed and worked to repress my anger. "Has anyone else come forward to file complaints against either of them? I'm sure we're not the only ones they've gone after."

"No."

I followed her as she exited the room. "You said my testimony was important in prosecuting Eric. What about Sara's against Jeremy?"

"We're waiting to hear from her parents and hoping to have their permission for her to testify after today's interview."

****

That afternoon, Kody and I were playing a video game in the family room when a familiar voice echoed from the doorway.

"There's my boy," Larry shouted. "How you doin', buddy?"

Dropping his controller to the coffee table, Kody reached a hand out to his friend. "Larry. Gosh. I haven't seen you since— I'm not sure the last time I saw you."

Larry shuffled a foot and hung his head. "I couldn't get to the hospital as much as I would have liked." He pasted on a smile. "But David got me there once. You were cuttin' z's."

"Yeah. I spent a lot of time sleeping. Come on in and sit down."

Larry sat on the edge of the leather sofa, his now-slightly soiled Giant's cap in hand. He looked around the room. "Nice place you got here."

Kody laughed. "It's not mine."

"It beats livin' in a tent. They treatin' you okay?"

"Yeah. Great."

"I understand from David, his folks got made your guardians. You okay with that?"

Kody's smiled. "Sure."

David took a seat next to me. "Larry, why don't you tell Kody what's been going on at home?"

"Oh, yeah. Lots of stuff."

Kody leaned in closer. "Like what?"

"Ole Frank last week found a hundred-dollar bill floatin' across the ground."

"No kidding."

"Nope. Got enough to feed all of us for a while. And Sasha—you remember Sasha? She's the one that had a crush on you."

I recalled the girl with the piercings and tattoos who seemed to hang close to Kody whenever I was near.

Larry grew agitated. "She went home."

Kody frowned. "Yeah? Was that a good thing?"

Larry sniffed. "No. That old man of her mama's took a swipe at her. They say she hit him over the head with something and killed him. They found his body in the closet and no sign of Sasha or her mama."

"She's missing?"

Larry shook his head. "They found her washed up on Treasure Island."

Kody's hand flew to his mouth. "Dead?"

"Yep. Nobody reported seein' anyone jump from the bridge. You know they've got those cameras to catch the jumpers. But she didn't show up on any of them. A lot of the jumpers end up out there on the island, you know. It took them awhile to identify her."

Larry apparently hadn't heard about me jumping, or he surely would have said something. My mind was incapable of absorbing that young girl's body washing ashore and nobody cared. The rancid taste of puke worked its way into my throat.

"Excuse me." I grabbed my hand over my mouth and hurried from the room as the realization enveloped me. That could have been me.

*"The most beautiful discovery
true friends make is they
can grow separately without
growing apart."*
-Elizabeth Foley

Chapter 35

The smell of turkey and pumpkin pies filled the house with a heavenly fragrance as Aunt Carol scurried about picking at the fall foliage the decorator had hung from the banister and on the walls. The dining room table held a huge cornucopia with colorful gourds, apples, and nuts tumbling onto a cream-colored linen tablecloth. Each of the twenty place settings held miniature cornucopias. Gold-rimmed china plates, set atop dark brown chargers, held coordinating colored napkins encircled with golden napkin rings that matched the cutlery.

I circled the table checking out the place cards when Aunt Carol wandered in. "Oh, there you are, Brittany. David was looking for you. He and the other gentlemen are downstairs."

As I drew close to the family room, the sound of laughing and hooting flooded into the outer hall. I found two uncles lying on the floor on their stomachs, arm wrestling. Kody and David cheered them on, Kody for Uncle Scott and David for Uncle Jim.

I had to shout to be heard above the roar of the crowd. "David. Aunt Carol said you were looking for me."

Several grunts and a thud from the floor captured his attention. He glanced at the two men on the floor then at me. "It can wait another couple of minutes."

I rolled my eyes and turned to leave.

He tore himself away from the action. "Don't go. I need to talk to you." A huge sigh confirmed the sacrifice he was making, but he motioned for me to follow.

We entered Kody's room, and David closed the door. This was the first time I'd been inside my boyfriend's domain. I'd looked in from the hall the day after we came home from the hospital to admire the skills applied by Aunt Carol's decorator. But she had asked that Kody and I not spend time together in either of our bedrooms. She said it wasn't proper, and I knew Mom and Dad would have set down the same rule.

David sat in the desk chair and gestured for me to sit on the bed. "It's about Sara." A tone of regret filled his voice. "She asked me to talk to you."

"Why can't she call or text? I've not spoken with her since we came home from the hospital. When I text her, she doesn't answer. When I call, she either doesn't answer or cuts me off making lame excuses."

"I know."

"So what's going on?"

"I don't know how to tell you this, Britt. And I don't want to hurt your feelings, but Sara's not allowed to hang out with you anymore."

"She's my best friend. Why doesn't she want to hang with me?"

"It's not that she doesn't want to. She feels bad about it. But her parents forbid her to spend time with you—or Kody."

"Kody?"

He nodded. "Yeah. They think you guys are a bad influence on Sara, and they said they believe Jeremy attacked her because she was with you."

I paced the room running my hands through my hair. "That's nuts."

"I'm sorry, Britt."

"We had nothing to do with her being attacked." Like an old wound that ached on a rainy day, the memory of my incident on the bridge reminded me that most people still believed I jumped. Most people—even Sara—and for sure her parents. "They think I'm crazy, don't they? They don't want their daughter hanging out with a crazy girl who would jump off the Golden Gate Bridge."

He sighed. "That's part of it."

Kody opened the door and came in. "What's going on?"

With tears streaking my cheeks, I paced and shouted, "Sara can't hang with us anymore."

Kody lay across the bed. He patted the end showing I should sit there. "Calm down. What's going on?"

Refusing his offer, I sat on the floor, my back against the footboard. "Her folks think I'm crazy because I jumped off the bridge, and they don't want her hanging out with me." I huffed. "Oh, and it's my fault Eric and Jeremy attacked us."

Kody brushed my hair from the back of my neck. "I'm sorry, Britt."

Bristling with indignation, I sputtered, "Fine. I don't need Ms. Goody Two Shoes in my life." I stood and faced the door.

Kody caught me by the hand. "You said she couldn't hang out with us. What did I do that ticked off her folks?"

My hurt turned into a white-hot anger as I faced my cousin. "Are you still dating her?"

David nodded. "I guess so."

I looked at Kody, my mouth forming a grim line, my jaw tightening and blood pounding in my head. My face had to be flaming by this point. "Guess we know where we stand."

Kody tugged my hand and pulled me back to the edge of the bed, then directed his gaze at David. "So Sara can't be near Britt or me, but she can date you? That's pretty much it?"

David straddled the desk chair. "Pretty much." He spread his hands in front of us and pleaded, "Please don't blame Sara. She cries a lot when her folks aren't around. She loves you guys. It's her parents."

My pulse calmed as I inhaled several deep breaths. "What do Sara's folks say about Kody?"

"Like many people, they're ignorant about a good many social issues, one being homelessness."

Kody sniffed and nodded. "I figured that was it."

I stomped to the door, and before leaving, I muttered, "They're stupid."

****

Several hours later, I'd calmed down enough to greet Aunt Carol and Uncle Jim's guests civilly. My Colorado family arrived the day before. Other than a few people I recognized from church, I didn't know many other guests.

The next couple of hours passed with good food and funny stories. Even the family tradition of going around the table and each person saying one thing they were thankful for went all right. When my turn came, I choked back tears, "I'm thankful for a family that loves me and for Kody and my recovery."

After dinner, people meandered about the house visiting, playing cards, or arm wrestling in the family room. It seemed my uncles started a new tradition catching on as a popular sport among the testosterone-carrying family members and guests.

Uncle Scott and Lisa caught up with me between card games. He dropped his arm around my shoulders and gestured for Lisa to join us. "We need to talk."

He didn't have to say anything more. I read it all over their faces. "You're getting married."

Lisa and Uncle Scott had so much in common. They loved living in the mountains, horses, hunting, and fishing. I looked up at Lisa. "You will be my aunt." Then I punched Uncle Scott in the shoulder. "It's about time. Mom always said this day would come if you ever came to your senses and realized what a great girl Lisa is."

He scratched his head and smiled. "Guilty."

Lisa wrapped her arms around my uncle's waist. "So you're okay with this?"

My smile broadened with approval. "Okay? I'm

167

thrilled! Can I be in the wedding?"

"Will you be my Maid of Honor?"

"Sure. When's the big day?"

She looked up at Uncle Scott. The warmth of his smile echoed in his voice. "December 28th."

I pressed in with relentless joy. "This year."

"Yeah. I think we've waited long enough. Don't you?"

I nodded and grabbed them both into a huge family hug.

****

Nana always shared my bed when they came to visit, and tonight I needed to talk with her. I missed sitting at her feet while she crocheted or brushed my hair or when we watched TV. We used to talk about everything. Even before Mom and Dad died, I spent several nights a week at Nana's house. We'd curl up together in her old wrought-iron bed, and she'd listen to my problems. Then she'd stroke my hair and hum "Mariah" until I fell asleep.

She got under the covers first. Propping her pillow against the headboard, she leaned back and sighed. "It's been quite a day. I guess Scott and Lisa shared their good news."

I rested my head in her lap. "Yeah."

"Are you okay with it?"

"Why wouldn't I be?"

She stroked my hair like old times. "It hasn't been that long since we lost your mom, dad, and Tiffany."

I fingered a ribbon on the sleeve of her nightgown. "It's what they would want."

She nodded. "I'm sure it is."

"Nana, do you think I'm crazy?"

She sat up, and my head slipped from her lap. "For heaven's sake, why would you ask such a question?"

"You know I didn't jump from the bridge, right?"

"You told me you changed your mind. Your foot slipped and you fell."

"And you believe me, don't you?"

The tone in her voice was sincere. "I do."

She assumed her previous position, and I plunked my head back in her lap. "Sara's not allowed to hang out with me anymore."

She stroked my hair. "I'm sorry."

"Her folks said I'm a bad influence, and it was my fault Eric and Jeremy attacked us."

"It's hard to be a parent, Brittany."

I lifted my head in defiance. "Are you taking their side?"

"I don't think there's a side to take here. You must try to understand how her parents feel. I wouldn't want you with someone I believed was dangerous or could cause you to get hurt."

I rested my head and yawned. "How can I change their minds?"

"I don't think you can."

"So Sara won't be my friend anymore?"

"Why don't we pray for your friendship with Sara. I'm sure if God wants you girls together, one day He'll make it happen."

*'Trust in the Lord with
all your heart and lean not
on your own understanding.'*
Proverbs 3:5

Chapter 36

Monday morning Uncle Jim, Aunt Carol, Kody, and I rode to the courthouse together to attend Jeremy's preliminary hearing. David was to pick up Sara.

We entered the front doors of a large building with great marble columns and marble floors. I crossed beneath the dome in the large hall and stopped and stared up.

Aunt Carol nudged me on. "It's beautiful, isn't it? It's amazing when you realize what's gone into the building and renovations after several earthquakes. They say it's now earthquake resistant." She tugged on Kody's jacket sleeve encouraging him to catch up. "I guess we haven't given you the grand tour of downtown San Fran, have we, Brittany?"

"Kody's gawking as much as I am."

He snapped his gaping jaw shut. "It's cool."

I slipped my hand into his. The two of us walking side by side healthy and strong proved God's providence through all that happened. "Real cool."

We entered a wood paneled courtroom with inlaid mosaics and swirling carved hardwood. Taking seats in the front row behind the prosecution, I continued to admire the workmanship in wood and stone. I glanced at the clock above the entrance. "Shouldn't David and Sara be here by now?"

Uncle Jim looked at his watch. "They should. The hearing

starts in a few minutes."

Moments later, David bumped through the doors. As he straightened his tie and hurried in, he didn't look like the crazy cousin I'd grown to love. With his hair styled and in his navy suit and dress shoes, he carried himself as a young professional. Kody, too, received a makeover by Aunt Carol. I sat in a gray pinstriped suit, simple white silk blouse, and black, three-inch heels. Dressed to perfection, not a hair out of place, my aunt and uncle presented their usual professional appearance.

Sneaking a peek at Jeremy sitting next to his attorney, he looked nothing like the boy I'd hated and feared for months. His black hair was styled, and he had no piercings, black nail polish, and eyeliner. He wore a suit and tie similar to the ones worn by Kody and David.

Expecting Sara to appear at any minute, I continued looking to the doors. David slid in next to me, leaned over, and whispered, "She's not coming."

I whispered back, "She has to."

He shrugged. "Guess not."

"She didn't explain?"

"She wasn't at home. Her mom said she was at school, and they wanted nothing to do with this nasty business. She said Sara would not testify. Then she shut the door in my face."

My thoughts spun. "What about the charges against Jeremy for attacking her?"

His jaw went tight then relaxed. "They dropped the charges."

My voice escalated beyond a whisper. "They what?"

Aunt Carol shushed me. "What's with you two? And where's Sara?"

I bent across Kody and whispered to my aunt, "She's not coming."

Her voice escalated. "What?"

She looked at Uncle Jim.

His jaw tense and he muttered, "I didn't think he'd do it."

"I thought you convinced him to let her testify."

The tone of his reply revealed obvious frustration. "They won't talk about it."

A man at the front of the courtroom announced in a booming voice, "All rise. The Honorable Judge Suzanne Ramos presiding."

Judge Ramos settled in behind the enormous, carved judge's bench. She wore her hair pulled back in a knot. The simple style accentuated her beauty. With her dark eyes and smooth coppery complexion, sitting high above the rest of us with the dark paneled walls and beautiful mosaic of the California State seal as a backdrop, she commanded respect.

We took our seats, and the courtroom was so silent that the sound of the judge flipping through pages of the file reverberated throughout the room. With her dark lashes sweeping across her cheekbones, she raised her head and smiled. "We are here today to hear the case of The People of California versus Jeremy Sherwood, case number 2019 CR 9898. Entry of appearances, please."

An imposing man in a well-fitted suit stood in front of us. "George Hankins for the People, Your Honor."

The defense counsel stood, a rotund man with a bad comb-over. "Michael Strauss for the defendant, Your Honor."

Judge Ramos continued. "Are there any matters to address before we take opening statements today?"

Mr. Hankins stood. "No, Your Honor."

Mr. Strauss half-stood, half-crouched. "Nothing from the defense, Your Honor."

Judge Ramos peered over her reading glasses at the defense attorney. "We expect formality in this courtroom, Mr. Strauss."

He straightened. "Yes, ma'am."

"Well Mr. Hankins, you have opening remarks?"

Mr. Hankins addressed the court. "Thank you, Your Honor. Today the prosecution will call four witnesses. First, we will hear testimony from the victim who will relate the facts about the unprovoked attack."

Mr. Strauss bounded to his feet. "Objection, Your Honor. Assumes facts not in evidence regarding the term 'unprovoked'."

Judge Ramos shook her head. "Mr. Strauss, this is just opening statements, not evidence, as you well know. Overruled."

Mr. Hankins continued. "An unprovoked attack. We will hear of the physical injuries, mental anguish, and loss of income suffered by the victim. Next, we will hear from the police officer who collected the report from the physician overseeing the victim's medical care, who will testify that the doctor signed the serious bodily injury form. David Harper and Brittany Masters who were at the scene will also testify. Thank you, Your Honor."

"Mr. Strauss?"

The defense attorney waited until Mr. Hankins resumed his seat before taking his place behind the lectern. He appeared bored with the entire procedure. I didn't like him already and not just because he was defending a scumbag like Jeremy. "Your Honor, as you will hear today, there is no eyewitness to this attack, and no evidence to align the serious bodily injury claim to my client. Thank you."

Judge Ramos smiled. "Thank you, Mr. Strauss. I believe that was the shortest opening statement I've heard you present in my courtroom."

Mr. Strauss returned the smile. "Thank you, Your Honor. I am always cognizant of the pressures of time on Your Honor."

I stifled a snort with my hands. He sounded like he was trying to butter up the judge.

Judge Ramos addressed Mr. Hankins. "Call your first witness."

"The prosecution calls Kody Alfonso Diaz to the stand."

Kody's hand was sweaty as he released mine then walked to the witness stand where they swore him in, and he took a seat.

The sound of the courtroom doors opening and closing

drew my attention. Settling into the back row were two young men I thought I recognized. One wore a white suit, light blue shirt, and a white tie. A white fedora dipped over his forehead, casting a shadow across his face. The other man wore a white and blue western shirt and white jeans. His white Stetson obscured his features.

The prosecutor began. "You are Kody Alfonso Diaz. Is that correct?"

"Yes."

"Mr. Diaz, where were you the night of Wednesday, August 26, 2018?"

"At Community Church."

"And why were you at the church on a Wednesday night?"

"I play drums in the youth worship band for midweek services."

"On that night what did you do after the service ended?"

He pointed toward me. "My girlfriend and I took a walk in the prayer garden."

The prosecutor turned and smiled at me then returned his attention to Kody. "What is this prayer garden, Mr. Diaz?"

"It is a walled-in area between the main church and the youth center where they have benches and trees and stuff."

"What did you and your girlfriend do in the garden?"

"We sat on a bench and talked."

"Is that all that happened that night?"

"No."

"What else happened?"

"Eric grabbed Britt and dragged her off between clumps of bushes. Then Sherwood hit me over the head with something and knocked me to the ground."

Mr. Strauss stood. "Your Honor, this assumes facts not in evidence. My client hasn't been found guilty of the crime of which they accuse him, and the witness should not say it was my client who perpetrated the attack."

The judge pounded her gavel. "Sustained. Mr. Diaz, you will refrain from saying Mr. Sherwood was the person who attacked you."

Kody nodded.

The prosecutor leaned against the lectern and tapped his finger on the top edge. "Please continue, Mr. Diaz?"

"The guy kept pounding me with his fists. I think he had brass knuckles." Kody cleared his throat as tears welled in his eyes. "I heard Britt scream, and I tried to get up and get to her, but he kept punching me." Kody cleared his throat again. "The last thing I remember was a sharp pain in my chest. Then I guess I passed out."

The prosecutor nodded. "What do you remember after that?"

"I woke up in the hospital. There were doctors and nurses all around me and they had me hooked up to a bunch of machines. They told me later that I coughed out the respirator, and the doctor smiled and said, 'Guess he's awake.'"

The prosecutor chuckled. "It sounds like you surprised the doctor."

"They told me I'd been in a coma and died."

The prosecutor glanced around the courtroom, smiled then returned his attention to Kody. "So you were dead?"

"They said I flat lined."

The prosecutor picked up a thick envelope from the table and took it to the judge. "Your Honor, we offer Exhibit A for the prosecution. This is a packet of photographs taken at the hospital from Mr. Diaz's admission through his release."

The judge took the envelope and pulled out the pictures. She cringed as she scanned through them. Once she'd finished, she handed the photos to the clerk who marked them and returned them to the judge.

"Mr. Strauss, any objection to Exhibit A being admitted into evidence for the preliminary hearing?"

Mr. Strauss stood. "Yes, Your Honor. A packet of photographs doesn't prove that my client inflicted these terrible injuries."

The judge nodded. "I will admit Exhibit A over defense

counsel's objection and give them the weight they are due. Continue, Mr. Hankins."

The prosecutor resumed leaning on the lectern. "I apologize for the graphic nature of those photographs, but the prosecution desires Your Honor to understand the brutal nature of this attack and see for yourself the severity of Mr. Diaz's injuries."

The judge replied, "I do not doubt that an attack took place, Mr. Hankins. Your job is to show me that the defendant committed this attack. Continue."

Returning to the prosecution table, he picked up another envelope and handed it to the judge. "I present this as Exhibit B for the prosecution, Your Honor. It is a summary written by Mr. Diaz's physician describing his injuries. Please note the serious bodily injury section of the report."

The judge did the same with the contents of that envelope she had done with the first and the prosecutor resumed his position at the lectern. "Your Honor, I would like to admit this report into evidence as Prosecution Exhibit B."

"Mr. Strauss?"

The defense attorney stood. "Same objection as before, Your Honor."

"Same response to your objection as before, Mr. Strauss. The court admits Exhibit B over objection for the preliminary hearing only. Continue, Mr. Hankins."

"I have no further questions, Your Honor."

"Mr. Strauss, did you want to cross-examine this witness?"

"I do, Your Honor."

With little success at buttoning his suit, the rotund attorney tugged his jacket together as he approached the witness stand. "Mr. Diaz. Please point to the man who attacked you."

With a shaking finger, Kody pointed at Jeremy.

"You're saying without a doubt in your mind Jeremy Sherwood was the assailant?"

Kody dropped his head.

The judge looked at Kody. "Mr. Strauss asked you a question, Mr. Diaz. Please answer him."

The attorney paced in front of the witness stand. "Let me rephrase the question, Mr. Diaz. Can you with no doubt identify Jeremy Sherwood as the man who attacked you?"

Kody rasped. "No."

At that single word, a gasp wove its way around the courtroom. I couldn't believe my ears. Kody knew who attacked him. We all knew.

Mr. Strauss raised his voice. "No? You are saying you cannot identify my client as the person who attacked you?"

"No. I can't."

"And why is that, Mr. Diaz? You said he beat you and stabbed you. Did you never see his face?"

"I couldn't see through the blood, and it was dark."

My heart sank along with my hopes for Jeremy's conviction. First Sara refused to testify and now Kody admitted he didn't see the person.

"Yet you have told this court that my client was the person who attacked you. Why would you say he is the guilty party if you can't identify him?"

"They followed us earlier, and I saw him in the truck when they drove by the church."

Mr. Strauss taunted Kody. "You saw him in a truck that followed you earlier in the day, and you jumped to the conclusion he was the same person who attacked you that evening?"

Kody nodded. "I know it was him."

"You know it was him, yet you told the court you could not identify him. I'm a little confused, Mr. Diaz."

The prosecutor stood. "Objection, Your Honor. The defense is badgering the witness."

She nodded. "Objection sustained."

The defense attorney looked at the judge. "No further questions, Your Honor."

The judge directed her question to the prosecutor. "Any redirect, Mr. Hankins?"

He shook his head.

The judge looked at Kody. "You may step down, Mr. Diaz."

The prosecutor called a police officer to take the stand. "Detective Murdoch, you were the investigator in charge of the Kody Diaz case, is that correct?"

"Yes."

"Did you collect DNA at the crime scene?"

"Yes."

"Did you identify the defendant's DNA at the crime scene?"

"No."

"What evidence led you to believe you arrested the right man?"

"We had the statements of Brittany Masters, Sara Alexander, and David Harper."

"Did you have any reason to doubt their statements?"

"No."

"Did you talk to the victim's treating physician?"

"Yes."

"I'm showing you what I have admitted as prosecution Exhibit B. Can you describe this, please?"

"This is the serious bodily injury form the doctor filled out."

"Now I'm showing you what I have admitted as prosecution Exhibit A. Can you tell me what this is, please?"

"These first four pictures I took at the hospital following the attack. The attending physician took the next three. Those are his initials in the bottom corner."

"Thank you, Detective. No further questions, Your Honor."

Then it was the defense attorney's chance to cross-examine. "Detective Murdoch, you've testified that you found no DNA, other than the victim's, on the broken statue alleged to be the object used to hit Mr. Diaz over the head. Is that correct?"

"Yes, sir."

"Did you find a knife or brass knuckles at the scene?"

"No."

Mr. Strauss looked at the judge. "No further questions, Your Honor."

The judge looked at the witness. "You may step down, Detective Murdoch."

After the detective left the courtroom, Mr. Strauss stood and addressed the judge. "Your Honor, the defense would like to move to dismiss the charges against my client based on lack of evidence, lack of identification, lack of foundation for admission of exhibits, and just the general lack of corroborating evidence or non-hearsay witnesses."

"Mr. Hankins, your response?"

"One moment, please, Your Honor."

A whispered conversation between the prosecutor and another attorney sitting at his table, peppered with numerous glances in Kody's and my direction, caused my stomach to flutter. Wouldn't a simple response saying Mr. Strauss was full of hot air have sufficed? My heart sank with every tick tock of the large clock on the wall.

"Your Honor, the prosecution calls David Harper to the stand."

Mr. Strauss stood. "Your Honor, although this witness was present during the alleged attack, he did not witness the attack itself, nor can he identify my client as the perpetrator of said attack. What purpose could his testimony serve?"

Mr. Hankins answered, "Mr. Harper witnessed Mr. Sherwood and Mr. Preston following him and Mr. Diaz two hours earlier and saw the same vehicle parked in front of the church at the time of the attack."

The judge shook her head. "There is no doubt Mr. Diaz suffered extreme injuries, and the Court is doubtful they are self-inflicted. However, if Mr. Harper did not witness the attack, he is not a credible witness to Mr. Sherwood being the person who attacked Mr. Diaz." She shook her head and looked at Kody. "I'm sorry. This must seem very confusing to you. We are not saying you weren't hurt. We say because you and none of your witnesses can positively identify Mr. Sherwood as your attacker and no other evidence exists to connect Mr. Sherwood to the crime, I cannot bind this case over for trial."

Kody gripped my hand so tight I cried out. My heart broke, knowing the agony he'd gone through over the past few months as he struggled through rehabilitation, as he worked to resume his life. I'd been there, walking alongside him, but I couldn't do it for him.

Now it seemed the justice system was about to fail him.

The judge continued. "I dismiss the charges against Jeremy Sherwood. Should the district attorney's office discover more evidence at a later date, they are free to file new charges. Mr. Sherwood is free to go. I conclude this hearing."

The defense side of the courtroom stood and shouted. Eric jumped and shouted from the back of the room. He'd been one of Jeremy's supporters, and as usual displayed a rude, devil-may-care attitude.

The judge pounded her gavel calling for order. Several moments later, she dismissed the court, and it was over.

"It's a funny thing about coming home.
Nothing changes, everything looks the
same, feels the same, even smells the same.
You realize what's changed is you."
-F. Scott Fitzgerald

Chapter 37

Mary suspended our weekly visits until after the holidays and I was determined to let no shadows of fear or shame cross my heart. I set aside the anxiety of returning to school and my disappointment with the outcome of Jeremy's hearing. I missed Sara terribly. But Nana was right, there was nothing I could do to change her parent's minds. Today was a new day and I was returning to my Rocky Mountain home.

Holiday travelers packed the plane to capacity, and even though we hit turbulence over Utah, I didn't care. With Kody to my left, David to my right, my aunt and uncle across the aisle, I couldn't ask for a better Christmas present. And, to top it all off, Uncle Scott and Lisa were getting married.

When we arrived in Denver, my joyful heart thundered like crazy as we pulled our carry-on luggage from the overhead compartment. Packed like sardines in the aisle, I twisted to look behind me at Kody and plastered on a grin of enthusiasm.

He wrapped me in a warm cozy way, cradling me with his arm, and chuckled. "I don't think I've ever seen you this excited."

"I can't wait for you to see the Bar-K. You will love it."

Following the line of people like a bunch of lemmings, we wove our way off the plane, onto the concourse, and descended the escalators to board the train. As we shuttled beneath the airport, the rapt faces of silent watchers faced the side of the car where we would exit when we reached the main terminal. Sitting on the bench at the end of our car, I leaned my head on Kody's shoulder.

He threaded his fingers through mine. "Tired?"

"A little. You?"

"Yeah. It's been a long day."

"We'll have about an hour's drive from the airport to get to the Bar K. We will get there around midnight."

The train stopped and people surged through the doors like socks in a washer. I led Kody and my California family up the escalator to the open area where I knew my Colorado family were waiting. Lisa's voice rang out, "Over here."

To the far left of the waiting crowd, Uncle Scott's black Stetson was a clear target, towering above all other heads. Gripping Kody's hand, I dragged my carry-on and forged ahead. Though my trip to San Francisco was my first time flying, it was far from my first time at Denver International Airport. It seemed every few months Dad or Mom drove down the hill to pick someone up or take them back. I had often accompanied them, so I was familiar with the area where waiting family and friends collected. But I'd never been there on Christmas Eve. Reaching the edge of a huge knot of people, Uncle Scott lifted me into a tight hug. "Welcome home, sweetie."

I exhaled a long sigh of contentment. "It's good to be back."

He took my bag, greeted the rest of the family, and led the way to the luggage carousels. Breathless from pushing our way past others swimming upstream, we circled the stainless, groaning mechanism, watching for our suitcases and duffle bags to pop out and spin past. As Uncle Jim recognized our bags, he pulled them off and set them behind him.

Kody's expression showed dazed weariness and confusion as he watched and waited. Then like a boy catching his first fish, he grabbed his duffle and shouted, "I got one."

We all laughed. David dropped his arm across Kody's shoulder, whispering something in his ear that set them both laughing so hard Kody dropped his bag.

Curious, I snuck up behind them and stuck my head between theirs. "What's so funny?"

Kody looked at David. "Nothing."

"A guy thing?"

David nodded. "Yup."

I stepped back, "I know when I'm not wanted."

Kody reached back and pulled me to him. "Never, beautiful."

He yawned, and I wondered if he felt as hollow as his voice sounded. "You can catch sleep on the way up the hill. That is if the adults don't keep you awake with their incessant chatter."

He pulled his phone and earbuds from his pants pocket. "I've got it covered."

****

We pulled up in front of main house on the Bar K just after midnight. David, Kody, and I slept most of the way home. Stretching and yawning our way out of the eight-passenger SUV, we stumbled toward the front door.

Uncle Jim shouted, "Where do you think you're going? We've got luggage to unload."

I moaned and leaned on David. "Can't it wait until morning?"

He pushed me up and held my shoulders, leading me back to the car. "Let's get it done. He'll leave us alone, and we can sleep."

Despite his weary state, Kody beat David and me to the back of the Sequoia, grabbed his duffle and carry-on then dragged them onto the pillared front porch. Grabbing my bags, I followed his lead.

Nana opened the front door. "It's about time you got here."

Kody was the first inside. He kissed Nana on the cheek. "Good to see you again, Mrs. Masters."

"You look dead on your feet, boy." She pointed to the staircase behind her. "You and David will be in the second bedroom on your right at the top of the stairs."

He looked back at me through red, sleepless eyes.

Tears streamed down my face as I whimpered. "That was Tiff's room."

Old feelings I'd long forgotten rushed in as I scanned the high-ceiling entrance hall, the staircase, the rustic furnished living room to my left, Dad's office to my right. Beyond the living room was the kitchen where I ate breakfast with Mom, Dad, and Tiff. I'd not been in the house since the accident. They'd closed it up before I got out of the hospital. After the accident, no one had the heart to remove Mom, Dad and Tiff's things. My eyes blurred, my mind swirled, and I collapsed.

It couldn't have been more than a few minutes later when the strong smell of ammonia brought me around. As I opened my eyes, Uncle Scott waved a nylon tube under my nose.

"Hey, girl. You gave us a start. You okay?"

Pulling back from the offensive odor, I pushed it away and sniffed. "Yeah. I'm okay, but I need to get to bed."

With his arms encircling me, Kody lifted me to my feet. "Easy girl!"

Nana pulled me into a warm embrace. "Why don't you stay with me tonight?"

I was the center of attention. And I didn't want to be. The thought of spending the night curled up next to Nana was the most comforting thought I could think. "I'd like that."

She took my hand in hers. "The rest of you can find your rooms. If you're hungry, there's coffee and donuts in the kitchen. You should find anything you need in the cupboards and refrigerator. I'll be over in the morning to fix breakfast. My girly here will be at my place. See you in the morning."

Uncle Scott jangled his keys. "We'll take you and Brittany home Mom."

As Nana and I climbed in the back seat of Uncle Scott's SUV, Aunt Carol and Uncle Jim said their goodbyes, while Kody and David dragged their bags up the front steps.

As my uncle climbed into the driver's seat of his SUV, he whispered to Nana, "Will she be all right?"

Nana patted my hand. "Nothing a good night's sleep and some TLC won't take care of."

****

The next morning, I awoke eager to sit on Nana's front porch and hopeful to see members of our resident fox family scurry by. Wrapped in an Indian blanket from the couch in the living room, I made my way to Nana's rocking chair and curled up to await my furry friends. A buck with a rack as large as I'd ever seen sprang across the open pasture as an eagle swooped low, caught something small and wiggling, and then soared over the forest.

Nana came out, wearing her suede parka and carrying a steaming cup of what I knew would be hot cocoa. "It's freezing out here!" She handed me the cocoa and pulled the blanket tight around my neck. "Don't stay out here too long. You'll catch your death."

"I won't. It's good to be back to the smells and sounds of the ranch."

She nodded and smiled. "I'm sure it is." Returning into the house, she called back. "It will still be there the rest of the day and tomorrow. Don't get a chill out there. You don't want to get sick and miss your uncle's wedding." She opened the door and stuck her head out. "Or Christmas."

I jumped to my feet. "Oh my gosh. It's Christmas." I hurried inside. "Where are my bags? Oh no! We left my bags at the main house."

She opened the door to a large closet off the living room and pointed. "Your Uncle Jim brought them over last night after you fell asleep."

I dragged my luggage into the guest room, dumped

everything out on the quilted twin bed then searched for something to wear. "Nana, is it okay if I take a shower?"

"It's fine. If you want to stay here through your entire visit, that's fine with me."

I grabbed two towels from the linen closet. As I turned to go into the bathroom, I recognized both. "These were Mom and Dad's."

She cast her eyes down. "I hope you don't mind. I wanted to have some of their things to keep them close." Tears welled in her eyes. "We took their clothes to the church clothing drive a few months ago. We left the linens and bedding, and most everything else we thought you'd need when you came back. I have your Mom's jewelry and family mementos. Special things I knew you'd want."

My breath caught in my throat. "That must have been hard."

She nodded. "It's your house now. You can stay here with me whenever you want, but some day when you're ready, you must claim it for your own."

Holding my clothes and towels close to my chest, I headed for the shower off the guest room. I stood in the doorway to the bathroom and looked back at her. "I'm not ready yet."

****

The family ate Christmas dinner at the main house. Then we opened presents beneath a large pine tree that exhibited Lisa's amazing decorating skills. A few moments of melancholy and memories drew my attention away from the others, but most of the time I was okay.

This was a new time and a new life. Mom and Dad would want me happy. They would want me to go on. I'd come to terms with owning the ranch and the house being mine. One day I would run the ranch just as they would. I would make them proud. For now, Uncle Scott had everything under control. I had to finish high school and then at least eight years of college and vet school. But today I didn't want to think about what was yet to be. I wanted to enjoy being back on the ranch and spending time with Kody.

Two hours later, I stood in the open doorway of the stables, my heart warmed watching the Christmas snow glisten and swirl across the open pasture. It began right after breakfast and with each passing hour grew heavier and deeper. Bundled in my warmest jacket, flannel jeans, boots, and riding gloves, I topped off my outfit with my white Stetson. My knit caps were warmer, but the wide-brimmed western hat worked best for keeping the snow off my head and neck.

Kody wandered about the tack room. "Is all this tack for your horses?"

Selecting one of Uncle Scott's warmest coats from a hook on the wall, I handed it to him. "Yeah. The boarders keep their stuff at the equestrian center." A lump formed in my throat as I lifted Dad's black Stetson from a hook on the opposite wall. "You'll need this to keep the snow off."

He plopped it on his head and grinned. "Where does your Uncle Scott live?"

"A few years ago, he built a log house about a mile down the lane. Before that, he lived with Nana."

"I like your Nana's house."

I gathered a bridle, saddle, and blanket then nodded for Kody to do the same. "Great-Great-Grandfather Masters built that house in 1920 something. The original ranch house burned down."

"Where was that?"

"Where Nana's house is now."

Walking down the center aisle of the stables, a sense of melancholy invaded my thoughts. I pushed it away and hung my tack on a sawhorse outside Draper's stall. I pointed to the paddock across the aisle. "Thunderbolt is a good horse for you." I chuckled. "He needs a rider that knows who's in charge."

As we exited the barn, the snow stopped and the sun

187

glistened on the freshly fallen blanket of white. Kody pulled Dad's Stetson down to shade his eyes, and I handed him a pair of sunglasses. "They'll help with the glare from the sun on the snow."

He didn't know the hat was Dad's, and for now, I didn't want to tell him. He looked good in it, and the realization hit me that this man had stolen my heart, the only man ever to claim it as his own since my daddy.

"He who finds a wife
finds what is good and
receives favor from the Lord."
Proverbs 18:22

Chapter 38

Saturday morning the main house fluttered with activity with all of us getting ready for the wedding. Kody, David, and I dressed in the new clothes we'd worn for court. It was nice to wear the outfits for something positive and fun instead of our dreaded time at the hearing.

We sat on the couch, keeping our wedding clothes neat and pressed. Uncle Jim entered and leaned back in Dad's old recliner. "What time does this shindig get started?"

I looked at the clock on the mantel. "We need to be at the church by ten. The wedding starts at ten-thirty."

"Are we driving?"

"Nana's driving us."

He nodded. "Is Scott picking up Lisa?"

I sucked in my bottom lip. "I suppose."

Nana came through the front door. "Nana's Taxi is waiting."

It was a short drive to the Episcopal Church where groups of people gathered in the parking lot. My grandmother arched her eyebrows. "I thought this was to be a small affair."

Leaning between the front seats to get a better view, I grinned. "Looks like all of Evergreen's here."

She fussed as she exited the SUV. "I hope we have enough food."

Uncle Scott and Lisa pulled in next to us. Uncle Scott was handsome in his rented tuxedo. With a red satchel in one hand and a David's Bridal garment bag slung over her shoulder, Lisa hurried toward the church in jeans and a green parka.

I caught up with her at the front entrance. "Need help?"

Breathless, she handed me the red bag. "Can you take this?"

My insides twittered with anticipation. "I've never been a bridesmaid."

She glanced back and grinned as she hurried toward the bride's room. "You look so grown-up."

"Not too citified?"

"Not at all."

Fifteen minutes after we got Lisa buttoned into her gown, the organ music started. I straightened the lacy veil that hung down her back. "This is beautiful."

Through tear-filled eyes, she smiled. "It was my mother's."

A knock interrupted our conversation. "You about ready?"

I opened the door to see Uncle Jim holding two pink bouquets, a matching rose boutonniere stuck in his lapel. "The organist started a few minutes ago. Let's get this show on the road."

Lisa took my uncle's arm. "Let's do this."

As we crossed through the vestibule, a rugged, gray-haired man, who looked like Lisa, stepped in front of us. His eyes brimmed with tears as he gazed upon the bride. He smiled at Uncle Jim. "Thank you, sir. I'll take it from here."

My uncle turned, offered me his arm, and led the way to the back of the sanctuary. As we waited for the bridal hymn to begin, he whispered, "That was close."

"What's going on?"

"He's Lisa's dad."

"I figured that. Why were you going to give her away?"

"Her mom died years ago and she hasn't had much contact with her dad. She wasn't even certain he would show up for the wedding. Scott asked me to stand in for him if he didn't make it. I'm sure glad he made it. Last night the best man called to say he was sick. So, Scott asked me to stand in for him."

I chuckled. "You're quite the man, Uncle Jim."

He sighed. "I'm just thankful he showed up."

Our music started, and my uncle escorted me toward the front of the church. As we parted to take our places as best man and maid of honor, he whispered in my ear, "One day I'll be walking you down the aisle to give you away."

As I kissed him on the cheek, a small, iridescent drop slid down his face.

"Here is a trustworthy saying:
If we died with Him we will also
live with Him."
2 Timothy 2:11

Chapter 39

Back at the house in San Francisco on New Year's Day, I sat with my tablet at the kitchen table. Checking my emails, I found the messages I'd been waiting for and squealed with delight. I'd scored 2500 on my SATs and 35 on my ACTs.

Coming up behind me, David teased when he saw my scores. "Guess we know who got the brains in this family."

"How did you do?"

"Good enough."

My competitive gene kicked in. "How good?"

He grinned. "Good enough to get me into Harvard."

I couldn't contain myself. "They accepted you?"

"Not yet. I should hear any day now."

"My cousin the high-powered lawyer. Who'd have thought it?"

"Have you heard from CSU?"

I sighed. "Not yet."

Kody joined us. "What's up?"

I didn't know how he'd feel about our doing so well on our college entrance exams.

He'd been waiting to hear if he passed his GED. Taking the high road, I shrugged in response to his question.

But David, reveling at the moment's glory, burst out. "Britt and I scored great on our SATs and ACTs."

Kody sat across from me. "That's awesome."

I took his hand in mine. "Have you heard anything on your GED?"

He grinned. "I passed."

David whooped. "Kody, that's great."

"Now I need to score well on the entrance exams before I can apply to OSU and start my scholarship and grant search."

I bent across the table and kissed him. "You'll do great."

He smiled as he laced his fingers through mine. "Nervous about tomorrow?"

For over a month, I'd existed in a dither of emotions about returning to school. "I want things peaceful and uncomplicated. But I'm not sure what to expect from my classmates."

David interrupted. "They're cool."

"Cool?"

"They know what happened, but it's been so long since your accident, they forgot. You know how kids are. That's old news."

I crossed my fingers of both hands. "I can only hope."

He nudged me. "I'm there for you, Cuz."

"I know. Thanks."

"Getting a little sappy, aren't we?" Kody teased.

"Anyone else hungry for ice cream?" David peeked around the kitchen doorway. "Coast is clear. Millie's at her brother's, and Mom and Dad are upstairs recovering from our flight."

He opened the freezer door, sticking his face into the swirling fog of cold air. "Chocolate, vanilla, raspberry crunch?" He moved items around and pulled out a half-gallon carton. "Come to Papa! We've got B&J's Triple Caramel Chunk."

He plopped the carton then laid two spoons on the table. With a spoon in hand, he dug into the creamy dessert and wiggled his eyebrows. "Enjoy."

As I crossed through the entry hall, a rapid knock came on the front door. I paused, not sure if I should answer the door as Millie always insisted on doing that. But she wasn't here. Looking through the peephole, I saw nothing. The rapid knock came again, so with caution I opened the front door and peeked out. A very short man with a crippled right arm stood on our porch. I held up one finger to the man and shut the door, leaving him outside.

As I backed away from the entrance, I slammed into David then jumped.

He laughed. "What's going on?"

I whispered. "There's a man on the porch."

"Who is it?"

"I don't know."

"What does he want?"

"I don't know."

With one bold movement, David jerked open the door. "Hey Petey. What are you doing here?"

He let the man in, and I hurried to put distance between me and the stranger. The man wore tattered jeans, a well-worn bomber jacket and smelled as if he hadn't bathed in months.

I found Kody napping in the family room and nudged him. "You need to come with me."

He stretched as he stood and then followed me down the hall. "What's going on?"

"Someone is here."

"Who?"

"I don't know."

"What do they want?"

Stopping in my steps, I turned to him. "You sound like David. There's a man in the front hall, and David called him Petey."

Kody whizzed past me. "Petey's here?"

As it turned out, Petey was Larry's longtime buddy who

lived under an overpass north of the city.

By the time I reached the front hall, Kody, David, and Petey sat in the living room where Petey cried, "Larry's real sick."

Kody knelt in front of the man and spoke in short, quipped sentences. "Okay Petey. What's wrong with Larry?"

"He's gonna die. I just know he's gonna die. Nobody comes out of that place 'cept in a box."

Kody laid his hand on Petey's good hand. "Where is Larry?"

"The hospital."

"What's wrong?"

By now, I realized Petey had more problems than just his crippled arm. With great patience Kody continued to drag information from the old man. "Petey, look at me."

The old man raised tear-filled eyes. "I went to the park to see him this mornin'. They told me Larry was real sick, and Charlie took him to the free clinic." His head bounced out of control, and he gasped. "They put him in the hospital."

David knelt next to Kody. "Petey, do you know which hospital?"

Petey nodded, "The big one."

David and Kody grinned.

Kody shrugged. "How did you get here?"

The old man sniffed. "I walked."

I interrupted. "Did he walk here from the Golden Gate Rec Area?"

Kody nodded. "He walks everywhere. Probably in better shape than most of us." He returned to questioning Petey. "Is it the hospital close to the bridge?"

Petey grew agitated. "You gotta get him out of there. He's gonna die. I just know he's gonna die."

Kody worked to calm the old man. "We'll go check on him."

David left the room and returned with his jacket and keys. "Come on, Petey, let's go."

Petey shot to his feet. "I ain't goin' to no hospital. I don't wanna die."

"We'll take you to Larry's place."

Petey wiped his nose with a grimy hand. "Yeah. That sounds good."

We all loaded into David's car and headed for the park. I grew edgy crossing the bridge. But I knew if I ever wanted to visit the places I loved around San Francisco I had to swallow my fear and move on.

After leaving Petey at the park, we drove to the hospital where Kody and I had spent weeks recuperating.

At the front desk, we asked for Larry's room number then took the elevator up to the third floor. As we approached the doorway, a nurse came out of the room. "Are one of you Kody?"

Kody raised his hand. "That would be me."

"He's been asking to see you since they brought him in. He's running a high fever and he's confused but he has moments of lucidity." Her lips formed a tight line as she shook her head. "He's undernourished, and when they brought him in, he looked and smelled like he hadn't bathed for quite some time."

Kody asked, "Why did they bring him in?"

"Whoever admitted him said he collapsed, and they couldn't revive him. We bathed him and put him on oxygen. Other than that, we're just trying to keep him comfortable."

One look at Larry and we knew Petey's fears were well founded. Our old friend was dying.

David sat on the edge of the bed, and Kody stood on the other side. The old man's eyes opened to slits, and he whispered, "I'm goin' home."

At first, I thought he was confused, but as his smile broadened and he gripped Kody's hand, I understood. He was going home to be with his Savior.

Larry coughed, and I cringed at the painful rasp. He winked at me. "You take good care of my boy here."

196

I pushed back the tears. "I will."

Dropping Kody's hand, he grasped mine and drew me closer. "He loves you a bunch you know."

I nodded. "I know."

He looked at David. "Hey there, Mr. Lawyer."

"Not for a while."

"Aw, you'll do it." He coughed. "I need you to take care of things for me. Can you do that?"

My cousin leaned in closer, as Larry's whisper grew softer. "Don't want no buryin'. Wanna be burned up."

David laid his hand on his friend's shoulder. "I'll take care of it."

With his last breath and last bit of strength, he took Kody's hand again. "Lighthouse."

And with an absolute peace, Larry left this world.

"Young love is wild and outrageous,
laughing at moderation and
blinding us to common sense."
-H. Jackson Brown, Jr.

Chapter 40

Six o'clock Wednesday morning my alarm jolted me from a sound sleep. "It's still dark," I mumbled as I pulled the covers over my head.

"Ms. Brittany? Are you up?" The familiar feminine voice resounded through the closed bedroom door. "Ms. Brittany? Time to get up."

I grunted as I tossed back the covers. "I'm up, Millie."

"Breakfast in thirty minutes."

How could she be so cheerful this time of day? Stumbling to my closet, I pulled out a pair of jeans and sweatshirt, grabbed shoes and underwear, and headed for the shower.

An hour later, with David's music blaring from the car speakers, we bee-bopped our way to school. As we pulled into the parking lot, panic overtook me, and a lump formed in my throat. "I don't want to do this. Take me home."

He climbed out of the driver's seat. With a teasing grin, he tossed me the keys. "Take yourself home. If I drive you back I'll be late for class."

I chucked him the keys and climbed out. "You know better."

His expression turned more serious. "You don't want to drive?"

"No. I don't have a California license."

With hesitant steps, I caught up to David as he entered the building.

He shrugged. "You have your Colorado license, don't you?"

"I cut it up."

Getting a new driver's license was not a subject I wanted to discuss, so I hurried away from him and toward my first class. I only needed one course to meet the California requirements for graduation, and I'd enrolled in two classes I needed to get into CSU. That meant I'd finish classes by noon.

Today Kody was picking me up, and we planned to spend the afternoon at the stables. Knowing I'd be with Kody and my beloved Mariah in a few hours made the morning somewhat bearable.

Most of the kids welcomed me back. No one asked questions about my time away, so I assumed they all knew where I'd been.

As I walked into my last class of the morning, sitting in the first seat by the door was Sara's friend, Kelly. "Hey gang, look who's back."

I cringed as I passed. "Hey Kelly."

She shouted as I took a seat in the last row. "I thought they put you in the loony bin."

She laughed and her clique of beauties joined her. I wanted to crawl in a hole, but within seconds, the bell rang. Ms. Webster took command of the classroom, shutting Kelly up. "Good morning class. Kelly, is there something you want to share with the rest of us?"

The blonde beauty tossed her hair over her shoulder in a gesture of arrogance. "No."

"Good. Then we'll get started."

I'd had Ms. Webster last semester and liked her a lot. She was one of the few who sent cards and flowers while I was in the hospital.

When the period bell rang, I waited for Kelly and her

friends to go. I was the last to leave. As I exited, Ms. Webster stepped up behind me and laid her hand on my shoulder. "It's good to see you back in school."

"I wish I could say it's good to be back."

She pursed her lips then sighed. "I'm sorry about Kelly. She started classes here last October, and it didn't take long for her take over that little group."

"I thought she went to Christian Academy."

"Her mom and dad split up, and her mom refused to drive her that far every morning." The teacher sighed. "She'll ease up on you after a few weeks."

I nodded. "I can handle it."

If I could survive those months of fearing Eric and Jeremy, dealing with Kelly was nothing more than an irritation.

According to the Kennedy grapevine, after I'd pressed charges and the school board learned one assault happened on school property, they expelled Eric and Jeremy from the school. The last news anyone heard was that both were at some private school on the other side of town.

****

Kody waited in his old Dodge with the big engine idling. I slid onto the bench seat, snuggled close and kissed him on the cheek. He smelled like a horse. "Been at the stables?"

He nodded. "We have a lot going on this week, and the boss wants everything squeaky clean for our guests."

"Guests?"

"I don't know. Some hot shots that want to invest in the stables."

I shrugged and snuggled closer.

A smile tipped the corners of his mouth. "Not that I don't enjoy the attention, but you need to fasten your seat belt."

I snuggled tighter. "Then I couldn't get as close."

"But I could keep my mind on my driving."

I giggled as I sidled across the seat and fastened in. "Better?"

His smile widened with approval. "Yes."

When we reached the stables, he parked the car behind the barn, gathered me into his arms, and ruffled my hair with his nose. "You smell good," he whispered as he cupped my face in his hand. "I can't get enough of you."

Carried away by my desire, I stared into the deep pools of russet that invited me to lose myself and forget the rest of the world. I gave into the warmth of his kiss. I wanted him and he wanted me.

Shivers of desire raced through me as he kissed the pulsing hollow at the base of my neck then covered my mouth with his.

He jerked back, and with a gentle grip pushed me away. "We have to stop."

I protested, tugging at the front of his shirt, I kissed his eyes, his nose, and his mouth. "I love you."

He pulled back again, this time opening the car door. "I'm sorry, Britt. This was my fault. I shouldn't have let it go this far."

Splaying my hands on my legs, working to stop the trembling, I nodded. "You're right."

As we entered the barn, Kody grabbed a bucket and mop. His voice held a tinge of regret. "Why don't you go visit Mariah? You haven't seen her for a while. She's getting lonely." He smiled. "Her treats are in the storage room in her bin."

Fifteen minutes later, I rode Mariah to the barn. Kody wasn't there, so I headed to one of the training rings. I dismounted, opened the gate, and led the way inside. For the next hour, I trotted and walked my horse around the ring. I recalled days on the ranch riding bareback. I sprawled forward across her soft neck, hugging her as she walked her rhythmic gait. "Sorry, it's been so long, girl. Between being in that stupid hospital, court hearings, and the rainy days, we've not seen much of each other." I sat up and breathed in the smell of horses and hay as I ran my fingers through her silky mane. "You'll see a lot more of me from now on. I promise."

"There you are." Kody sat atop Sharazad. "Been looking all over for you."

I slid off Mariah and led her out of the ring. "I've been right here."

"David and Sara are up at the barn."

I hesitated, torn by conflicting emotions. "Sara?"

"She talked her mom into letting her take lessons. I don't think her folks know we're here. You want to see her?"

"Does she want to see me?"

"Yeah. She asked me to find you. David said we should meet them at the lake in thirty minutes."

I climbed on Mariah. "Let's go."

"Aren't you going to saddle up?"

"No."

He huffed. "Okay."

When we reached the lake, we dismounted and waited for David and Sara. I leaned against Mariah, kicking small stones with the toe of my boot. "You sure they meant here?"

"This is the closest lake to the stables."

From the other side of the water, a girl's voice called, "Britt."

I'd recognize that squeal anywhere. As she dismounted, I hurried toward her, and she ran toward me. She threw her arms around my waist and giggled.

When she stopped hugging the breath out of me, she stepped back. "You're not mad at me, are you? Please say you're not mad at me."

I chuckled. "Who could stay mad at you, twerp?"

"It's my folks."

"You need not explain. David told me."

We spent the next hour catching up before David brought up our SAT and ACT scores.

Sara's face scrunched into a mass of confusion. "I don't know what you're so excited about. They're just tests."

David guffawed. "Just tests? Are you crazy? I need those scores to get into Harvard. And Britt's going to CSU."

202

"You're leaving?"

"Not until September. But Britt and Kody will leave in June. She wants to spend time at the Bar K before she leaves for school, and Kody scored a job at a stable in Columbus, Ohio. He starts the middle of June."

Sara slumped to the ground at the edge of the lake, pulled her knees to her chest, and cried.

David sat next to her. "What's wrong?"

She jerked upright and stormed back to her horse. He ran to catch up.

Kody faced me with fingers spread and eyes open wide. I shrugged.

Sara mounted her horse and David gripped the reins. "What's wrong?"

She sniffed, wiping her hand under her nose. "You're leaving. That's what's wrong. I'll never see you again."

"Don't be silly. You'll see me again. I'll be at school for seven years then I'm coming back to San Francisco, and I hope to join a law firm here. Come on, Sara. You know I could never leave this town for good. It's home. I'll be back."

She jerked the reins from his hands. "You've got this all figured out, don't you?" She swung the horse's head around. "And what about me?"

Urging her horse into a gallop, she headed toward the stables. David looked at me, spreading out his hands. "What did I do?"

"To the well-organized mind,
death is but the next
great adventure."
-J.K. Rowling

Chapter 41

A small group of Larry's friends and the Harper family gathered in the park where for the past fifteen years Larry pitched his tent and called it home. The enormous redwoods, with their sparsely pined branches, dripped with sorrow as the day fit the moment. It rained incessantly for the past three days, and though it had stopped pouring, a misty cloud of fog enveloped us. Pastor Kyle read from the Bible and prayed with us. Larry's *family* mumbled through the two hymns we sang.

An hour later, we returned to the parking lot with Kody carrying the small oak box that held Larry's ashes. Aunt Carol dabbed a handkerchief at tears on her cheek as she climbed into the passenger seat Uncle Jim slipped behind the wheel. No one spoke for several long moments. On the ride home, I watched raindrops drizzle down the window, and held tight to Kody's hand.

David tapped on the box in Kody's lap. "What are you going to do with that?"

"Point Reyes Lighthouse. When he could get a ride out there, it was Larry's favorite place to hang out. He talked for hours about watching the whales as he stood at the top of the lighthouse and looked out over the Pacific."

"Are you going out there today?"

Kody sucked in his bottom lip and his eyes glistened with

unshed tears. "I'm not ready yet."

****

Spring in San Francisco came to life with fragrant flowers, greening trees, and blooming shrubs. I couldn't pass down the streets without inhaling deep breaths, allowing the sweet fragrances to devour my senses. My step was light as I jogged around the block I now called home. The early morning fog had lifted and the sun glittered on the bay, bathing the bridge in an opalescent glow. As I rounded the corner, Kody exited the house carrying Larry's ashes.

I hurried to catch up with him as headed toward the garage. "You going today?"

He grinned. "Yeah. It's time.

"But it's Easter."

"Yeah, so what?"

"Aren't you going out to dinner with the rest of us?"

"No." He walked on.

"Want company?"

"You want to go?"

I glared at him. "Of course I want to go."

He shrugged. "Okay."

"Let me get ready and we can leave."

Aunt Carol lounged in the living room reading DiAnn Mill's latest book, "Fatal Strike." Uncle Jim napped on the couch with his newspaper scattered across his legs and the floor.

I leaned against the doorframe and spoke softly to Aunt Carol. "Is it okay if I go to Point Reyes with Kody?"

She peered over her book as her reading glasses teetered on the tip of her nose. "You aren't going to dinner with us?"

"Is it okay?"

She grinned. "You tired of hanging out with us old folks?"

I sat on the footstool in front of her. "No. It's not that."

She rolled her eyes. "It's okay. I understand. Too much of a good thing." She poked me in the belly. "Go on with you."

As I left the room I turned back to face her. "Services were beautiful this morning."

"Even if you did have to get up at four thirty?"

"Nana likes to go to Easter sunrise services at the top of the mountain."

"I bet that's beautiful."

"Probably. But she could never convince me it was worth getting up that early."

Showered and changed, I joined Kody and David in the garage. David sat in the backseat of Kody's car where he held the oak box on his lap.

Kody buckled in, adjusted the mirror, and burst out in wild laughter. "You guys look like someone died."

I didn't understand his joviality. "Someone did. Your friend Larry."

He shook his head. "Nah. Larry's alive and well with Jesus. He's at the marriage feast of the Lamb, scarfing down as much food as he can. We're the ones who are mourning, not him. We need to get over it."

Taken aback by his reaction, I turned to him with mouth open wide then popped it shut. "What's with you?"

"Larry was a happy guy. He's in a great place. That box is all that's left of him here. He'd want us to have a good time."

The two-hour drive passed quickly as we sang along to old songs on the radio and talked about Larry.

Kody shared the story he'd told to Ms. Deering the day I interrupted them. "It's a hoot." He said. "Larry came to Point Reyes with some guy he met on the wharf. They struck up a conversation, and the guy told him he was going out to Point Reyes that afternoon and asked if Larry wanted to go along. Seeing how Larry didn't have a schedule to keep, that was no problem. The man drove a fancy sports car, and Larry was convinced this guy was some big movie star. He had a British accent and spent money like it was water."

I interrupted. "I can't believe he'd trust a stranger enough to get in his car and fall for some story about going to Pointe Reyes."

Kody laughed. "Larry didn't trust folks coming around where he lived, but away from there, he'd talked to anybody. Anyway, this guy took Larry with him to the Point Reyes Lighthouse. Larry knew his way around the place. He loved to tell stories about the sea lions on the beach and the whales off the point. So, this guy tries to keep up with Larry, right? Not an easy task. The old guy moved slow this last year, but before that, he walked all over town. Up and down all those steps at the lighthouse? It didn't bother him."

I nudged him. "So, get to the good part. What happened to Larry?"

"I'm getting to it. So, they're hanging out on the overlook above the lighthouse when four police officers rush this guy, handcuff him, and take him away." He laughed. "So, there's Larry, miles from home with no way to get back. He's shuffling around the overlook and notices the guy dropped his car keys when the cops grabbed him. So, Larry grabs the keys, hustles to the parking lot, jumps in the fancy sports car, and drives himself back home."

"What did he do with the car?"

Kody laughed. "He parked it in the lot at the Rec Area, dropped the keys on the floor, and locked it." He chuckled. "The media was all over the story about this guy's arrest. The cops never could figure out how the guy's car got parked in the Rec Area with the keys locked inside."

*"The truth always comes out in the
end, no matter how hard anyone tries
to hide it or stop it. Lies are just a
temporary delay to the inevitable."*
-Anonymous

Chapter 42

The following week, we had Eric's preliminary hearing. I sat
with my California family and Kody behind the prosecution,
just as we had at Jeremy's hearing. But today Ms. Deering
was the prosecutor.

Looking professional in a tailored navy pantsuit, she
greeted us with handshakes and smiles all around. "I apologize
for all the delays. Maybe now we can lay this case to rest."

I hoped she was right. I wanted it finished as much as
anyone. They scheduled Eric's hearing for the week after
Jeremy's, but as the court dockets backed up and the defense
attorneys filed motions, the court pushed the date back twice.

Ms. Deering coached me on my testimony on all the things
Eric did. I'd met with her last week to practice direct-and
cross-examination. It surprised me to learn that watching
television hadn't prepared me for the reality of how the hearing
would go. Ms. Deering assured me she would be on my side.
But she said I should expect the defense to confuse me and
have me back down on my facts. She said he might even press
me enough to cause me to break down into tears.

I knew my facts. I only needed to communicate the truth to
the judge, who would determine whether the prosecution
introduced enough evidence to bind Eric over for trial.

It didn't surprise me to see Eric dressed and groomed to the nines—clean-shaven, hair cut short, and no obvious tattoos or piercings. The suit he wore resembled David's. He looked like the clean-cut, perfect young man I was certain the defense would make him out to be. Two men sat at the defense table with Eric. The one with the strong chin and piercing eyes looked to be Eric's dad.

The same court official who spoke at Jeremy's hearing stepped in front of the judge's box. "All rise. The Honorable Judge Suzanne Ramos presiding."

We stood and waited for the judge to take her seat and smack her gavel before we sat.

"We are here today for the preliminary hearing in the People's case of the State of California versus Maurice Eric Preston 2019 CR 9899. Could I have an entry of appearances, please, from counsel?"

I clamped my hand over my mouth to stifle a laugh when I heard Eric's name called as Maurice Eric. No wonder he went by Eric.

Ms. Deering stood and addressed the judge. "Andrea Deering for the People, Your Honor." She resumed her seat.

The two men at the defense table stood, the one who didn't look like Eric speaking first. "Franklin Dickerson for the Defense, Your Honor. And with me is my esteemed Co-Counsel, Thomas Jefferson Preston."

Mr. Preston nodded. "Good morning, Your Honor. Nice to see you again."

The judge acknowledged Eric's father with a nod then continued. "Are there any matters we need to address before we begin with evidence, Ms. Deering?"

"No, Your Honor. Thank you."

"Mr. Dickerson?"

Eric's attorney stood. "No. Thank you, Your Honor."

The judge scanned the papers before her. "Your opening statement, Ms. Deering?"

Ms. Deering gathered papers from the prosecution table

and approached the lectern. A slight change of the position of the microphone and she began, "Your Honor, today the prosecution intends to show that the defendant attacked the victim in this case, Ms. Brittany Masters, with intent and malice. He did so not on one occasion, but on four separate and distinct occasions. His actions, despite what the defense may contend, were unprovoked, were not a casual friendship, and were not the result of a teenage romance gone wrong." She flipped a page. "The defendant knew what he was doing and did it anyway. In fact, Your Honor, the defendant attacked the victim in concert with another—"

Mr. Dickerson bolted to his feet. "Your Honor, objection. No co-conspirator has been proven."

Judge Ramos peered over her bifocals. "Sustained. Ms. Deering, you know the rules. You cannot bring in anything unproven in this court or any other."

Ms. Deering dropped her gaze to her papers. "My apologies, Your Honor. It won't happen again. Your Honor, the evidence will also show that the defendant inflicted harm on the victim and caused her severe emotional trauma."

Again, Mr. Dickerson was on his feet. "Your Honor, objection. The potential outcome of these chance meetings between my client and Ms. Masters is not the focus of this preliminary hearing."

"Sustained."

My heart sank. Having the defense's objections sustained couldn't be a good thing, right? I glanced at Ms. Deering. The corners of her mouth turned upwards in the tiniest of smiles. Far from being overwhelmed, she knew what she was doing.

Hope surged through me as the hearing continued.

"Your Honor, thank you." Ms. Deering picked up her papers and returned to her seat. A short, whispered conversation with the assistant counsel sitting at the prosecution table followed, then she glanced at me and mouthed, "You ready?"

I nodded and drew several steadying breaths.

The judge addressed the defense. "Mr. Dickerson, please present your opening statement."

Empty-handed, the defense counsel strode to the lectern and began, "Your Honor, my client is being maligned by a girl spurned by unrequited love. This child chased my client, a boy intent on his studies and college, and when he told her he was concentrating on his future and not on his hormones, this girl set out to destroy his reputation. My client comes from a good family, well known in this area, and has never been in trouble before. Thank you, Your Honor."

I bit my tongue to hold back my response. Good family. Rich family, he meant, and judging by Mr. Preston's familiarity with the judge, influential to boot. My hope seeped away once again.

"Ms. Deering, you may call your first witness."

"The People call Brittany Masters."

Aunt Carol squeezed my hand and whispered, "You will be great."

Uncle Jim winked and offered a nod of encouragement.

As I walked to the witness stand, it was impossible to steady my erratic pulse. I repeated to myself, "Go with me, Lord."

Standing beside the witness stand, I scanned the courtroom, amazed at how different it looked from up here. There at the back of the room sat the two men I'd seen at Jeremy's hearing. Who were they? How did I know them? I returned my attention to Ms. Deering.

At the clerk's instructions, I raised my right hand and swore to tell the truth. I sat on the wooden chair behind the small raised enclosure. My California family smiled at me, and I took heart in their support, praying for the right words to say.

Ms. Deering took her place again at the lectern and began by asking me my name and address. I rather went on autopilot as she unfolded the facts of the case, following the questions she'd worked with me on last week.

When we came to the details of the first attack, I sharpened my focus, not wanting to make any mistakes.

"I want to take you back to the first attack."

I nodded as I swallowed a lump in my throat.

"Tell the court what happened to you and your friend at the Golden Gate Recreation Area following a barbecue for the homeless held by your church on Saturday, April 29th of last year."

I shared the entire story as I'd told it to David, to Kody, and to the police more times than I could recall.

Ms. Deering faced me again and smiled. "Thank you. Now please tell the court what happened to you and your friend, the evening of Wednesday, July 4th of last year, as you exited the ladies' room at the Marin County Fair."

I started the story, but a wave apprehension swept through me when I came to the part about using the stun gun on Eric. I recalled what she said in the living room the day of our interview about not bringing this up. She said we should wait to see if the defense brought it up. I couldn't tell the story without including the stun gun. I stared at Ms. Deering then whispered. "Do I?"

The judge leaned toward me, offering a reassuring smile. "You must speak up, Ms. Masters. The court can't hear you."

Ms. Deering looked to the judge then nodded. "Go ahead, Brittany. Tell the court what you did when Mr. Preston grabbed your arm."

The words popped out before I could even think. "I—I stuck him with a stun gun."

Heat rose up my neck and my cheeks burned with the pulsing of my heart. The sneer on Eric's face made me whimper. I forced my attention toward Ms. Deering. "Sorry."

The court erupted in tittering and outright laughter.

The judge pounded her gavel. "Order in the court."

The courtroom went silent, and Ms. Deering lowered her voice a notch. "It's okay. Go on. Tell us what happened."

I finished my story just as it had happened, including how Eric dropped to his knees when I stunned him, then how I found Jeremy struggling with Sara and used the gun on him.

Ms. Deering asked to approach the bench, and the judge agreed. "Your Honor, my witness is rattled, as you can see. Could we have a ten-minute recess for her to recompose herself?"

The judge nodded and recessed the court. At Ms. Deering's instruction, I waited until Eric and his attorneys left the courtroom. Aunt Carol walked with me to the restroom where I checked my makeup and got a drink of water. I joined Ms. Deering, the rest of my family, and Kody in the witness room, glad to receive hugs all around.

Kody cupped my face in his hands. "You're doing great. I'm so proud of you."

I nodded as words stuck in the back of my throat. Ms. Deering asked everyone else to leave.

When it was just the two of us, she sat across from me at the table. "Kody's right. You are doing great. I know I told you we would wait and see if the defense brought up the stun gun, but now it's out in the open, I think we can use this information to our advantage. I'll ask you questions about your frame of mind when you bought the gun and when you used it, and then we'll move on to the other incidents. Okay?"

I nodded. I didn't feel okay, but I couldn't let her down.

"Good, because then the tough part starts."

If this wasn't tough, then I couldn't imagine how much worse it would get. "Tough?"

She nodded. "The defense will tear apart your story. He'll try to confuse you, mix up your story, and question your motives. You need to stay calm. If you think you will cry, you don't understand a question, or you don't want to answer a question, ask for a break. As the victim in this case, you will come across as more sympathetic if you don't repeat the story and the facts verbatim. A little emotion is okay, but you don't want to look like a basket case either. That will make their allegations more believable."

I drew a deep breath. "I'm ready."

With court back in session and me in the witness stand, Ms. Deering resumed her questioning. "Now Brittany, please tell the court what you mean by you stunned him with a stun gun."

"I pressed the end of the stun gun to his shoulder. He squealed and fell to the ground."

"And is that what you did to Jeremy as well?"

I nodded.

The judge leaned over her bench. "Ms. Masters, you need to answer louder because we're recording this hearing, and the transcriber cannot hear your response."

I raised my voice. "Yes."

Ms. Deering continued. "When did you buy this stun gun?"

"After the first attack."

"Why did you buy this stun gun?"

"Because I feared they would come back and hurt us again."

"Did you know owning this weapon without parental consent was illegal for a minor?"

"Yes."

"But you bought it anyway?"

"It seemed everywhere I turned I saw them. They made disgusting remarks and threatened to finish what they started. I didn't know what else to do."

The judge pulled her mouth into a straight line as she watched me. Was that a good or bad thing?

Ms. Deering moved on to the next incident. "Tell the court what happened to you in the hall of Kennedy High School the afternoon of Wednesday, September 12th of last year."

As I told the court about Eric and Jeremy attacking me at my locker, memories of that day and that night filled me with rage and frustration. I straightened and glared at Eric. He would not win this one. I had right on my side and Jesus next to me. I spared not one detail from the time Eric slammed me against my locker until David came to my rescue.

Finishing my testimony and holding my head high, I glared at my attacker one more time.

Ms. Deering's eyes grew wide as she studied me. "Are you okay, Brittany?"

I replied with a clipped, "Fine. Thank you."

"Would you like few minutes before we go on?"

"No."

She looked at the judge then back at me with an odd lifting of her brows. "Okay, Brittany. The evening of the same day of the attack at school—that evening you attended midweek services at Community Church. Is that correct?"

The defense attorney stood. "Objection, Your Honor. Ms. Deering is leading the witness."

The judge sighed. "Sustained. Ms. Deering, please re-phrase your question."

"Tell the court what occurred the evening of Wednesday, September 12th of last year in the prayer garden of Community Church."

Just as I'd reported to the police, I told the gruesome details of Eric's attack on me and Jeremy's attack on Kody.

Mr. Dickerson stood. "Objection, Your Honor. The court dismissed all charges against Jeremy Sherwood because of lack of evidence. This is all hearsay."

Ms. Deering addressed the judge. "Your Honor, I am eliciting this statement not for the truth of the matter, but to show the victim's state of mind."

The judge closed her eyes for a moment. "Sustained. Move on."

Ms. Deering continued. "Brittany, can you identify the man who attacked you on each of these four occasions by where he's sitting in the courtroom and an article of clothing he's wearing?"

"Yes. It's Eric Preston, and he's sitting beside his attorney and his father, and he's wearing a dark suit, a blue striped tie, and white shirt."

"Your Honor, let the record reflect the witness has identified the defendant."

The judge nodded. "So noted. Anything else?"

Ms. Deering nodded. "Just two more questions, thank you." She continued. "Brittany, why didn't you come forward and report the first attack?"

I hung my head, tears burning. "It embarrassed me. They threatened to hurt us if we told. And Sara feared what her parents would say."

"Afraid of her parents?"

"Well, she's two years younger than the rest of us, and she thought they might not let her hang out with us if they knew what happened."

"And what about the other attacks?"

Facing the judge, I straightened. "I wanted to get through my senior year with no problems, no trouble, then go to college. If they would have stopped and left us alone, we wouldn't be here today."

"Did you think if you didn't tell anyone, the assaults would stop?"

I nodded then remembered the judge's instruction from before. "Yes. I hoped they'd lose interest and leave us alone."

"No further questions, Your Honor."

The judge directed her gaze at me. "Ms. Masters? Would you like to take a break before cross-examination?"

I shook my head. "No, thank you."

My intensifying rage and frustration squelched the fear and anxiety I carried into the witness box. Eric hurt me, and Jeremy hurt Kody and Sara in a way greater than the physical attacks, which were bad enough. For months, Sara and I lived with fear and near paranoia every time we went out. I'd lost the ability to enjoy hanging out with my friends and classmates. Kody carried guilt because he couldn't save me that night. We'd lost the feeling of invincibility most kids carry throughout high school. They stole something precious from us we could never reclaim.

Eric whispered to his father and then addressed the people sitting behind him. When he turned back to face me, his smirk conveyed his position: he would walk away from these charges a free man. Jeremy, who sat front and center behind Eric, sneered with the smugness of a victor.

The defense attorney stood before me. "Ms. Masters? Did you say Kody was your boyfriend?"

"Yes."

"Is he here today?"

"Yes."

Ms. Deering objected. "Your Honor, I'd like to know where Mr. Dickerson is going with his line of questioning. Mr. Diaz is not on trial here."

The judge glared at the defense attorney. "Objection sustained. Mr. Dickerson, get to the point."

"The point is, Your Honor, Ms. Masters is a sexually active young woman."

Ms. Deering objected. "Your Honor, the defense is making a huge assumption that if Ms. Masters has a boyfriend, she is sexually active. I don't see the relevance in this line of questioning, and I object to Mr. Dickerson's assumption."

The judge sighed. "Objection sustained based on relevance." She raised her voice. "Mr. Dickerson, do you have questions for the witness that pertains to your client?"

He smirked. "Your Honor, I am only trying to establish that Ms. Masters is a normal young woman who flirted with my client over the time in question then filed charges against him for sexual assault when he did not return her affection."

I gasped. Between clenched teeth, I muttered, "That's not true."

Ms. Deering eyed me and zipped her lips showing I should not speak.

Mr. Dickerson continued. "Your Honor, we were all young at one time. Most of us have experienced unrequited love. We know the pain and humiliation when our affections are unreturned."

Ms. Deering stood. "Your Honor, again defense counsel has moved on to closing arguments."

"Sustained. Mr. Dickerson, do you have a question of the

witness?"

He bowed to the judge in submission to her authority and then turned his beady eyes on me again. "Ms. Masters, moving on to the next fairytale you concocted. You told the court my client again attacked you several months later at the Marin County Fair. I believe you said you used a stun gun on him. Is that correct?"

"Yes."

He laughed. "Has this alleged stun gun been presented as evidence?"

"No."

"Do you have it with you?"

"No."

"You do not own a stun gun, do you?"

"Yes."

"Where is it?"

Ms. Deering objected. "Your Honor, he's badgering the witness."

"Sustained."

"And as to your boyfriend and you being hospitalized because of attacks at your church, isn't it true that the court found my client's friend, Jeremy Sherwood, not guilty of the attack on your so-called boyfriend?"

I retorted in cold sarcasm. "The court did not find him *not* guilty."

He blinked several times then sighed. "Ms. Masters, was Jeremy Sherwood found guilty?

"They dismissed the charges."

"Ms. Masters, this entire process is ridiculous. My client never laid a hand on you. You fabricated this story because he rejected you. Isn't it true you were so traumatized by my client's rejection that you tried to kill yourself by jumping off the Golden Gate Bridge?"

Gasps went through the courtroom, and I crumbled beneath his lies. "No. That's not true."

"Did you or did you not on Thursday, September 27th of

last year throw yourself off the Golden Gate Bridge?"

In almost a whisper, I answered his accusation. "I fell."

"What's that, Ms. Masters? You fell from the bridge?" He faced the court and, with a ridiculing laugh, said, "Ms. Masters, people do not fall from the Golden Gate Bridge. Jump? Yes. Fall? No."

I straightened. "I changed my mind, and I fell."

"No further questions, Your Honor."

The judge looked at Ms. Deering. "Any more questions of this witness?"

"No, Your Honor. Thank you."

The judge dismissed me and released the court for a two-hour recess.

*"And when you stand praying, if you
hold anything against anyone, forgive
them, so that your father in heaven
may forgive you your sins."*
Mark 11:25

Chapter 43

My family, Kody, and I left the courthouse, and strolled through the downtown plaza, while I composed myself. We paused outside a café, and my aunt scanned the menu posted in the window. "How about we have a light lunch?"

Still fuming from the comments made by Eric's defense attorney, my stomach twisted in a knot. "I'm not hungry. Just the thought of food nauseates me. You guys go on." I sat on a park bench in front of the café. "I'll wait for you."

Kody sat next to me. "I'll stay with her."

Under the warm glow of his smile, my anger eased. "Go on. I'll be okay."

He shrugged. "I'm not hungry either."

My family disappeared through the darkened doorway as Kody took my hand in his. "I'm sorry you have to go through this."

"Not your fault."

"I know, but it hurts all the same."

We sat in silence for some time when I noticed a sidewalk vendor selling frozen yogurt. "That might help."

He followed my gaze. "Ice cream?"

I chuckled. "It's frozen yogurt, but close."

Hand in hand, we strolled toward the vendor cart where we

bought two cups and returned to the bench. We were finishing our treat when the rest of my family exited the café.

Aunt Carol smiled. "I'm glad you're eating something."

Uncle Jim glanced at his watch. "We need to get back." He smiled at me. "You ready?"

Back in the courtroom, the trial resumed. The judge denied the prosecution's request for the opportunity to present character witnesses. Judge Ramos said I wasn't on trial today and no evidence or testimony from another witness called my credibility into question. I breathed a sigh of relief at her decision. I'd felt as though I was the one on trial during the defense attorney's questions.

Ms. Deering stood at the lectern. "The prosecution calls Maria Rodriguez to the stand."

I'd seen the girl at school, but I didn't know her. Why would she step forward as a witness?

They swore the girl in and Ms. Deering stepped to the lectern. "Maria, will you tell the court what happened to you after your swim meet on November 12th of last year?"

The dark-haired girl appeared to force back tears as she scanned the courtroom. Her gaze landed on Eric, at which time her mouth drew into a firm line and she pointed at him. "Eric Preston molested me."

A low rumble passed through the room.

Ms. Deering waited until the onlookers quieted. "Ms. Rodriguez, can you identify this person you named?"

Maria nodded. "Yes."

"Please tell the court where he's seated and an item of clothing he's wearing."

"He's seated at the table with the two men, and he's wearing a dark blue suit."

"This is the man who molested you on November 12th of last year?"

"Yes."

Ms. Deering addressed the judge. "Your Honor, let the record reflect the witness identified the defendant."

The judge nodded. "Subject to cross."

Ms. Deering resumed her questioning. "And did you report the molestation?"

Maria bowed her head. "No."

"You told no one?"

"No."

"And why are you coming forward now?"

"Brittany is the first girl to stand up to Eric. And it's about time someone did."

"What do you mean?"

"There are a lot of girls he's messed with. I've heard them talking in the restroom."

Ms. Deering spread her hands in mock frustration. "If Eric has been doing this to other girls at school, why hasn't anyone reported him?"

Maria glared at Eric. "We all lived in fear of what he and Jeremy might do to us."

"Jeremy?"

"Jeremy Sherwood. He's done it too. And he likes to beat up the boys. I guess Eric prefers picking on girls. We don't fight back as good." Her eyes met mine. "You go, girl. Zap him!"

Several titters of laughter echoed through the room.

Ms. Deering continued with her line of questioning. When she finished, she smiled at me then turned her attention to Maria. "Thank you for coming forward, Ms. Rodriguez." She faced the defense attorney, her mouth curved in a triumphant smirk. "No more questions, Your Honor."

"Mr. Dickerson?"

The attorney stood behind the lectern and took an extra minute to organize his papers. He leaned his elbows on the top surface as if trying to close the distance between Maria and him. Maria shrank back in her chair at his tactics, and I tossed her a quick grin. She saw me, nodded, and leaned forward again.

"Ms. Rodriguez, Eric Preston is an attractive young man,

would you agree?"

She shrugged. "I guess if you like the bad boy look."

"The bad boy look?"

"Yeah. The black eyeliner, the tongue piercing, the tattoos on his arms."

Mr. Dickerson turned to face his client. "I'm sorry, Ms. Rodriguez, but I see none of those intimate characteristics you mentioned. You must know him well."

Once again, Eric's supporters snickered at the defense counsel's wit. I saw nothing funny. I knew the Eric Preston Maria described.

Mr. Dickerson turned to face the witness once more. "He is popular at school, and his family is very wealthy. I can understand why young women would throw themselves at him."

Ms. Deering stood. "Your Honor, my esteemed colleague is testifying."

The judge shook her head. "Mr. Dickerson."

He smiled at her. "Objection sustained, I presume?"

Judge Ramos fixed him with a steely gaze. "You are bordering on contempt, Mr. Dickerson."

"Noted, Your Honor. I have no further questions for this witness."

The judge made notes then addressed the prosecutor. "Ms. Deering?"

"No other witnesses, Your Honor. We rest our case."

"Mr. Dickerson, do you intend to call any witnesses on behalf of your client?"

"Your Honor, I have several character witnesses prepared to tell the court a different story than the one concocted by the prosecution witnesses."

"Mr. Dickerson, this is a preliminary hearing. I must determine whether enough evidence exists to bind the defendant over for trial. As you know, the threshold of proof is low in a preliminary hearing, and I must hear all evidence in the light most favorable to the People. Unless one of your witnesses can place the defendant in another location at the time of each of these incidents or call into question the credibility of the two witnesses, their testimony is of little benefit."

"One moment, Your Honor." Mr. Dickerson returned to the defense table and whispered to Mr. Preston and Eric.

Eric's face twisted into a frown, and he spat a reply to his attorney. Mr. Preston laid his hand on Eric's forearm, and Eric pulled from his grasp. A heated discussion followed. It seemed there was a lack of agreement on the defense team.

Ms. Deering turned and smiled. "I think we've got him."

The district attorney's announcement cheered my heart, and I shrugged the kinks out of my neck while we waited for the defense to decide what to do.

After several minutes, the judge tapped her gavel on the bench. "Mr. Dickerson, do you intend to present evidence or call any witnesses?"

He returned to the lectern. "Your Honor, we have one witness. She is not a character witness for my client. She is a rebuttal witness to contradict the testimony of both of the prosecution's witnesses."

I couldn't imagine who this witness could be, since only Sara and Kody were present at any of the attacks on me, and Maria had said she and Eric were alone. I turned at the sound of the door to the courtroom opening and gasped. Her auburn hair shimmering, she strutted to the witness stand wearing a fitted, cashmere dress. The school counselor who tutored me while I recuperated sent a provocative smile toward Eric's dad.

For the next fifteen minutes, Ms. Chatham sang Eric's praises, elaborating on his academic accomplishments and popularity at Kennedy High School. Under Mr. Dickerson's expert examination, Ms. Chatham perjured herself saying how I hung around Eric, sought him out, giving times and dates to back up her testimony. She continued by spinning a web of lies implying Maria Rodriguez had chased Eric, threatened him when Eric broke up with her, and had damaged Eric's car in her rage over their relationship.

When Ms. Deering cross-examined, she went for the jugular. "Ms. Chatham, how long have you known the defendant?"

The guidance counselor smiled. "About ten years."

"So are you a friend of the family?"

She wiggled in her seat. "I guess so."

"A good friend?"

She smiled and batted her eyes. "A great friend."

"You and Eric's mother are friends?"

I couldn't imagine Mrs. Preston being friends with a school counselor. Eric's mother stood erect, straightened her designer suit, pushed her way into the aisle, and hurried from the courtroom.

The prosecutor cleared her throat. "Ms. Chatham?"

The counselor quirked her head to one side. "Yes. I know Mrs. Preston."

"Are you a friend?" Ms. Deering followed the witness's gaze to the defense table. Picking up a sheet of paper in one hand, she stood beside the lectern.

Ms. Chatham shifted in her seat.

Ms. Deering continued. "Let me rephrase. Do you and Mrs. Preston spend time together?"

The defense attorney objected because the relationship between Ms. Chatham and his client's mother was not pertinent to the case.

Judge Ramos replied, "Your response, Ms. Deering?"

"Your Honor, I am seeking to establish the relationship between the witness and various members of the defendant's family to determine if there is undue bias."

"Overruled."

Ms. Deering proceeded. "Answer the question, please, Ms. Chatham."

"I don't spend time with Mrs. Preston. We're more like acquaintances. I know of her."

"Are you a guidance counselor at Kennedy High School?"

"Yes."

"And is Eric Preston currently a student at Kennedy High School?"

She squirmed. "He was."

Ms. Deering feigned surprise. "He was?"

"Yes."

"He's no longer a student there?"

"No."

"Did he graduate?"

"Not yet."

"Why is the defendant no longer a student at Kennedy High School?"

The perky redhead stared at the defense table as though waiting for them to tell her what to say. "He enrolled at another school."

Ms. Deering threw up her hands. "Why would he leave during his senior year?"

Ms. Chatham shrugged. "Why not?"

"Was he expelled?"

"No. The school asked him to leave."

"Perhaps the line between being expelled and being asked to leave is fine for you, Ms. Chatham. Why was he asked to leave?"

"For bullying."

"Bullying? Didn't you testify under oath that Eric Preston was a model student?"

"Yes."

Standing next to the lectern, holding her hands to her chest, Ms. Deering ended her performance with a bang. "Ms. Chatham are you telling this court you lied under oath?"

The witness stammered. "Uh—no."

Ms. Deering returned to stand behind the lectern. "Perhaps you'd like to amend your previous testimony?"

Ms. Chatham nodded. "I guess."

"So was Eric Preston a model student?"

"No."

"Did Mr. Preston's defense counsel ask you to provide testimony here today as a favor to the defendant's father?"

Ms. Chatham didn't respond, her eyes wet and her lips trembling.

Ms. Deering glowed in triumph as she returned to the prosecution table. "No further questions, Your Honor."

I wanted to burst out in applause, but I held back my enthusiasm. As the attorney returned to her seat, I squeezed her shoulder. "Great job."

The defense rested its case and asked for a brief recess before the judge made her ruling, which the judge granted. Mr. Dickerson requested to meet with Ms. Deering.

I leaned forward to whisper to the prosecutor. "What's going on?"

"I think they may want to make a deal."

"Nothing less than time in prison, okay?"

She nodded. "Let's see what they offer."

While the attorneys were gone I fidgeted in my seat, scanning the contents of my purse, wishing for a glass of water. I pulled my phone from my purse to check for messages, but Aunt Carol shook her head. "No phones in the courtroom."

As I thought of slipping away to the restroom Ms. Deering and Mr. Dickerson returned to the courtroom. Ms. Deering crooked a finger showing I should follow her into the hallway. Uncle Jim and Aunt Carol followed.

I waited until we gathered around a table in a small room. "Well?"

"They're willing to plead guilty to a reduced count of sexual assault and go to sentencing on the one count." She held up a hand to stop me from interrupting. "I know it's not what we wanted, but it will mean you won't have to testify in court. You won't have to go through another round of insinuations."

I considered her words before replying. "You're the one with the expertise in the law. What do you think?"

"I feel this is the best course of action. If we go to trial and we get a conviction, which I think we will, Eric's family has the money to appeal forever. You and your family will relive this nightmare for years. I don't need your permission, but if we accept the plea agreement, it ends today."

I looked at Uncle Jim and he nodded as did Aunt Carol.

Gritting my teeth then relaxing my jaw, I considered what she was saying. "How long will he be in jail?"

"I will demand he gets the maximum fine and jail time."

"What is that?"

"Forty-eight months in jail and a $10,000 fine."

I nodded. "He stole a year of my life, seems only fair he repays with four years of his."

Ms. Deering returned to the conference room where the defense council waited. A few minutes later, the attorneys came back into the courtroom.

Ms. Deering stood. "Your Honor, we have agreed with the defense regarding a plea agreement."

Judge Ramos nodded. "What is the agreement?"

"The defendant will plead guilty to one count of sexual assault, a class one felony, with a mandatory sentence of four years' incarceration in a federal institution and a $10,000 fine. In exchange for this agreement, the court will defer the other three charges pending completion of sentence and payment of a fine."

The judge looked to Mr. Dickerson. "Is this your understanding of the agreement?"

"Yes, Your Honor."

Judge Ramos looked at Eric. "Will the defendant please stand?"

Eric stood.

"You have heard the agreement as outlined by the district attorney and your defense counsel. Do you agree?"

Eric looked at his father, who nodded. "Yes."

Judge Ramos looked in my direction. "Thank you, Ms. Masters, for your appearance here today and for your bravery in these unpleasant circumstances. You and your family are free to go. We do not require your presence for the rest of this hearing. We will reconvene after lunch. I want to confirm case law in this matter, and we'll proceed to sentencing. Court is in recess until one o'clock."

After court dismissed, I pressed my way toward the defense table, where Eric stood in the bailiff's custody, his hands cuffed behind his back. I faced my attacker and smiled. "I forgive you, and I'll be praying for you."

Through red eyes, Eric whispered something to the officer escorting him. The officer dug in Eric's jacket pocket and pulled out my watch—the watch Mom and Dad had given me for what became our last Christmas together. I thought I'd lost it the night he attacked me.

Eric motioned for the officer to give it to me. "I was keeping it as a souvenir."

I choked back a whirling hurricane of emotion as I accepted the token. "Thanks."

As the officer escorted Eric away, he whimpered, "I'm sorry."

"It's times like this my
Buddy Timon here says: you gotta
put your behind in the past."
Pumbaa

Chapter 44

It was three weeks before Senior Prom. I had not yet asked Kody to escort me nor did I have a dress, but I bought the tickets the day they went on sale. David was taking Sara, and it would be a great opportunity for me to spend a few hours with her.

How difficult could it be to find a simple little something to wear? Aunt Carol had other ideas.

I entered the house, breathless and sweating, and headed for the stairs. Aunt Carol stepped in from the living room. "Did you forget we were going to the mall this morning to get your prom dress?"

I checked my watch. "It's only eight-o'clock."

"The stores open at nine."

I hurried up the steps. "Give me ten minutes to shower and change."

According to my aunt, we had to be there when the stores opened, because finding the perfect prom dress and accessories would take the entire day.

We started at Nordstrom's, where we couldn't find a dress we agreed on. We then stopped at Ann Taylor. I tried on ten dresses, and I liked two of them and Aunt Carol approved of only one that was not too short, nor too revealing, but still cute.

As we entered Yes Style, Sara and her mother were exiting. Aunt Carol smiled at Sara's mom. "Nice to you see you, Prudence. It's been awhile."

The woman glared at me then returned her attention to my aunt, who she greeted with a smile and a handshake, lamenting her distress at not seeing my aunt for so long. "You must be busy, what with raising three teenagers, Jim traveling so much, church activities—I never see you at the club anymore."

Aunt Carol smirked. "Yes, we have our hands full with the kids, but they are a true blessing."

Prudence stammered, "Is that right?"

Holding her finger aside her cheek, my aunt rolled her eyes upward. "Last Saturday the family played a round of golf and had lunch in the club dining room. We saw you on the patio, and Jim waved to your husband, but he walked the other way. He seemed to be in quite a hurry to leave. I guess he didn't see Jim."

Prudence shrank. "That must have been it."

Aunt Carol smiled at Sara. "We haven't seen you in ages. What have you been up to?"

The elephant in the mall grew larger with each passing word. No one mentioned the hearings, my accident, Kody, Sara's parents splitting me up from my best friend and allowing Jeremy to walk around a free man. That was not acceptable conversation.

"We must be going. Brittany needs a prom dress." Aunt Carol nudged me into the store and whispered, "That woman infuriates me."

"Now she knows I'm going to prom and will assume I'll be going with Kody. I wonder if she won't allow Sara to go with David."

Aunt Carol grinned. "Prudence would never go that far. She will lecture Sara not to spend any time with you, then attempt to worm her way in with the Kennedy School Board to be a chaperone."

"You're kidding."

"Don't worry. With Sara attending Christian Academy and David at Kennedy, I have a little more pull with the board than she does."

I found nothing we could agree on at Yes Style, so we moved on to Talbots. As I tried on dress number five, or number twenty-five if you count the ones at all the other stores, Aunt Carol sighed. "I like it. What do you think?"

I checked it out in all the mirrors, smoothed my hands over the satiny cobalt blue and smiled. "I like it."

Taking me by the shoulders, Aunt Carol turned me one direction then the other, eyeing the length and checking out the dip of the neckline. "We could wait until next Saturday and see what we can find at Niemen Marcus."

I didn't want to spend any more time looking at prom dresses. "Let's take this one." I hugged myself. "I love it."

After lunch we found matching shoes, and Aunt Carol insisted she had a perfect string of pearls with matching earrings that would accessorize the outfit.

Now I had to ask Kody to go with me. One hurdle over, a big one to go.

When we got home, I found Millie in the backyard clipping herbs. "Have you seen Kody?"

She straightened and arched her back with a grimace. "He said he needed to work on the Dodge, something about putting on new brakes."

"I didn't know he knew how."

She chuckled. "The longer I know that boy, the more he surprises me. I swear he's a jack-of-all-trades."

I entered the garage and Kody's feet stuck out from under the car. I nudged his foot. "You want to go to the prom with me?"

A muffled voice returned. "Can't."

I pursed my lips into a pout. "Why not?"

"Got a date."

I leaned down and looked under, but all I could see was a body in gray coveralls on a mechanic's dolly. I tugged at his foot, "What do you mean you have a date?" My temper flared. "Who with?"

232

He pushed the dolly out and stood. Beneath the grime and grit, David smiled. "Sara."

I punched him in the shoulder. "Where's Kody?"

"He went to get an oil filter."

"What are you doing here? You know nothing about fixing cars."

"Who do you think taught Kody? And do you think the Chevy ran like it does when I got it?"

I shrugged.

"I took auto mechanics my freshman year and got hooked. Dad and I built the engine in that baby, and I do all my maintenance."

Kody came through the door and tugged me into a tight hug. "Hey Beautiful. What are you doing here?"

David returned to his original position on the dolly, but before sliding under he told Kody, "She came to ask you to the prom."

My cousin, Mr. Tact.

Kody kissed me on the nose. "I wondered when you would get around to asking."

"So you'll go?"

"I already rented a tux. Can't have my girl going stag to her senior prom, or worse yet, taking another guy."

****

Standing in the center of the amazing four-story atrium, I gazed up through the open skylight of the Galleria Events Center. The night was crisp and beautiful.

Kody's muscles rippling beneath the fitted tuxedo jacket quickened my pulse. His strong thighs and slim hips fit the pants as if they were custom-made.

He'd not let go of my hand since we entered the building. Turning me to face him, he fingered a tendril of hair on my cheek. "You look amazing."

I'd never worn my hair up and curled in such a creation as

Aunt Carol's stylist had designed.

That morning, at the spa, my aunt and I had massages, skin scrubs, pedicures, and manicures. I felt like the girl in *The Princess Diaries*.

I stroked Kody's close-shaven cheek. "You're not bad yourself, handsome."

As I looked over his shoulder, a streak of red came running toward us. "Britt, Kody." Sara threw her arms around my neck. "I'm so glad you're here."

David caught up to us. "She's been looking all over for you."

She tugged me by the hand and led me into the ballroom. We crossed the inlaid wood dance floor and found a table away from the DJ and out of the main flow of traffic. Three stories above us glittering lights twinkled. Voices carried down from kids who had made their way to the upper stories. At the front of the room, a stage rose, supporting a DJ on one corner and a king and queen's throne on the other. The decorating committee had arranged cutouts and backdrops from the Pride Lands of Africa in every available space. Full-sized figures in papier mâché of Pumbaa and Timon stood in dioramas throughout the hall. Behind the stage hung a banner proclaiming *Kennedy High School Junior-Senior Prom. Welcome to Hakuna Matata 2019.*

Kody took my hand in his and bowed. "May I have this dance?"

I giggled as we walked onto the dance floor but melted in his arms as he swept me away. He whispered in my ear, "You think we lost them?"

I nuzzled my head in his chest. "Who?"

"David and Sara."

I bent my head back to meet his gaze. "Are we trying to?"

"Yeah."

We spent the next two hours dancing. We'd stop occasionally, and I'd introduce Kody to a classmate. Then we'd be off again, gliding through the night, oblivious to anything or anyone outside of our own private world.

Kody interrupted the moment. "Hakuna Matata, huh? Whose idea was that?"

I shrugged. "Don't know. I wasn't on that committee."

"I've forgotten. What does it mean?"

"It means 'don't worry'."

He nibbled my ear. "I won't."

Sobs came from behind me. I turned to see a small streak of red running in the restroom's direction. Seconds later David ran past.

He stopped, came back to us, and asked me, "You want to go check on her?"

"What happened?"

Throwing up his hands, he sighed. "Looks like we broke up."

I pushed past people as I struggled to run in high heels. In the restroom, Sara huddled in the corner, sobbing. I hiked up my tight skirt so I could squat down in front of her.

She reached out and grabbed me, pulling me to sit on the damp, wet paper towel covered floor.

"Oh, Britt. What am I going to do?"

"What happened?"

"I broke up with David."

"You broke up with David!"

"Yes." A torrent of sobs followed.

"If you dumped him, why are you crying?"

Through broken sobs, she said, "He said...he said—"

****

Kody and I arrived home to find David in the family room playing his latest video game. "Hey guys. Did Sara get home okay?"

Dropping his tuxedo jacket on a chair by the door, Kody plopped into a beanbag, pulled off his tie, and slipped out of his vest. "Yeah. Her dad picked her up. You want to tell us what happened?"

My cousin continued jerking and punching the controller in his hand. "Didn't she tell you?"

"She told Britt she broke up with you."

"Guess that says it all."

Kicking my shoes off and curling up on the sofa, I tossed a pillow at David. "You don't seem too broken up about it."

He turned off the TV "You guys don't understand. Sara and I never had a romantic relationship. Did you ever see me kiss her?"

Kody twitched his lips. "Can't say I ever did."

I agreed. "No. I guess not."

"Did you ever hear me say I loved her?"

I shook my head. "Nope. You didn't."

"We hung out together when I was in eighth grade and she was in sixth. We were in the middle school youth group at church. Our fathers worked together, and our moms were on a lot the same committees. Our families spent a lot of time together, and I enjoyed hanging out with Sara. She's fun to be with. But she was like a little sister."

I picked at a raised spot on the pillow next to me. "I don't think she thought of you as a big brother."

"Until about a year ago, she treated me like a big brother. Then she got clingier and acted weird. She told people she was my girlfriend. It was easier to go along with her."

"What about other girls?"

"I haven't met anybody I wanted to date. Kody or Sara are always around, and I hang with them."

"I'm surprised she broke up with you. But I never did think you felt about her the way she felt about you. It's too bad. I hate to see her get her heart broken. I wish I could call her. I sighed then glanced at my watch. "It's two a.m. and past my bedtime. See you guys tomorrow."

*"As you start your journey, the
first thing you should do is
throw away that store-bought
map, and begin to draw
your own."*
-Michael Dell

Chapter 45

Three weeks later, dressed in cap and gown at the massive
Civic Center Auditorium, I confirmed my tassel was in the
correct position as I waited in line with my classmates for the
first notes of "Pomp and Circumstance." I couldn't find David
in the crowd of 525 graduating students, and I didn't recognize
most of the kids.

The guy behind me tapped my shoulder. "Do I know you?"

"I'm Brittany Masters."

His eyes grew wide. "You're the girl who jumped off the
bridge." He pointed at me and shouted to someone behind him,
"She's the one who jumped off the bridge."

A low rumble of conversation moved down the line. I
wanted to crawl in a hole.

The Kennedy High School Band started up a tune, that
drowned out the chatter around me. For now I wouldn't have to
talk to anyone. But I'd have to sit beside this jerk for the next
three hours. If he'd had an ounce of decency, he would have
kept his mouth shut when he recognized who I was.

We moved forward in our line until we reached our seats. I
sat upright in my chair and stared straight ahead. I didn't look
at the guy beside me, but I heard him whispering to the girl

next to him, who whispered to the guy next to her, and so it went.

After more than an hour of listening to our principal, assistant principal, mayor, and several other noted figures from San Francisco, Pastor Kyle took the stage. He asked everyone to please stand as he offered a prayer. His familiar face and encouraging words brought me a bottomless peace.

I'd not paid much attention a few weeks ago when they announced the top students in our class. With missing so many days over the past year and a half, my 3.8 GPA was good enough for me. An easy smile played at the corner of my mouth as Marie Rodriguez, the girl who testified at Eric's hearing, took the stage as our valedictorian. She spoke with confidence and pride as she shared with the class the importance of overcoming obstacles in life.

I was certain she couldn't see me sitting far in the back of the auditorium, but when she finished, I flipped the thumbs up sign and nodded.

The guy I'd been trying to avoid nudged me and whispered, "Good speech."

My focus remained riveted to the front.

"Sorry about before. I shouldn't have done that."

Locking my gaze on his, I smiled. "It's okay. I forgive you."

"Sometimes I put my mouth in gear before my brain checks in."

I smothered a chuckle as I returned my attention to the stage. "Foot in mouth disease?"

"Yeah."

I nodded. "It's going around."

"I don't care what they say. You're cool."

Oh, the drama of high school. I couldn't wait to have it all behind me.

****

That afternoon, our house and backyard bulged with people. Millie oversaw the servers from the catering company, who kept trays of hors d'oeuvres and crystal glasses of sparkling cider moving among the guests.

Earlier that morning, Aunt Lisa and Nana announced that they had no intention of sitting around doing nothing while everyone else worked. After several moments of discussion, Aunt Carol conceded. She asked them to greet the guests as they arrived and put the gifts in the family room. This seemed to pacify my new aunt and Nana, at least for the moment.

Printed banners with "Congratulations! David" and "Congratulations! Brittany" strung throughout the house. One banner in particular made my heart soar. Above the staircase for all to see as they entered hung a banner printed in scarlet and gray: "Congratulations! Kody."

Certain all the guests had arrived and settled in, Aunt Carol corralled the rest of the family and led a blindfolded Kody into the family room. She had posted Harvard and Colorado State pennants on the wall above the gift table.

My aunt led Kody to the couch where she sat him down. He reached behind his head and fingered the knot in the scarf. She took his hand, put it in front of him, and shoved a gray envelope into his palm. "Don't take that off yet," she warned.

She guided me to the couch and plopped me next to him. "Okay. You can take it off now."

I took the envelope while he worked to untie the silk scarf from around his head. Curiosity getting the best of me, I had to look. I gasped, then handed the mailer back to Kody.

His eyes flew open wide. "This is it?"

Aunt Carol nodded. "What else could it be?"

He glanced around the room. "If this isn't good news, I'll be embarrassed."

David leaned over the back of the couch. "Ohio State?" He gripped Kody's shoulder. "Way to go, man."

"I haven't opened it yet."

"What are you waiting for?"

With trembling fingers, Kody ripped one end of the envelope and pulled out a folded sheet of paper, dropping it, and then catching it before it hit the floor.

Uncle Scott teased. "You a little nervous, old man?"

Kody grinned. "Just a little."

The tension and joy in the room was unmistakable, and all grew quiet as Kody read the letter.

Jumping to his feet, he lifted me from the couch, crunching the letter in his hand. "I'm accepted!"

With no thought of my family surrounding us, I smothered Kody's last words with my lips, holding the kiss for several seconds.

Hooping and hollering, the family closed ranks around us creating a huge group hug. My cheeks warmed with the realization that I'd kissed Kody in front of my entire family.

In a huge bear hug, Uncle Scott lifted Kody from the floor. "Never any doubt. We knew you'd do it." He looked at me and winked. "Great kiss, Britt. I'm surprised the man can still think straight."

As the family quieted, Nana read Kody's letter and Aunt Carol pulled something off a shelf. She held an Ohio State pennant then faced the rest of us. "Guess that's a wrap. By next fall, we'll be empty nesters." She wiped away a tear. "Yep, we'll have the house all to ourselves."

Kody flopped back on the couch. "I was getting worried. You and David got your letters weeks ago."

I hung the pennant on the wall next to mine. "I knew they'd take you. They'd be nuts not to. You'll be the best equine vet ever to grace their halls."

Guests drifted into the family room, congratulating Kody and filling the room to the point I had to squirm my way out.

Millie made each of us our favorite flavor of cake, but in place of her normal eight-inch layer cakes, she'd decorated three large sheet cakes. Mine was lemon flavored with fluffy lemon frosting.

As I sat on a lower step in the front hall and balanced a large piece of cake on a small paper plate, I heard Sara's voice on the front porch. She entered with her mom and dad on both sides. When she saw me, she ran over and caught me up in a hug. My dessert, icing and all, spiraled across the room and landed on her mother's blouse.

Mrs. Alexander squealed, flipping her hands in a comical gesture down the front of her Versace blouse. What remained of the mess splattered across the toe of her Chanel alligator high heels.

Aunt Carol stood in the doorway to the kitchen with both hands in front of her mouth, her eyes brimming with tears of restrained laughter. "Millie," she shouted.

Millie entered from the back hall, and upon witnessing the frantic Mrs. Alexander, assumed a near identical expression to Aunt Carol's smirk. "Yes, ma'am."

My aunt took Sara's mom by the arm and led her to Millie. "Please take Prudence to the kitchen and help her clean up."

I grabbed a stack of napkins and attempted to clean the mess from the marble tile floor. With the toe of her shoe, my aunt pulled a small oriental rug from the other side of the entry hall and covered the sticky smear. With her head held high, Aunt Carol turned to leave the room. "Millie can take care of that later."

Sara and I slipped away to my bedroom. Once the door was closed, she collapsed on the floor in a fit of laughter. "I can't believe that happened. Did you see her face?"

I fell on my bed, giggling. "That couldn't have been funnier if I'd planned it."

"Wonder if anyone got that on their phone. It would win *America's Funniest Videos*."

I sniffed. "You think she'll be mad?"

Sara fell into a new fit of laughter. "Did you see her face?"

I nodded.

"Yeah. She'll be mad. She'll make Dad take her home."

241

My laughter subsiding as I laid across my bed. "Won't you have to leave with them?"

"With all the people here and the size of this place, it'll take them awhile to find me."

"I've missed you."

Still sitting on the floor, she leaned her back against the bed. "Me too."

I ran my hand through her hair and gave it a shake. "How am I supposed to get along without my little sidekick?"

Her words tumbled out with a clipped edge. "You're the one that's leaving. Not me."

"I have to go."

She faced me, her eyes brimming with tears. "I know. But I don't have to like it."

"Maybe your folks will soften up and let you come for a visit."

She chuckled. "And maybe the moon will turn to cheese."

Rolling onto my back, I stared at the high ceiling. "You've got to grow up sometime. They won't always be able to tell you what to do."

She plopped next to me on the bed. "That's an eternity from now."

"Do you know where you're going to college?"

She shrugged. "Mom wants me to go to SFU."

"San Francisco State?"

She smirked. "Then I won't have to leave home."

"I hear it's a good college. What do you want to study?"

She spread her hands wide above her head. "I don't know."

"Nothing interests you?"

Rolling to her stomach, she giggled. "They have a Department of Human Sexuality Studies. Maybe I should become a sex counselor."

I shoved her. "Get real."

"When do you leave?"

"For home?"

"Yeah. I guess Kody and the family are going with you?"

"They're only going for a visit. David will be here all summer."

"Yeah," she said in an unconcerned tone.

"Sounds like you're over the breakup."

"I guess there was never anything to break up."

"So, you're okay?"

She sat up and pushed her feet under her butt. "I'm more than okay."

I swirled my hand in front of her face. "Okay girl. Give it up. What are you holding back?"

"He was right there all the time, and I never noticed him."

"Who?"

"Joshua."

"Who is Joshua?"

"He's a classmate at Christian Academy. Guess he's had a crush on me since fifth grade."

"That's great."

Sara swiped away a tear. "You didn't answer my question. When are you leaving?"

"In two weeks."

She flopped across me and ruffled my hair. "I'll miss you."

I pushed her over then rolled to my back. "We don't have to say goodbye yet."

She nodded. "Yes, we do."

"We can meet at the stables. They're picking Mariah up tomorrow, but I can ride one of the other horses."

"We're leaving tomorrow."

"Where are you going?"

Strutting around the room, one hand behind her head and one on her hip, she announced in a mocking, arrogant tone, "Mother thinks I need a season in Europe."

A sharp rap at the door heralded someone outside, and Mrs. Alexander barged in. She grabbed Sara by the arm and tugged her out the door. "I might have known I'd find you here."

Sara jerked her arm from of her mother's grip. "We were saying goodbye. Can't I even tell my best friend goodbye?"

I giggled. "Nice outfit, Mrs. Alexander."

She stomped her foot. "It's that smart mouth of yours that gets you and anyone close to you in so much trouble. Someone needs to take you in hand."

Before I could retort, Aunt Carol appeared in the hall. She winked at me then dropped an arm around the irate woman's shoulders. "Calm down, Prudence. You found your daughter, and now you can go home."

"Wearing this?" By now Sara's mom trembled and tears brimmed in her eyes. "Someone might see me. Carol, don't you have something else I can wear?"

"You'll be fine. And you need not be in any hurry to return the clothes."

"I can't believe you wear such things." She tugged at the front of the oversized, faded and tattered denim shirt then with both hands pulled on the thighs of a pair of tattered jeans. "What if someone sees me?"

Aunt Carol led a frantic Prudence down the steps. "Come along, Sara. Your mother needs to get home."

*"A great horse will change your
life. The truly special ones
define it . . ."*
-Anonymous

Chapter 46

Two weeks later, pulling two rented carts filled with our luggage and duffel bags, my California family, Kody, and I resembled a small version of the McAllister family in the movie *Home Alone*.

How could I accumulate so much stuff in one year? I arrived in San Francisco with two duffels. Here I was returning to Colorado with three duffels and two suitcases. The rest of my traveling companions made do with one suitcase or duffel each.

I scanned the luggage. "I hope Uncle Scott has room for all this?"

Uncle Jim chuckled. "I told him we'd meet him here at pickup, and it would be best if he came alone." He scanned the pile of canvas and leather. "That Sequoia might be an eight-passenger vehicle, but that pile is three passengers."

A squeal of excitement broke from my lips when the black SUV rolled through the entrance to the pickup area. "There he is."

Kody took my hand. "Calm down. We saw him two weeks ago."

I jiggled like a puddle of Jell-O. "But I'm going home. Do you understand? I've waited more than a year for this day!"

He grinned. "I understand."

While David and Kody helped me drag my luggage into my old bedroom in the main house, the downstairs grew quiet. "What's going on down there?"

David shrugged. "Why?"

I started toward the open doorway. "It's quiet. Where is everyone?"

Grabbing my hand, he tugged me toward the window seat. "A little different view than our place?"

I sighed as I surveyed the open pastureland and forested hillside. "Yep." Sitting on the floral cushion, identical to the one in my other bedroom, I cranked open the side windows. "That's better." I inhaled. "Smell that?"

David sniffed. "Smells like horses."

I grinned. "It smells like home. What do you think, Kody?" When he didn't reply, I turned. "Where did he go?"

David shrugged. "Don't know." He started for the door. "Are you coming?"

"You go on down. I'll be there soon."

Opening the duffel that held my jeans, T-shirts, and boots, I grabbed clean clothes then headed for the shower to wash away the travel crud.

Feeling refreshed, with my wet hair pulled back, I hurried downstairs and found the living room devoid of people. No voices echoed from the kitchen. No TV blared in the family room. No one was in Dad's office.

"Where did they all go?" The sound of my voice echoed beneath the cathedral ceiling.

Aunt Carol and Uncle Jim wouldn't be in the stables. Maybe Uncle Scott took them up to the equestrian center. But surely they would have told me.

I giggled as the realization hit me. Today's my birthday, and they're up to something.

Exiting the front door, I laughed aloud. Pickup trucks,

SUVs, and several four wheelers filled the lane to beyond Nana's house.

I followed the sound of voices to the old barn. The doors stood open. Inside I found my Colorado family, my California family, and all the friends and neighbors I'd missed so much over the past year.

"Happy Birthday, Brittany."

We mountain folks don't hold back when we get excited. Yahoos followed the birthday greeting then a local country band with a sweet mountain twang led everyone in a round of *Happy Birthday to You.*

"Happy Birthday, Ms. Brittany."

I turned in shock. "Millie? Where did you come from?"

"Ha. You thought I went to my brother's yesterday."

"You came here?"

She pulled me into a hug, "Couldn't miss my girl's eighteenth birthday."

****

As the sun slipped behind the mountains, Kody and I sat on the top rail, at the edge of the pasture. Mariah grazed between clumps of aspens.

Kody grinned. "She's happy here."

"Who wouldn't be?" I nudged him. "You think you could be happy here?"

"Someday."

"I'm not ready to talk about someday yet."

He surprised me as he dropped to the ground inside the fence then lifted me from the rail. Cupping my chin in his hand, he searched my upturned face. "Love you."

I brushed his lips with mine. "Love you too."

Something I'd given no thought to before crossed my mind. "When's your birthday?"

He chuckled. "Where did that come from?"

"I've had two birthday parties since we've been together.

247

David had his birthday festivities at the beach last August. We've never celebrated your birthday. When is it?"

"December 25th."

"Christmas?"

He chuckled. "Yep. I share my birthday with Jesus. Good of me, don't you think?"

I nudged him. "Why didn't you tell us?

Taking me by the shoulders, he pressed his forehead against mine. "This past Christmas was the greatest birthday present I can ever remember getting. I had you and your family, and we rode horses through the snow. Why would I want anything more?"

I shrugged. "I guess. If you're okay with it, then I am too."

"I am."

For the next thirty minutes, we shared few words as we walked hand in hand across the pasture. The mountains loomed in the distance as shadowy outlines while the moon glowed brighter in the darkening sky.

With a little coaching, Kody mounted Mariah then pulled me up in front of him.

"I can't believe you've never ridden bareback," I teased. "It's the only way to ride."

"How do you get her to do what you want?"

I shrugged. "She knows where I want to go and how fast I want to get there."

He pulled the elastic band from my hair and brushed it to the side where it fell over my shoulder. "I hope you're not in a hurry to go back."

The touch of his lips on the back of my neck sent a shock wave through my body as I leaned against him.

With a slow gait, Mariah walked toward the barn. I giggled. "I'm not in any hurry, and she doesn't seem to be, but I think she's telling us we need to get back."

As I trotted Mariah around the equestrian center arena, I couldn't believe Uncle Scott convinced me to ride English. He said he needed an instructor for the summer, and he didn't want to pay someone when he could get me for nothing. The fancy duds and cute little hat, with a wannabe saddle, was not my thing, but there I was prancing around like little Ms. Princess. "I can't believe it's been a week already."

Kody trotted by my side on Thunderbolt. "Me neither. Next week this time, I'll be riding horses in Ohio. Who'd have thought it?"

"It's been quite a year."

He chuckled. "You think?"

"Six months ago, if someone had told me we'd be riding, laughing, and making plans for our future, I wouldn't have believed them."

At the entrance to the arena, I reined Mariah to a stop.

Still mounted on Thunderbolt, Kody opened the gate. A melancholy smile tugged at his lips. "I'm just glad it's behind us."

Back in the barn, with the horses fed and watered, Kody joined me in Mariah's stall. He sat on the wooden box where I stored my grooming tools, rope halters, snacks, and other necessities. "It's time, Britt."

I continued brushing my horse, tears coursing down my cheeks. "I don't want to say goodbye."

"You picked her feet yet?"

I shook my head.

He came up beside me, a hoof pick in his hand. "You mind?"

I shook my head again.

"We'll see each other, you know. Nana informed me in no uncertain terms that I am to spend school break with your family." He grinned. "I think she likes me."

I giggled. "You won her over when you asked her if you

could marry me someday."

"She told you about that, huh?"

I nodded. "Nana and I don't have many secrets."

He jerked his head up, his eyes wide. "You tell her everything."

I kicked a pile of straw at him. "Not everything."

"Guess both of your families like me."

"Now you don't even have to marry me. You're part of the family." I flipped the brush over Mariah's rump and teased, "Have you decided if you'll change your name to Masters or Harper?"

In one swift movement, he took me his arms and locked his eyes on mine. "Someday I plan to make you Mrs. Kody Diaz."

I laughed. "And if I don't want to change my last name?"

He jerked back and released me. "You don't want to marry me?"

I tugged at the front of his shirt and grinned, "I've already got the sign designed and I know right where to put it."

"Sign?"

I laid the imaginary signage out in front of us and pointed. "Diaz and Masters Equine Veterinary Clinic—Boarding and Lessons—English and Western."

His arms held me tight as he covered my lips with his. Raising his head, he chuckled. "You've got this all figured out, don't you Ms. Brittany?"

I huffed. "Don't you start. Millie's the only one I let call me that."

He sighed. "Eight years is a long time."

"We'll make it."

"That's got to be one of the longest engagements in history."

I laughed. "We Masters work slow. Look how long it took Uncle Scott to marry Lisa."

We walked hand in hand through the stables and sat on Nana's front porch. Kody leaned against a weathered oak railing. "How comfortable are you with getting engaged as young as we are?"

Leaving the rocking chair, I leaned against the upright rail. "I'm not comfortable with getting engaged at our age." Wrapping my arms around him I snuggled my face into his shoulder. "I can't imagine ever loving anyone else. But we have eight years of school ahead of us, and we both know things happen. If I've learned anything this past two years it is that life is full of twists and turns, ups and downs, good and bad. I think we should wait and see if we still feel the same way in four years.

He squeezed me tighter. "You are wise beyond your years. I don't like waiting but I know you're right."

*"Goodbyes are not forever,
are not the end; it simply
means I'll miss you until
we meet again."*
-Anonymous

Chapter 47

Early the next morning, Aunt Carol joined me on the window seat as I watched the morning mist lift over the mountains. She took my hand in hers. "I wanted to talk to you about some things before we leave."

I grinned. "You sound serious."

"What I want to talk about is serious." The corners of her lips lifted for a brief second. "It's about your faith."

She surprised me. I thought she wanted to talk about my relationship with Kody, or school, or staying in touch. "My faith?"

She nodded. "I prayed for years that Cali and Josh would find a personal relationship with Jesus. And I have peace they are with Him now."

"I'm sure."

"But if they had only known Him years ago, their lives and yours would have been so much richer, more fulfilled."

My first impulse was to defend my parents and tell my aunt they had a wonderful life. We had a great family. They were happy. But now I knew the amazing feeling of knowing with no doubt that God loved me, that Jesus was always with me, and that the Holy Spirit would lead me. I couldn't in good conscience disagree with her. "I know."

She pulled my head to her chest and held me. "You've been such a blessing to us. You're more than a niece. I think of you as my daughter. I love you more than you can imagine."

Wrapping my arms around her, I snuggled close. "Love you too, and I know what's bothering you."

"You do?"

"You're concerned that since I'm back on the ranch, away from you and Uncle Jim and the church, that I'll drift away. I'll become a lost lamb." I took both her hands in mine and inhaled a deep breath. "That won't happen. I promise."

She kissed me on the cheek then on the nose. "Good."

"I have a question, though."

"What's that?"

"Those two guys?"

"Two guys?"

"The guys that saved Sara and me after the barbecue. I'm certain it was one of them that pulled me from the bay."

"Oh, those guys."

"I said nothing because it still worried me that people thought I was crazy. But those men were in the courtroom at Eric and Jeremy's hearings."

She smiled. "I thought that might have been them."

"You saw them?"

She nodded.

"Do you think they're angels?"

"What do you think?"

"Yes."

****

It was the one trip to Denver International Airport I dreaded with all my heart. At the departure curb, Uncle Scott, Lisa, Nana, and I said goodbye to my California family. Uncle Jim collected their luggage and smiled back at us as he entered the sliding glass doors. "See you in September, Scott."

Surprised by his statement, I turned to Uncle Scott. "What

did he mean?"

He chuckled. "Hunting season."

My Colorado family loaded in the SUV, leaving Kody and me standing on the sidewalk. Lisa rolled down the passenger's side window. "We're heading over to Heidi's to grab sandwiches and drinks. You want something?"

My stomach churned, but I knew I'd get hungry on the way home. "Tuna salad on whole wheat and a bottle of water."

"Got it. We'll park in the waiting area. Call us when you're ready, and we'll pick you up here."

I nodded then followed Kody into the airport. We took the elevator to the ticket counter level then headed toward the security gates. I inhaled a deep breath when we arrived at the top of the escalators. Wrapping my arms around his waist, I nuzzled his chest. "I don't want you to go."

He kissed my forehead. "I don't want to leave, but I have to."

"I know." Forcing back tears, I gripped the handrail of the escalator and stepped onto the grated moving step. "Grab snacks down here. It's a long flight to Columbus."

He chuckled. "How long?"

I stepped off the escalator, interlacing my fingers in his. "Long."

"You don't know how long, do you?"

"No. But it must be a long flight. Ohio's more than a thousand miles."

He tugged me into the ice cream shop. "Ice Cream?"

I chuckled. "I hope we don't make a habit of this."

His mouth twisted in a questioning smirk.

"Remember? That day during Eric's trial? You bought me ice cream."

"Oh yeah. I remember."

"The day before I went back to school. We were talking about ACTs, SATs, and GEDs. We were all stressing about scores and passing. David brought out the Ben and Jerry's."

He chuckled. "Yeah, I remember."

"If I eat ice cream every time I'm stressed or sad, I will get as big as a barn by the time I graduate from college."

He eyed me up and down and grinned. "Not a chance."

It was time. Kody's flight to Columbus was leaving in an hour, and he needed to get through security then out to the concourse.

His lips captured mine, more demanding this time, sending the pit of my stomach swirling in sadness and regret. How long would it be? How long would I wait until once again I'd feel the caress of his lips on mine?

For the next hour, I stood at the two-story window watching planes leave and arrive. A United flight headed west, disappeared over the mountains, and my heart ached thinking of my California family being so far away. The family who would forever be an intricate part of my life.

About the time Kody's flight should have taken off, a Frontier jet roared into the sky. I'd see Kody again; of that I was certain. What life held for us, what God had planned, only He knew.

My recent past, filled with grief and heartache few girls my age encounter, flashed through my memory. I knew God pulled me from the car the day of the accident. He protected me through the attacks by Eric. He lifted me from the waters of San Francisco Bay because He had a purpose for me. A purpose only He knew. I would be okay. More than okay. I was riding the wind with God carrying me to His chosen destination.

-The End-

Epilogue

Ten Years Later

We buried Nana this morning, and I'm at peace knowing she's gone to be with Jesus. She grew frail over the past few years, and it was a great blessing to have her at our wedding last year. When I returned home from college and moved into the big house, I insisted she come and live with me so I could keep an eye on her.

Uncle Scott and Aunt Lisa continue to run the ranch and equestrian center. I try to help where I can.

Aunt Carol and Uncle Jim sold the big house in town and retired to the beach house. They invited Millie to join them. But she said there wouldn't be enough to do there to keep her busy. Her brother's health has been failing, so she moved in his house to take care of him.

David was made partner in a prestigious law firm in San Francisco. He married a girl he met in law school. They have a two-year-old daughter and another child due in six months.

Sara appeased her mother by attending San Francisco State University where she earned her teaching degree. She met Tony her junior year and they were married soon after her graduation. He recently finished serving his residency in infectious disease. They are to leave in a few weeks to serve for three years with a Christian outreach organization in Ethiopia.

Nana left me her little cabin to use as a veterinary office. We haven't yet opened for business for small animals, but we have built a large practice working with horses and other large animals. The interior renovations are nearly completed and yesterday the enormous sign with gold and blue lettering arrived. It reads, "Diaz and Masters Equine Veterinary Clinic—Boarding and Lessons—English and Western."

Kody and I lead the youth group at our church and have become involved with a suicide prevention ministry that works with teens dealing with depression and anxiety as a result of bullying and a variety of traumatic life events.

Remembering back to the early months following the loss of my parents and sister, blaming myself, feeling lost and broken and hiding behind the smile everyone saw, I wish I had reached out to someone who may have been able to stop me from doing the unthinkable. Someone who could encourage me to see beyond the moment and know the hope I eventually found in Jesus Christ.

It is my prayer that through this ministry we will reach young people before it is too late. To be there for them. To encourage. To support. To listen. To love.

If you or a friend are suffering from depression, you need to know the warning signs of suicide:

- Threatening to hurt or kill oneself or talking of wanting to hurt oneself; and or, looking for ways to kill oneself by seeking access to firearms, available pills, or other means; and/or talking or writing about death, dying or suicide.
- Increased substance abuse (alcohol or drug use).
- No reason for living; no sense of purpose in life.
- Anxiety, agitation, unable to sleep or sleeping all the time.
- Feeling trapped—like there is no way out.
- Hopelessness.
- Withdrawal from friends, family, and society.
- Rage, uncontrolled anger, seeking revenge.

- Acting reckless or engaging in risky activities, seemingly without thinking.
- Dramatic mood changes.

If you, a friend or family member are exhibiting any or a combination of these warning signs and are a member of a church, speak to your pastor or youth leader immediately. If not, contact a mental health professional or call 1-800-TALK (8255) for a referral.

Linda Abels also publishes historical fiction under the pen name of Maggie Magoffin. She holds a bachelor's degree in English and Professional Writing and completed Christian Writers Guild's Master Craftsman program. Linda and her husband live in Colorado, along with their golden retriever. For more information about Linda and her work go to www.maggiempublications.com and www.lindaabels.com.

www.ingramcontent.com/pod-product-compliance
Lightning Source LLC
Chambersburg PA
CBHW031711170626
46808CB00005B/1706